TROLLHUNTERS

written by

Guillermo del Toro

&

Daniel Kraus

illustrations by

Sean Murray

jacket by

E. M. Gist

HYPERION

Los Angeles   New York

Visit www.hyperionteens.com

To my children and the time of dreams and hope.

May it last us all a little longer.

—GDT

For Craig Ouellette

—DK

First Hardcover Edition, July 2015
1 3 5 7 9 10 8 6 4 2
Printed in the United States of America
G475-5664-5-15142

Library of Congress Control Number: 2014935103
ISBN 978-1-4231-2598-3

Visit www.hyperionteens.com

SUSTAINABLE FORESTRY INITIATIVE   Certified Sourcing
www.sfiprogram.org
SFI-00993

THIS LABEL APPLIES TO TEXT STOCK

They call me Troll;

Gnawer of the Moon,

Giant of the Gale-blasts,

Curse of the rain-hall,

Companion of the Sibyl,

Nightroaming hag,

Swallower of the loaf of heaven.

What is a Troll but that?

—Bragi Boddason the Old, ninth-century poet

PROLOGUE

The Milk Carton
Epidemic

You are food. Those muscles you flex to walk, lift, and talk? They're patties of meat topped with chewy tendon. That skin you've paid so much attention to in mirrors? It's delicious to the right tongues, a casserole of succulent tissue. And those bones that give you the strength to forge your way in the world? They rattle between teeth as the marrow is sucked down slobbering throats. These facts are unpleasant but useful. There are things out there, you see, that don't cower in holes to be captured by us and cooked over our fires. These things have their own ways of trapping their kills, their own fires, their own appetites.

Jack Sturges and his little brother, Jim, were oblivious to all this as they sped down a canal bed on their bikes in their hometown of San Bernardino, California. It was September 21, 1969, a perfect day from a vanished era: the dusk light spilled over the peaks of Mount Sloughnisse to the city's east, and from the nearby streets the boys could hear the buzz of lawn mowers, smell chlorine from a pool, taste the hamburger smoke from somebody's backyard grill.

The high walls of the canal kept them secret and provided perfect cover for their gunfights. That afternoon, as usual, it was Victor Power (Jack) versus Doctor X (Jim), and they swerved around piles of rubble to take shots with their plastic ray guns. Victor Power, also as usual, was winning, this time decisively because of that new bike: a cherry-red Sportcrest so new the birthday ribbons were still attached. Jack was thirteen that day but rode his present as if he had been riding it all his life, up suicidal banks, through grasping weeds, sometimes without hands so that he could fire off a particularly good shot.

"You'll never catch me alive!" cried Victor Power.

"Yes, I will!" panted Doctor X. "I'm going to . . . wait . . . hey, Jack, wait up!"

Jim—or "Jimbo" as his brother called him—pushed his thick glasses, broken but taped together with a Band-Aid, up his sweaty nose. He was eight and small for his age. Not only was his battered yellow Schwinn a lesser bike than the Sportcrest, but it was so large that Jim had yet to discard the training wheels. Dad had sworn to Jim that he would grow into it. Jim was still waiting for that to happen. In the meantime, he had to stand up on the pedals to really make it go, which made it difficult to shoot his ray gun with any accuracy. Doctor X was doomed.

The Sportcrest shot through a pile of litter. Jim followed moments later, training wheels squeaking, but when he saw the crumpled milk carton, he swerved around it. The face of a smiling little girl had been printed on the side of the carton along with the words LOST CHILD. It gave Jim the creeps. This was how they advertised missing children, and there were a lot of them.

It had been a year earlier when the first kid had disappeared. San Bernardino had organized search parties, rescue teams. Then another kid went missing. And another. The town tried for a while to search for each one. But soon it was a child missing every other day and the adults couldn't keep up. That had been the scariest part for Jim, seeing the resignation in the faces of the sleep-deprived parents. They had surrendered to whatever evil was taking their children, and when they poured milk for their families, they tried to ignore the faces on the sides of the cartons stamped with those dreadful words:

HAVE YOU SEEN ME?

The last count Jim had heard was 190 missing kids. The number would have seemed like fantasy if not for the evidence he saw everywhere: a higher fence around the school, larger numbers of parents patrolling the playgrounds, the police crackdown on kids being on the streets after dark. It was unusual that Jim and Jack would be allowed to be out on their bikes this close to sundown, but it was Jack's birthday and their parents couldn't say no.

Jack had wasted no time in making a single improvement to his bike. He had taken his transistor radio and fixed it with wire to the shiny red handlebars. Then he had turned it on as loud as it could go, and their entire afternoon had been orchestrated to the bounciest songs of the day: "Sugar, Sugar," "Hot Fun in the Summertime," "Proud Mary." You wouldn't think those songs would be the perfect sound track for the laser-blasting volleys of Victor Power and Doctor X, but they were. As long as Jim could keep his mind off those milk cartons, this just might be the best afternoon of his whole life.

Up ahead on Jack's bike, the radio changed to a new song: "What's Your Name?" by Don and Juan. It was a love song, not Jim's favorite, but for some reason the wistful crooning captured the mood of the dying day. The sun was going down fast, school started up again the next day, and this final half mile of riding might be the last flare of summer before fall classes snuffed it like a candle.

Jim squinted into the sun. He could make out Jack pedaling so fast that birds threw themselves out of the way, not to land until they had gone south for the winter. Jack whooped and dry leaves danced in the Sportcrest's wake. In just a few seconds, Jack would pass under the Holland Transit Bridge, a monolith of concrete and steel. A couple of cars were traveling across it up above, but beneath were shadows so deep and dark they made your eyes hurt.

He had to catch up to his brother. When they got home, he wanted it to be as equals, Jack and Jim Sturges, instead of the perennial winner and loser, Victor Power and Doctor X. Jim stood on his pedals and pushed with all of his might. The training wheels protested—SQUEAK, SQUEAK, SQUEAK!—but he kept on cycling his legs, willing them to be longer and stronger.

When he looked up again, Jack was gone.

Jim could see the Sportcrest lying beneath the bridge, silhouetted by the falling sun, its handlebars bent and the front wheel still spinning. With the bridge coming up fast, Jim reversed the direction of his legs and his Schwinn came skidding to a halt a few feet outside the bridge's shadow. He straddled the center bar and panted, searching for his brother in the blackest corners.

"Jack?"

The Sportcrest's front wheel kept spinning, as if the ghost of his brother still pedaled.

"Come on, Jack. Don't be dumb. You're not going to scare me."

The only response came from Don and Juan. Echoes twined their sweet harmonies into an eerie wail:

"I stood on this corner, / Waiting for you to come along, / So my heart could feel satisfi-i-i-ied. . . ."

With muffled firecracker pops, the streetlights next to Jim switched on, one after another, filling the canal with a yellow sodium glow. That meant it was night: there was no more time to fool around.

"If we don't get home right now, Dad's gonna ground us for weeks. Jack?"

Jim swallowed, stepped off his bike, gripped his ray gun in his sweaty palm, and walked alongside the bike until he was within the bridge's darkness. There it was ten degrees cooler, and he shivered. The training wheels turned slower now, but still complained:

SQUEAK. SQUEAK. SQUEAK.

He came upon the Sportcrest. The front wheel was beginning to slow its revolutions. Suddenly, he felt as if that wheel were Jack's heart, and if it stopped moving, his brother would be gone forever.

Jim peered into fathomless shadow. Ignoring the drip of moisture, the scurry of what might be rats, the thud of car tires passing overhead, and Don and Juan's death moans, he raised his voice.

"Jack! Come on! Are you hurt? Jack, I'm serious!"

He cringed at how the words reverberated back. The yellow streetlights, the violet skies, the clammy temperature, the mocking echoes of his panic—how had the transformation from dream to nightmare happened so fast? He spun around, looking into one shadow, then another, faster and faster, his chest hitching with sobs, his cheeks burning with fear, when he thought of the one direction he hadn't yet looked.

Slowly Jim craned his neck so he could look up into the underside of the bridge.

It was black. Nothing but black.

But then the black *moved*.

It happened naturally, almost gracefully. Giant, powerful limbs differentiated themselves from the concrete as they adjusted their clinging grip. Something the size of a boulder—a head—rolled about until Jim could see eyes burning orange like fire. The thing took a breath and it was like the entire belly of the bridge rippled at once. Then it exhaled and the force of putrid air blew Jim's body back.

The thing let go of the bridge and dropped to the ground. Dirt billowed and trash flew into the air, and in that swirl of debris Jim saw milk cartons, two, three, four, five of them, cavorting and twirling, the grins of missing children mocking their own deaths. The thing reared back like a grizzly and the street lamps gleamed off of two horns, which tore through the overhead concrete. A mouth opened, glistening with huge, mismatched teeth. Orange eyes locked on Jim. Then arms—long, muscular pythons of matted fur—reached out.

Jim screamed. The underpass made it ten times louder, and the thing paused for just a second. Jim took that second and leapt astride his Schwinn, pushing off from the pavement. His left foot kicked past Jack's radio, killing Don and Juan once and for all, and then he was out from under the Holland Transit Bridge, still screaming, legs churning.

He heard it behind him: the gallop of a colossal thing, chasing after on all fours like a gorilla.

Mumbling with terror, Jim pushed his pedals harder than ever before. The squeak of the training wheels became a shriek. Still the thing closed in. The ground shook with each landing of monstrous feet. It snorted like a bull and the expelled air reeked of sewage. The plastic ray gun dropped from Jim's grip; never again would he feel the cunning strength of Doctor X. The thing behind him growled so near that the entire frame of the bike vibrated. The streetlights threw a horrifying shadow of the thing's arm, reaching for Jim with long, sharp claws.

Jim pulled off to the left, hopping the edge of the canal, bursting through ditch weeds, and exploding onto a sidewalk. There was a fire hydrant right in front of him, red like Jack's birthday bike—oh, Jack, Jack, what had happened to Jack? Jim tore around the hydrant and shot down the middle of the street. A car honked and veered out of his way. Jim ignored the angry shouts. He was speeding like his brother, learning how to properly ride at last, and the training wheels tore off and went bouncing down the street, useless little pieces of rubber.

Home was *right there*, just seconds away, and he strained down the home stretch, screeching for air, tears streaming horizontally across his cheeks. The bike lurched up the curb and collided with the white fence. Jim went head over heels before crashing down on the front lawn, his face scratched by Mom's manicured bushes, his glasses unfastened from their Band-Aid binding.

The dog was barking from inside. He heard footsteps, the front door opening, the commotion of his mom and dad hurrying down the steps. Jim realized he was still screaming, and that reminded him of the beast. He scrabbled for both halves of his glasses and held them before his eyes. Nothing.

He scanned the front yard, the quiet suburban houses, the mailboxes, the flower beds, the sprinklers. There were no monsters, but at his feet he saw something else.

It was a bronze medallion connected to a rusty chain. It was engraved with a foreboding crest: a hideous, snarling face; indecipherable markings of a savage language; and a magnificent long-sword across the bottom. Jim's sobs caught in his chest and he reached out for it.

"Jim! What's wrong?"

It was his mom, falling to her knees beside him, brushing dirt clods from his ears. His dad came next, kneeling in front of him, taking him by the knee and shaking it to focus Jim's attention. They were saying his name, over and over: *Jim*. How horrible it was that no one would call him "Jimbo" ever again.

"Buddy, look at me," his dad said. "You all right? You okay? Buddy?"

"Where's your brother?" His mother's hoarse whisper suggested that she somehow knew. "Jim, where is Jack?"

Jim did not respond and instead leaned to the side to see past his dad. The imprint in the grass was still there, but the medallion was gone, if it had ever been there in the first place. He felt a strange sense of sadness at its absence and an even more powerful sense of failure. He collapsed into his parents' arms, crying, shuddering, and knowing that he had now experienced the nature of true fear, the pain of true loss.

Jim Sturges was my father. Jack Sturges was my uncle. The story I just told you I wouldn't learn myself until forty-five years later, when I was fifteen. It was then I learned that Uncle Jack was the very last kid to disappear in the Milk

Carton Epidemic, which ended as quickly as it had begun. The destroyed Sportcrest became a family relic; I've seen it a hundred times. It was also when I was fifteen that I learned how my dad spent the following decades, all of his youth and most of his adulthood, visiting the Holland Transit Bridge at night with flashlight in hand, searching for clues as to what happened to his older brother. There was never a trace of Jack aside from the milk cartons that would depict his brave, smirking face along with the word *MISSING*.

What a perfect way to describe my dad in the years to come.

PART I

Down the Drain

1.

Contemporary accounts state that the historic and decisive Battle of the Fallen Leaves took place in the final two minutes of the fourth quarter on Harry G. Bleeker Memorial Field at San Bernardino High, with our beloved Saint B. Battle Beasts up by only six points and our starting quarterback out with a concussion. It was then, during the most important game of the year, and there, upon that dewy sod, that a brave hero fell and an unexpected victor arose. To this day, tales from that night fuel the bedtime stories and dreams of children of all ages—human or otherwise. So read carefully these pages you hold. Go ahead, believe every word. After all, you may one day want to tell this story to your own kids.

Stranger things have happened. Just wait and see.

My name is James Sturges Jr., but you can call me Jim, same as my dad, and I used to be just like you. I was fifteen when my adventure began. It was a Friday morning in October and the alarm clock went off at its usual rude time. I just let it beep; I had learned to sleep through it. Unfortunately, my dad, Jim Sturges Sr., was the world's lightest sleeper. A gust of wind against the side of the house was enough to wake him up, and then he'd come check on me, waking me up, too. I guess you'd have to attribute it to what happened to his older brother, Jack. That kind of thing messes you up.

He came in and turned off my alarm. The silence that came next was even worse because I knew he was standing there looking at me. He did that a lot. It was like he could barely believe that I had survived another night. I cracked my eyes open. He was wearing a too-tight dress shirt, dirty around the collar, and was trying to get that left cuff buttoned, something he did every morning until he broke down and asked me for help.

He looked old. He *was* old. Older than most of the dads I'd met, going by the wrinkles pinwheeling from the corners of his eyes, the bushiness of his eyebrow and ear hair, and his almost total baldness. He also had a slumped posture I didn't see in other dads, though I doubt that had to do with age. I think it was other stuff, weighing him down.

"Rise and shine." He didn't sound particularly shiny. He never did.

I sat up and watched him take hold of the steel shutters over my window. He plucked his glasses from his pocket, broken as always and held together with a Band-Aid, and squinted at the key code. After punching in the seven-digit number, he yanked upward and the steel panels accordioned to reveal a sunny day.

"Don't bother," I grunted. "I'm just going to have to lock them again when we leave."

"Sunshine is important to growing boys." It didn't sound like he believed it.

"I'm not growing." I took after my dad when it came to size and was still waiting for that growth spurt everyone kept raving about. "In fact, I think I'm shrinking."

He fussed with the left wrist button some more before heading out the door.

"Up and at 'em," he said. "Breakfast is important, too."

It didn't sound like he believed that either.

After showering and getting dressed, I found Dad right where I expected him, standing in the living room entrance by the altar to Uncle Jack that was arranged above our electric fireplace. I call it an altar because I can't think of a better word. Every inch of the shelf was filled with Jack memorabilia. There were school photos, of course, of kindergarten Jack beaming above a *Lone Ranger* shirt, second-grade Jack happily displaying his various missing baby teeth, fifth-grade Jack sporting a black eye and looking darn proud of it, and eighth-grade Jack—the final Jack—tan and healthy and looking like he was ready to conquer the world.

Other objects on the altar were weirder. There was the thumb-operated bell from Jack's Sportcrest, speckled with rust. There was the bike radio that played its last song in 1969, a weird-looking contraption sporting a crooked antenna. There were other things that had a brotherly significance only to Dad: a broken wristwatch, a wooden Indian figure, a little chunk of fool's gold. Most unsettling, however, was the object right in the center of the altar: a framed milk carton picture of Jack, a black-and-white replica of his eighth-grade photo.

Dad noticed me in the glass reflection.

He forced a smile.

"Hi, son."

"Hey, Dad."

"Just . . . tidying up."

He held no cleaning liquid, no towels.

"Sure, Dad."

"You want to eat?"

"Yeah, whatever. Okay."

"All right." He pushed that fake smile to its breaking point. "Let's do breakfast."

Doing breakfast meant cold cereal and milk. There was a time when we ate actual cooked food in the morning, back before Mom had her fill of Dad's insecurities and walked out. Dad was doing the best he could, I told myself. We crunched and slurped across the table from each other, faces to our bowls. On occasion he threw glances about the room to ensure that the house's steel shutters were locked tight. I sighed and poured myself some more milk. It came from a jug. Dad never bought cartons.

He kept checking his watch until I was guilted into tossing the rest of my cereal down the garbage disposal. As he tapped his foot by the front door, I hurried into my room, threw on my jacket and backpack, and punched the key code into the shutters to lock them. Only when I was at his side did Dad begin to unlock the front door.

It was a ritual I knew by heart. The door had ten locks, each one more impressive than the last. As he shifted bolts and turned keys and slid chains, I whispered along to the same lonely percussion solo I had been hearing for fifteen years: *click, rattle, zing, rattle, clack-clack-clack, thunk, crunch, whisk, rattle-rattle, thud.*

"Jimmy. Jimmy!"

I blinked and looked at him. He stood in the doorway, looking vulnerable in that ill-fitting shirt, a hand clutched to his stomach where his ulcer was acting up right on schedule. I wanted to feel bad for him, but he was motioning at me with impatient gestures.

"Get off the porch or the pressure sensors will go off. Now, now, now."

I shrugged an apology and made my way past him onto the lawn. I heard the electronic noises of the alarm system being armed, followed by the computerized female voice: "Home zones all clear." Dad exhaled, as if this outcome had been in doubt, and secured the external physical locks before leaping off the sensored porch. He landed beside me, the patches of hair above each ear damp with perspiration.

The poor old guy was winded; he was in no shape to fight the personal demons that had grown to dragon size in his mind. His chest beat up and down, drawing my attention to the vinyl calculator sleeve inserted into his front pocket and stamped with the logo of San Bernardino Electronics. Legend had it that Dad invented the Excalibur Calculator Pocket worn by science nerds the world over, but Dad denied it. My theory is that his bosses screwed him out of the credit. That's what happens to guys like Jim Sturges Sr. It made me feel like crap.

He escorted me across the lawn. The front-door security camera whirred as it followed our progress. His feet tangled with my own and I noticed that his socks, as always, were stained green. To make up for the promotions and bonuses that he didn't get at work, Dad mowed lawns on the weekends—town parks, cemeteries, even the football field at Saint B. High—and always dressed like a freak with goggles and gloves. It made me even more popular at school, believe me. He pushed me with a hand that smelled of grass.

"You'll miss the bus, Jimmy. And if you miss the bus, I'll have to turn around and drive you to school, and then I'll be late for work."

"Can't I just walk?"

"And you know how hard it was to arrange my schedule so we could both leave at the same time. The boss gave me heck, Jimmy, real heck."

"You didn't have to do that. Only babies take the bus."

He gave me a stern look.

"You can never be too careful. Look at my brother, Jack. How independent he was. How full of spirit. He used to tell me, 'Jimbo, *nothing* can hurt me.' But things did hurt him, despite the fact that he was—"

I recited it with him: "The bravest kid you *ever* saw."

Dad turned around in front of his San Bernardino Electronics company van (a.k.a. "the safest vehicle in San Bernardino"), which doubled as transport for his mowing equipment, and sighed. I noticed his unbuttoned shirt cuff flopping outside of his jacket. He deserved to go to work like that if he wasn't going to let me grow up and do simple things like walk to school on my own.

"Well," Dad said after a moment. "He was."

He walked over to the van and began to unlock it. I kicked the ground. He was right; the bus was coming. I could hear it over on Maple Street, and I was going to have to run if I wanted to catch it. But that wrist button stopped me. I kept imagining the younger guys at Dad's office making fun of the disheveled, anxious man with the Band-Aid glasses who wore his Excalibur Calculator Pocket like a badge of honor. One victim in this family was enough.

I stepped over to the side of the van, yanked the shirtsleeve free, and in a few swift moves buttoned it. I offered a weak smile. He blinked down at me through dirty lenses.

"The bus, Jimmy. . . ."

I sighed.

"I'm on it, Dad."

2.

The school was lined with pumpkins. I tallied them and was up to forty-one before the bus pulled to its usual stomach-lurching halt. Lunch boxes and books went spilling across the grimy floor and kids took to all fours to fetch the runaway thermoses and escaping pencils. I sat back and stared at the sign outside San Bernardino High.

THE 102ND ANNUAL
FESTIVAL OF THE FALLEN LEAVES
ALL WEEK LONG
SHOW YOUR SPIRIT!
GO BATTLE BEASTS!

You didn't grow up in Saint B. without the Festival of the Fallen Leaves figuring into your memories in one way or another. Maybe you dressed up like a princess or a robot and marched in the Kids' Jubilee. Or maybe you volunteered alongside your parents to help wipe down syrupy tables during the Kiwanis Pancake Blowout. The whole thing originated from a pretty cool story about some sort of legendary banishing, but I always forgot who was banishing whom and for what.

It didn't really matter, because the festival had evolved over time as a way for the town to sell itself to itself. For seven days, there were art walks with overpriced masterworks slopped together by local artisans; there were racks filled with unsellable clothing at bargain prices; there were free band concerts under public park gazebos; there were special deals at car dealerships, restaurants, and insurance offices. And it all ended right here at Saint B. High with a big football game followed by *Shakespeare on the Fifty-Yard Line*, an abridged production done right on the field. You got your sports and your culture in one place, without even having to set down your chili-cheese dog.

That year promised to bring them out in droves, and not just because the team was undefeated. Off the western end of the school was Harry G. Bleeker Memorial Field, your typical goalposts-and-floodlights deal with plenty of nooks for kids to smuggle in beer and make out. The next Friday, however, was to be the debut of our jumbotron, a freakishly large video screen that had been under wraps for weeks as workers completed the installation. Already that morning they were atop the high scaffold, adjusting their hard hats.

The whole moronic festival, which I could not have cared less about, began on Saturday—the next day—which meant that these were the final precious hours before everyone went nuts decking the town in Saint B. red and white. It was the worst time of year for kids like me, who weren't good at sports, or drama, or anything, really.

I exited the bus last, and got no farther than the sidewalk before a kid I knew from the unpopular table at lunch came barreling out of the main entrance. He grabbed hold of me to stop his momentum. We both swung around like we were ballroom dancing. He jabbed a finger at the school.

"Tub . . ." he panted. "Trophy Cave . . ."

That was all he needed to say. If there was one spot in school reserved for the darkest acts of bullying, it was the Trophy Cave, a third-floor hallway that housed the school's trophy collection. It had once been the location of the French and German classes, but those electives had been cut. The fluorescents had long before either burned out or been tampered with, and the hall existed as a dim channel of evil to be avoided at all costs, even if it meant being late for class or clenching your bladder for another period. On a regular basis you could hear the blubbers of underclassmen receiving their first (or fourteenth) wedgies.

Some kids were cursed enough to have their lockers located in this torture chamber. Tobias "Tubby" D., my best friend, was one of them.

Before I reached the Trophy Cave, I knew the identity of the assailant. A steady *SMACK, SMACK* was booming through the hall—the patented sound of Steve Jorgensen-Warner. Steve dribbled a basketball wherever he went. Classes, the cafeteria, the restrooms, the parking lot. Some teachers, coaches mostly, even let him bounce the ball in class to help him concentrate on schoolwork while other students ground their teeth in silent irritation.

Steve, obviously, was not just another student. Yes, he was captain of the basketball squad. And yes, he was the star running back of the football team. That still doesn't give you a complete picture. He was handsome in the oddest way. His eyes were too small and his nose piggish; he had a ridiculous amount of hair and a couple of teeth that looked like fangs. Yet somehow in combination these features were sort of mesmerizing. His unnatural muscular bulk and odd way of speaking—crisply, politely, as if he were a foreign student who had learned English in a class—completed the strange package. There was nobody else like Steve Jorgensen-Warner. What the teachers didn't know is that there was also nobody crueler.

A crowd had gathered. I hopped to my tiptoes and saw Tub on his knees, his freckled face beet red, gasping for air around a left-arm half nelson. With his right hand Steve continued with the basketball, simultaneously carrying on an easygoing conversation with one of his teammates. I pushed to the front of the crowd. A runner of spit was hanging from Tub's bottom lip and he clawed at Steve's bicep.

"Air," Tub gasped. "Need . . . air . . . for breathing. . . ."

Steve apologized to his friend for having to pause their pleasant chat and turned his attention back to the overweight sophomore writhing in his grip. Warped fun house reflections of Tub's face were caught in each burnished bronze plaque, championship cup, and framed photo of young adults lined up in identical jerseys, each of them happier and healthier than my wheezing best friend.

SMACK, SMACK. SMACK, SMACK.

Steve's fanged smile never touched his eyes.

"You know the deal, Tubby. Five bucks a day. I regret if this wasn't clear."

"You were . . . unbelievably . . . clear. . . ."

"Five bucks is a real bargain. I challenge you to find a better deal anywhere."

"Gave you . . . all I had . . . yesterday. . . ."

"Well, if that's true, then why aren't you apologizing?"

"Trachea . . . crushed . . . words . . . difficult . . ."

"Sorry is such a little word. Why don't you just say it?"

"*Sorry . . .*"

"That sounds halfway genuine, Tubby. Apology accepted. Just have that five bucks by the end of the day and we'll forgo any further nastiness. Until next time, of course."

I would have given anything to be the kind of kid who barged from the crowd to push Steve away from my friend. But that fantasy would just get both of us killed. In fact, I began to go in the opposite direction, but it was against the tide of pressing kids and my feet got tangled. I sprawled backward, to my horror, and fell down inside the circle of torture.

Steve blinked down at me with his beady eyes. He released Tub, who flopped to the floor in a puddle of his own saliva. Steve turned. The basketball smacking slowed to the pace of the whale heart we'd listened to once in a biology class video. Time stretched out. I felt like one of those athletes caught in the trophy case for all of eternity.

"Ah, Sturges," Steve said. "You want in on this, too? Great news."

Over the years I'd taken my share of abuse from Steve Jorgensen-Warner, beginning with a legendary Indian burn in third grade and leading up to a sprained wrist freshman year after I'd "tripped" down the school's back steps. None of those beatings, though, had been my fault. Even Tub, locked in fetal position, looked aghast.

"Oh, wow," I said from the ground. "I should get to class. We should all get to class. Shouldn't we? I mean, isn't it time for class? I mean, wow."

The Trophy Cave amplified my blather.

SMACK, SMACK! The ball sounded positively invigorated. It was a predictor of mood as reliable as a dog's tail. A resplendent grin spread across Steve's face as he came at me with the ball, dribbling behind his back and between his legs. The guy was in his element. Had there been a hoop, he would have dunked it.

3.

All in all we got away lucky. We both got the "trash compac-tor," this nifty procedure in which you are shoved into a locker far too small to fit a teenage human, then smashed repeatedly with the door until you somehow fit anyway. It's more pain-ful than it sounds. The coat hooks gouge your scalp, the sharp corners bruise your shoulders, and if you're stupid enough to try to stop the door from slamming, you can break a finger. I've seen it happen.

Lucky for me, I'd been trash compacted enough to learn how to open lockers from the inside. I relaxed until I heard the smack of the basketball fade, and then let myself out. Tub was whimpering from the next locker, and I can't say I blamed him. He was a big guy, and simple physics meant that his extraction wasn't going to be an easy one. First I told him what he needed to do to jog the mechanism. That took a while because of the constant stream of swear words coming from the slots in the locker. The bell rang. I sighed. Now we'd be tardy.

Ten minutes later we were recuperating in the boys' room. Neither of us had any intention of walking into class late with bloodied lips and elbows. So we took our time, washing our wounds with cold water and blotting them with scratchy brown paper towels.

"Those towels are for brutes," Tub said. He ducked into a stall and came back with a fistful of toilet paper. He patted it against a scraped elbow. "Ah, now I'm being properly pampered. Is this a spa? Are we in a spa? When do we get the salt scrubs? The erotic hot-stone rubdowns? Jeeves, our itinerary, please!"

I forced a grin, which segued into a wince. Already my cheekbone was bruising. I ran through my options of concealing it from Dad. Oversize sunglasses? A jaunty scarf? Fantasy face paint? He did not react rationally when my safety was threatened.

Tub leaned in to the mirror and frowned. I'd like to tell you all about how real beauty is on the inside, because if that's the case, Tub's innards must make surgeons swoon. You could call Tobias Dershowitz chubby, if you were being cute, or husky if you were being diplomatic. The fact is he was fat, and that was only the beginning of his problems. His hair was a thick, orange, out-of-control hedge. His face spilled over with the kind of freckles that make kids like Tub look like overgrown toddlers. Worst of all were his braces, marvels of modern torment: whips of stainless steel crisscrossing each tooth separately and lashed to a dozen silver fasteners. The braces clicked so much when he spoke, you expected sparks.

He was, at least, tall, which is more than could be said for me. He stood before the mirror ramrod straight as if adjusting his military regalia, then looked around the bathroom to make sure we were alone.

"Check this out." He squirreled a hand up under his shirt and withdrew from his armpit the sweatiest five-dollar bill I'd

It was black. Nothing but black. But then the black moved.

ever seen. He held it out as if I might like to fondle it. "I had a fiver all along! The asshat didn't know where to look!"

"You really showed him, Tub."

"I know, right?"

He chuckled, folded up the bill, and inserted it back into his pit.

In the midst of pulling his shirt back over his gut, his smile faltered. Tub was a kung fu master when it came to covering up injuries with jokes. But there were moments when he ran out of steam and seemed to acknowledge, for just a moment, the bitter truth. And the truth was that the insertion of a clammy five-dollar bill into his armpit was the closest thing he had to a victory.

I hit the button on the automatic hand dryer so it might drown out my next question.

"Did you cry?"

"Nah. Not this time." He paused and shrugged. "Not a lot."

Our silence extended too long. Good old Tub knew how to remedy that. He hocked a loogie and spat it into the urinal. Then he slapped me on the back and started for the door. For a second I lingered, watching the bloody wad of snot dissolve into someone else's piss. It said a lot about our lives, I thought. When I followed him out, I resisted turning back. I could have sworn there was a rumbling coming from inside the urinal drain, somewhere far beneath the tile floor.

4.

Math was out to kill me. I'd always known it. Overall I was an average student, but multiplication and division signs were like bayonets against my brain. That Friday it didn't help that Ms. Pinkton was in a foul mood. The morning announcements were read by our student council president, who could not conceal her excitement about the Festival of the Fallen Leaves, *Shakespeare on the Fifty-Yard Line*, the game versus the Connersville Colts, and the big unveiling of the long-awaited jumbotron. All of it put Pinkton on edge.

"A scoreboard," she muttered. "What about Bunsen burners to replace those fire hazards in the lab? New calculators for calculus? A Wi-Fi signal that actually works? Have any of you seen the fetal pigs they're dissecting in anatomy? Half are deformed and the other half are freezer burned."

She was right, of course. The school's priorities could be summed up in that noise two classrooms down: *SMACK, SMACK*. Pinkton's opinions ought to have endeared her to a loser like me, except that she took out her frustrations on her students. My only hope for the semester was to slow the bleeding so I could squeak through the class with a D. Pinkton had been reminding me all week that I needed an 88 percent on next Friday's test if I had any chance of that.

Public humiliation was an important part of Pinkton's psychosis. She wasted no time calling a series of victims to the chalkboard to be struck down by a kamikaze battalion of quadratic equations. I hid behind my book, pretending that my naked fear was total absorption in a spellbinding text. It worked for thirty-five minutes but I couldn't help but peek over the top. Claire Fontaine was at the board, after all, and I couldn't miss that.

Everything Claire did was worthy of slow-motion replay, and math was no exception. The chalk swooped upward and fluttered downward. Her pilled sweater stretched this way and that. She tucked her long dark hair behind her ear and left it with an adorable smudge of white dust. I thought she was beautiful, though she wasn't in the classic sense. The popular girls would say she wasn't skinny enough. They would also point to the fact that she didn't wear makeup or do anything to tame that hair. And her clothes—well, what could be said about her clothes? Her boots were not sexy and knee-high; in fact, they were ankle-high and rubber-soled and looked suited for hiking. Her clothes were beyond vintage; they looked picked from military surplus racks, an array of pea-green coats and sand-colored skirts and multi-pocketed slacks, all of which looked as if they'd been through actual World War II combat. And that beret she wore before and after school wasn't of the look-at-me-I'm-French variety; it was more in the style of I'm-going-to-invade-your-country-and-be-your-new-dictator.

Only one thing didn't make sense: that bright pink, exceedingly girlish backpack that inexplicably hadn't one anti-establishment patch sewn onto it, nor a single permanent-marker defacement. Most thought the spotless backpack made her even weirder. To me, it meant that she just didn't care. A good backpack was a good backpack.

None of that was to say that she wasn't feminine. Believe me, she was. It just wasn't her whole deal. Though she'd only been at our school a single semester, it was obvious that she had other stuff going on in her life. That was considered a violation by the cool crowd, but she seemed ignorant of those rules, maybe because she wasn't from California. She came from across the pond. Oh, I forgot to mention that. Claire Fontaine came from the UK. That's right—the girl had an accent. I think you're starting to get the picture here.

All I can say is that Europeans must be way ahead of us in math. That's the only explanation for the way Claire tore apart equations. You could see the chalk crumbling to dust in her fist. When she was done—it never failed—she slammed a period on the end of the equation like she was finishing a sentence.

"Punctuation remains unnecessary," Pinkton said. "But nice job, Claire."

She exhaled like she'd just pinned an opponent. As she took up the eraser and wiped the board clean, Pinkton wrote a new line of gibberish and began surveying the class for the next casualty.

"We've got time for one more. Volunteer, folks. It's the American way."

I cocked my head to make myself look even more engrossed with the textbook. Pinkton's gaze swept past me and I felt a rush of pride in my acting. Then disaster: Claire was strutting back to her desk, clapping her chalky hands in front of her so that she emerged again and again from smoke like a rock star, and she happened to glance my way. I, of course, was ogling. Her lips twisted into a wry smile.

"Cheers, Mr. Sturges," she said.

That accent never failed to turn my body parts traitor. This time, it was Mr. Right Hand who betrayed me. It shot up in an overzealous wave, as if Claire were a mile away, and Señor Stupid Mouth got in on the act, too: *"Cheers to you, too, Claire!"*

"Is that you, Jim?" Pinkton asked. "What a nice change. Let's see if you can untangle this knot."

My grin wilted and I faced the equation. It looked as if both the alphabet and the number system had puked all over the board. I grimaced; the bruise on my cheek stung. I considered displaying my wounds and explaining how I could not possibly walk all the way to the board without breaking into wails of the greatest suffering. Instead I gave Pinkton my best pleading look.

She "gave me the chalk," as we called it, holding up the chalk in her fist like a middle finger.

I steeled myself, stood, took the chalk, and walked until my nose practically touched the board. Without having any idea what I was going to do, I raised my arm before realizing that Pinkton had written the equation at Claire's upmost reach, which was a good four or five inches above my own. I couldn't even reach the problem, much less solve it. I bore the laughter rising behind me and let my vision lose focus so that the eraser-swirls of chalk became a fog. A London fog, where girls like Claire Fontaine walked around kicking ass in berets and solving dangerous calculations in between forceful kisses with short, courageous men.

5.

It has been confirmed again and again throughout time that nothing strikes fear into the hearts of uncoordinated kids like a rope dangling from a gymnasium ceiling. Tub went so far as to lodge a formal complaint with the front office last year, scheduling a meeting with Principal Cole and everything. It was barbaric, Tub insisted. And a liability, too—what if some kid fell twenty feet and became paralyzed for life? Baseball, fine. Volleyball, okay. You might conceivably run across those sports later in life. But when you're an adult, when the hell are you going to encounter a rope that desperately needs to be climbed? According to Tub, he had Principal Cole in the palm of his hand until he let that *hell* slip. Cole had a no-tolerance policy for cussing. Tub was out the door and the ropes remained.

Tub and I were the only two who had yet to reach the obligatory halfway point on the rope. While the rest of the boys shot hoops, I floundered four feet off the ground, trying to figure out how the Steve Jorgensen-Warners of the world operated all four limbs independently. I held my breath and shimmied up a couple more feet. My palms burned and my legs wobbled. All I could think about was how to protect my sensitive parts if I fell.

"That a way, Sturges!" Coach Lawrence shouted. "Momentum is the key to success!"

I heard a grunt and checked the rope to my right. As opposed to my unpredictable lurches, Tub was moving steadily, though at a glacial pace. Sweat popped from his every pore and he bared his metal teeth in strain. His entire body was trembling as if it might explode.

"That's it, Tub!" In his excitement, Coach Lawrence had forgotten to use Tobias's proper last name. "You're going to kick this rope's butt! Don't you give up! Men do not give up!"

"Please, Lord, take me now," Tub whimpered. "Or Satan, anyone."

"Four more feet," I grunted. "Put your shoulders into it."

"The hell's that mean?"

"No idea."

"Then quit with the motivational speaking."

"Okay," I rasped. "Man, I wish this rope had a noose."

"Oh, wow, that'd be great. Quick, easy death, no pain."

Below us had arisen a chant: *Tub! Tub! Tub!* I glanced down and caught Coach Lawrence wincing; it was his use of the nickname that had set it off. I turned my attention back to the rope. The halfway point was marked with a red bandana just ten or twelve inches out of reach. All I had to do was touch it and then I could limp over to the bleachers and weep over my ruined muscles. I took an unsteady breath and reached up for the bandana with a sweaty hand. The threads of rope were hot iron wires in my palm.

"Sturges!" Coach Lawrence cried. "Go for the gold!"

I was drunk enough with exertion to think I could do it. Then Tub yipped. I looked and he was wagging his head around as if trying to evade a bee. It was hard to see because both of our ropes were in motion, but I saw the problem: a thread of hemp from the rope had gotten caught in Tub's braces. I knew from his cross-eyed panic just what he was envisioning: when he fell, his entire jaw would come flying out the front of his face.

Tub's rope began spinning. I lashed out with an arm to try to steady him but only felt his fingers grasp frantically at mine for an instant before his weight dragged him down. Naturally the thread of hemp snapped immediately and Tub went down on his ass, right in front of everyone.

The arm I'd used to help Tub never made it back to my rope. It pinwheeled, my feet slipped, and then I dangled from one arm. Unlike Tub, I tried to hold on and instead slid all the way down, the rope scorching my palm until I struck the floor with both knees. It hurt all the way up into my skull.

Coach Lawrence offered both of us a hand. Tub looked miserable, wounded, resigned to his fatness. The chant of his name, which for a while we could have pretended was serious, had broken apart into hoots and howls. A single basketball continued its steady SMACK, SMACK. Eventually Tub made it to his feet, rubbing his sore butt, and that's when the basketball looped over the crowd and bounced off the side of his face. You couldn't deny that it was one hell of a throw.

6.

For the second time that Friday, Tub and I found ourselves cleaning our wounds. There was little either of us could do this time to lighten the mood. Both of us had lingered in the shower, where our blood ran into the central drain. Now we were the last two guys in the locker room. I was almost dressed, but Tub sat motionless and dripping on the far end of the bench, facing away from me, still wearing his towel.

It sounded like something a teacher would say, but I couldn't come up with anything better.

"Don't let them get to you, Tub."

"Gee, thanks for that totally sound and utterly useless piece of advice, Mr. Guidance Counselor."

"They're not our friends. Who cares what they think?"

"Then who are our friends, Jim? Go ahead and list them. I'm sure I can spare the zero seconds that will take."

"Don't be dumb. We have friends."

"I'm not talking about friends that only exist in chat rooms. Or friends of the feline or canine variety. I'm talking about real, human friends who do human-type stuff, like talk and hang out and eat with silverware. Wouldn't that be great,

Jim? Some friends who knew how to use silverware? That'd be a real step up for us at this point."

Tub's eyes glowered over his bare shoulder.

"Trying to cheer me up just makes it worse," he said. "We have to accept who we are. And before you ask, I'll tell you. We're nobody. We have no life. We have nothing to look forward to. We're not special. I just want it to go away. All of it. The stupid being scared. Doesn't it seem we've been scared forever?"

"Look, remember when I was scared of monsters in my closet?" I asked.

"Now *that* was dumb. Everyone knows monsters live under the bed."

"Yeah, well, I was pretty sure it was the closet. And then I couldn't take it anymore, being afraid all the time like my dad, and so one night I got out of bed and opened the closet and got inside and spent the whole night there. Eventually I fell asleep and then it was over. I mean, it's all got to end sometime, Tub."

He didn't respond. I finished tying my shoes, too tight. The whole room felt too tight, squeezed in against my shoulders like the locker I'd been inside a few hours earlier.

"Least we've got each other," I offered.

"So true," he said. "Where you think we should set up our wedding registry?"

Though constructed with sarcastic words, the sentence had the tone of an apology. I sighed in relief and checked the clock. The bell would be ringing soon. It had been a long day for me and an even longer one for Tub.

"I bet someone gets us a nice china set," I said. "And a bread maker."

"Awesome. When the zombie apocalypse strikes, that bread maker will save our asses." He took an unsteady inhale and cleared a phlegmy throat. "You need to give me a minute, or I will never finish dressing. You got no idea how hard it is for me to put socks on."

Tub hated changing his clothes with someone else in the room. He was going to have to accept his weight at some point, but this was not the time for pushing that agenda. I ambled over to the next aisle.

The coach's office was in the far corner. The lights were off. In fact, Coach Lawrence must have hit most of the lights on his way out. Darkness lay over the locker room like a tarp. Aisles looked too long and were notched with unexpected crannies. I hesitated before going any farther. Locker rooms were places stained with bad memories: snapping towels, underwear tossed in a toilet, tennis shoes burned through a locker grill with a lighter. It was no wonder that shadows there loomed larger.

I reminded myself of the nonexistent closet monster and kept walking. I got about three steps before I saw the thing.

It was crouched in the farthest corner. I took a deep breath and leaned in, but it did not go away. It was amorphously shaped and taller than me but did not move or make a sound. In the distance, I heard the sighs of Tub getting dressed and felt a surge of protectiveness. I couldn't let this thing chase my naked friend into the hallway. That was one humiliation too many.

There was a light switch just five feet away, right between me and the thing, and I edged in that direction, my shoes splishing through some foul locker room liquid. Reaching for it felt like reaching for the red bandana on the rope. I paused, afraid to see the truth behind the thing's multifaceted folds of skin and pungent odor.

I slapped at the switch. It winked on, a single, weak bulb.

A mountain of damp gym towels sat piled in the corner. It stunk, but it wasn't exactly going to leap out and kill me. My face went hot and I almost starting kicking at the pile, except that, with my luck, that would cause a landslide and I'd be smelling like one hundred underarms for the rest of the day.

There came a clanging noise from the shower room.

I glanced over, expecting another false alarm, but noticed that the grate over the center drain had been moved aside. The streams of water leading into the drain were splattered about as if disturbed by feet. Pink daubs of Tub's blood and my own were mixed in there, too. I took a step back to try to get a better look, and my peripheral vision caught a dark shape lumbering across the opposite end of the locker room.

It was Steve; it had be Steve, out to collect from Tub his overdue five dollars. This time, I wouldn't let it happen. I lunged into the next row of lockers and just caught the back end of what might be a foot, though it looked too large for Steve. And there was a sound, a glottal, huffing snort so resounding it had to have come from a colossal chest.

I sprinted, my sneakers cracking through shallow puddles. Away from the light bulb, it was even more difficult to identify what was passing the aisles on the opposite end of the room. I saw what looked like giant, hunched shoulders dragging thick arms. But hadn't I thought the towels were a murderous blob? I sped for the next row and arrived there with a bold, terrified "AHA!"

Tub wrapped his arms around his shirtless torso. He was still working on those damn socks.

"What? Jesus! Come on! Privacy, Jim! Privacy!"

Heavy footsteps crossed somewhere behind me with such force that the tiled floor vibrated. I turned, dashed three steps, and then heard a clanging noise from the shower. I tore around the corner. The grate was back over the drain hole. Had I been wrong before? Had it been in place all along? I grabbed the mildewy wall for support, tried to catch my breath, and thought I saw the grate still shuddering, just a bit.

7.

Few Fridays had been longer. What I didn't suspect was that it was only beginning.

I exited the school alongside Tub. Predictably, several of the pumpkins lining the front entrance had been kicked in, and the two of us had to step around the scattered guts. Tub made some quip, but the orange gore turned my stomach. I was still stricken by what had happened in the locker room. Naturally I had said nothing to Tub. Either I was going crazy or the athletes of our school had been taking too many steroids. Neither possibility was going to put my best friend in better spirits.

My foot hadn't hit the sidewalk before a group of girls accosted the both of us. This being a highly suspicious event, we started searching for the bucket of pig's blood about to be dropped on our heads. But instead there were flyers in neon colors being thrust in our faces. Three of the girls were classic drama dorks decked out in the most calculatedly uncoordinated of outfits. But the fourth wore the colors of army fatigues. It was Claire Fontaine.

"Play tryouts tomorrow." She bit off the end of a licorice

whip and downed it with a swig of cola held in the same hand. "Either of you gentlemen interested?"

Gentlemen—it sounded so musical that I wished I was wearing a tuxedo with a carnation on the lapel. I looked at the hot pink flyer that Claire was holding. No surprise that the play was *Romeo and Juliet*. The drama coach, Mrs. Leach, had learned her lessons when it came to *Shakespeare on the Fifty-Yard Line*. Tradition held that the short, half-hour play was cast and rehearsed in a single week, so to keep things simple she cycled through the same four abridgments: *Hamlet, A Midsummer Night's Dream, Macbeth,* and *Romeo and Juliet*. The last had been performed so many times that it had its own nickname: *RoJu*.

"Free donuts?" Tub investigated the fine print. "It says here free donuts. How can that be true in this economy?"

Claire let out a chuckle. Her cheeks were red and the fall breeze whipped her hair out from under her beret. She hitched up her immaculate pink backpack and took another chomp of licorice. It was well known that she was a junk-food fiend; it was probably what kept her from the waif physique of the most popular girls. Personally I didn't care what kind of saturated fats and granulated sugars were to blame for that excellent figure.

She had a laugh like the pounding of random piano keys.

"See!" Tub pointed at her and gave me a victorious look. "It's a trap!"

"I'm laughing at the *word*, Mr. Dershowitz," Claire said. "They call them 'doughrings' where I'm from. I don't understand the 'nuts.' There are no nuts involved."

"Oh," Tub said. "In that case, let's reconsider this. I've got a dentist appointment tomorrow. They're putting on new braces. You probably noticed I have braces. I'm hoping the new set will be a little more dashing. But maybe I can make it afterward. I'm always up for doughrings. Nuts get stuck in my braces anyway. I guess that's not need-to-know information. I don't know why I'm still talking, to be honest. But here I am. Talking. Still."

Claire offered up the same funny lip twist she gave me in math class, the one that made me feel like we were sharing a secret. She began saying something about how there were never enough "blokes" at tryouts, and how the drama club needed "new blood," as her "da" would say. I nodded along but my attention wavered. Not many things could distract me from a direct encounter with Claire Fontaine. In fact, I could only think of one.

SMACK, SMACK.

I snatched the flyer from Claire's hand and turned up the wattage on my asinine grin.

"I'll be there," I said.

Tub shrugged and took a canary yellow flyer from one of the drama dorks.

"I'll come for the doughrings," he sighed. "Assuming I still have teeth."

"Smashing, then!" Claire popped onto the toes of her hiking boots for a moment. "Noon, right here at Saint B. You chaps practice your sonnets and work on your brogues!"

"You know it!" Tub said.

More unsuspecting males were loping down the steps, and the girls swept over to woo them with the magic of *RoJu*.

"I have no idea what she just said," Tub remarked.

I took him by the shoulder and shoved him down the

sidewalk. Tub complained, but I held tight and focused on the goal of getting us out of the parking lot. Clutches of kids obstructed our path, but I kept weaving. The sound was closer now, faster, but I couldn't pin down its origination point.

SMACK, SMACK!

Tub's protests snapped off like a busted twig.

"Oh, crap. Crappity crap-crap."

Tub pointed. Steve Jorgensen-Warner was wending his way across the parking lot, the basketball beating patiently against the pavement. Cars were making U-turns and peeling out and ripping around without mufflers, a driver's ed film come to life, and yet somehow Steve never had to disrupt his gait. He saw us and put on a chilling, placid smile.

"Tell me you still have that fiver," I hissed.

Tub shook his head.

"Vending machine. Sixth period."

I gave him an aggrieved look.

"The human body needs food, Jim!" he cried.

I scanned for a safer route. A line of school buses idled along the front courtyard. Usually I walked home, a secret I didn't share with Dad, but it would be easy to sneak Tub aboard. The driver was famously encumbered with cataracts. The only problem was that Steve and his basketball of doom were right in our path.

I dropped to my stomach and rolled under a parked truck.

"Jim? This isn't shop class! No time for oil changes!"

"Get down here!"

His transition to belly took longer than mine, but the motivation of that smacking ball worked wonders. Greasy machine parts banged against our heads while our world narrowed to a cinematic rectangle: gray sidewalks, a sliver of grass, tires crunching over broken glass, and hundreds of disembodied feet hurrying by in all directions.

SMACK, SMACK! The noise approached the rear of the truck.

"Move!" I hissed. "Next car, next car!"

My elbows and knees throbbed from the day's previous miseries, but nevertheless I used them to power me past the truck's front wheels, into the blinding light of day for a couple of seconds, and then beneath the frame of a filthy four-door sedan. Tub was at my heels, gasping for air, pouring sweat. Bumpers and springs and exhaust pipes had already torn his shirt and pulled his pants down to crack level.

Steve's ball was belting against the curb to our right. We could see his unscuffed designer shoes, the cuffs of his tailored pants. He stopped, as if detecting our position. I looked left at the thoroughfare being abused by cars. It was a dangerous, shifting maze—but then one of the cars paused to let another vehicle pull out.

"Now!" I hissed. "Now, Tub!"

I crabbed leftward, rolled through the sunlight, and then was under the idling car. Tub followed, panting. Wind blew the car's exhaust our way and we coughed and fanned it aside. There: the buses were a short sprint away if we could just get a little closer. The car above us honked and we both jumped and banged our heads on the front axle. We heard the gear shift into drive position.

We scrunched up against each other, almost hugging, and let the car pull away. As soon as we cleared the back license plate, we scrambled out of the way of an oncoming convertible, tripped across a speed bump, and went somersaulting into the next row, right between two parked cars. Steve must have glimpsed part of our blundering because the basketball picked up its pace, that awful sound like a fist into flesh.

I scuttled beneath the car to the right, Tub to the left. My fingers locked into the slots of a manhole cover. The buses were close. We could make it. I located Steve's sneakers. He was just far enough for me to dare to get Tub's attention and gesture for us to break for it. But Tub was looking at me in terror.

I'm stuck, he mouthed. *I'm stuck!*

The car above me sunk as somebody got inside of it. My body went numb and I forgot how to breathe. The car started; in seconds, it would pull away and reveal my location. The ball blasted against pavement and I saw both it and Steve's shoes moving toward our location in effortless harmony. He was five feet away, four, three, two. I clapped a hand over my mouth to keep myself from squeaking.

Metal scraped across cement, and I felt the manhole cover bounce beneath my elbow. I looked at it, expecting nothing more than vibration brought on by the car's thrumming engine. But the cover was ajar and fed into the blackness of a sewer. I blinked for a moment, confused.

And then a massive, gnarled paw reached out from the depths.

I would have screamed had my terror not been so absolute. The paw was the size of my torso, the gray skin of the palm divided into leathery segments by the scars of untold battles. The fur that covered the back of the paw was black but hardened with the brown of congealed sewage. The hand oscillated like a radar until it faced me and then pounced, wrist and finger bones crackling. I contracted into a ball, and the paw scraped across the ground. Jagged yellow claws the size of my forearm pulverized the parking lot concrete as easily as if it were Ms. Pinkton's chalk.

Far away, I heard the first bus pull away from the curb, followed by the rest.

I tried to squirm away from the manhole but was caught up by the back axle. The paw extended on an arm that just kept going, the muscles getting thicker, white scars crisscrossing the fur in gruesome glyphs. I looked to Tub for help, but he had his fists tight against his eyes, and I dimly realized that the basketball was right between our cars, beating out its patient, psychotic rhythm. I had bigger problems: the giant paw crawled at me like a spider. I curled between the rear wheels.

In a day devoid of luck, the luckiest thing saved us. The driver's side door of the car above flew open and hit the basketball, and I watched the orange sphere strike awkwardly off a nearby bumper before rolling all the way across the lot.

"Oh, man, I didn't see you," said the driver. "I'll get it. I'm so sorry. I'll get it."

There was a festering pause.

"No problem," Steve said. "I got it." But I could imagine his icy grin.

The spiffy shoes turned and went after the ball, and I rolled out from under the car and backed away on hands and knees until I was squatting against the rear bumper of a truck several spaces away, wheezing for breath, every inch of my skin tingling in the open air. My inadvertent savior drove away. After that I heard the pained hisses of Tub maneuvering himself from his undercarriage prison.

He walked over to me, dragging his weary feet. His face

was smeared with oil and his jeans were torn, and yet he was laughing.

"You know how to throw a party, Jim Sturges Jr., I'll give you that."

"Is it . . . can we . . . is it safe?"

Tub checked the lot, but he seemed unconcerned.

"Coach Lawrence nabbed him for practice. We live to fight another day, soldier."

"No . . . I mean, the *thing* . . . is it . . . ?"

Tub frowned.

"The thing. Hmmm. Can you be more specific?"

I clutched at the bumper and raised myself to unsteady feet. I patted the truck bed, taking solace in the cake of dust. It was real; I was not caught in a nightmare. I smeared the dust with my fingers and smelled it.

"If you lick that, we're no longer friends," Tub said.

With utmost caution I edged over to the empty parking space where I had been trapped. I didn't want to get too close and so skirted out into the path of exiting cars. I was met with honking and various colorful curses, but I ignored them. The cracks on the pavement that had been made by those vicious claws moments earlier looked like the unassuming marks that came with wear and tear and age. The innocent manhole cover was right where it was supposed to be.

"That." I pointed. "Look at that."

Tub leaned over the disc of iron.

"This right here?"

Tub kneeled down and brought his eye as close to the cover as his gut would allow. I tensed my stomach muscles and braced for the worst.

"I *see* it," he said.

The blood drained from my face.

"You do?"

"I sure do. You want me to get it?"

"What? No! Just get away!"

He pointed at a small pink spot on the manhole cover.

"Looks like Bubblicious to me. Let me tell you a secret: I've got gum in my pocket that's *never even been chewed*, which is a big part of what I look for in a gum. But far be it from me to stand between a man and his cravings."

8.

I didn't say a word to Tub about what I'd seen. The fact that I had no proof to show him bothered me less than that I had no proof to show myself. There were no claw marks anywhere on my skin, no tufts of fur caught in my jacket zipper. For a long time I'd worried about the mental stability of my father. It was why Mom had left us, why we lived alone in a homemade prison. What if, printed in my genetic code, was a similar insanity? Tub might abandon me, too.

I looked past the football field, where the jumbotron workers were packing it up for the day. To the east, the crags of Mount Sloughnisse were bathed in peach light. To the west, a different kind of mountain had slipped into shadow: the towers of totaled vehicles at Keavy's Junk Emporium, a legendary spot for late-night teen trespassing. I scanned the darkening sky to estimate the time. To Dad, getting home after dark was the worst possible offense.

"Hey, Pocahontas." Tub chomped at a stick of the gum he'd offered me a few minutes earlier. "If you're a few minutes late the old man will live."

"You still don't get it."

"I get that he needs to put a couple more links in your leash."

"He just worries. About a lot of things."

"Congratulations, you are today's winner of the Understatement Award! Honestly, I don't know how a guy that wound up sleeps at night."

The truth was that he didn't sleep at night. Tub knew it, too, and grimaced at his own comment. I was going to tell him not to worry about it when he perked up his head and slapped my shoulder.

"Shortcut time?" His braces flashed in a mischievous grin.

The building closest to Saint B. High was the San Bernardino Historical Society Museum, a columned edifice mostly ignored by the local population but, if rumors were to be believed, celebrated by rare-artifact aficionados all across California, whose deep pockets made it possible for the society to announce new acquisitions annually. Much more popular was the expansive garden that surrounded the museum. Rare was the weekend that you didn't see a woman in a white dress being photographed while the rest of her wedding party milled about and yawned. The garden was cordoned off by a mile-high fence, though, confounding any high schooler who wanted to save time going north.

Tub and I, though, knew a different route.

"I don't know, Tub. We're going to run out of luck one of these days."

But he was already walking backward toward the museum, wagging his eyebrows and blinding me with those metallic choppers. Even in my current mood, I couldn't help but laugh. He knew he had me and ran as fast as he could toward the front entrance. I hiked up my backpack and took

off after him. Our shoes thumped down the hedge-lined sidewalk and up the grand marble stairs, and we passed beneath
the jade owl that glared down at us from the frieze carved
over the entryway.

Weekday afternoons were dead at the museum, and we
laced through the empty queue line until we were passing
Carol, our favorite cashier. She was older than us, probably in
college, and always had an uncapped highlighter in her hand.
She glanced up at us over the tops of her glasses.

"Picked a bad day, guys."

"Good afternoon, my sweet," Tub said.

"Lempke's on the lurk. He's all pissed about some late shipment. I strongly suggest you turn back."

"No time, my dear, no time."

"It's your ass," Carol said.

Tub held out his hand as he passed the admissions window, and without looking up Carol high-fived it.

"Thanks," I said as I followed.

"You got it, good-looking."

Through the turnstiles we ran, cutting a hard right to take
a side staircase. We passed framed pieces we'd seen so many
times we no longer registered them: some royal guy in a blue
suit and a feathered cap surrounded by sporting hounds; two
lines of soldiers heading at one another with rifles a-blazing;
one of those omnipresent buckets of fruit that artists of yesteryear were so enamored with. At the top of the stairs was a
gargantuan taxidermic bison head. Tub never failed to leap up
and scratch the wiry under-beard. I didn't even try—it was too
much like the fur I'd seen coming out of the manhole.

Our path never changed. First we crossed through the Sal
K. Silverman Atrium, a skylit dome kept empty so it could be

filled with chairs for fundraisers and events. The floor was kept waxed, and we both took full advantage of the six-foot skid range. We slid out the other side of the atrium and sped past stuff that had once transfixed us: glass cabinets filled with ancient tridents; spooky masks from a dig in Ancient Mesopotamia; the reconstructed skeleton of an allosaurus.

We were giggling; the danger of this trip never failed to thrill. Straight ahead was a door marked STAFF ONLY, but we knew it was unconnected to an alarm. Tub pushed through it and we emerged into the same old ugly stairwell, onto the same old unpainted concrete steps. What was different this time was that Professor Lempke was standing half a flight above us, clipboard in hand, staring at us in shock.

Kids could talk all day about the backbreaking Ms. Pinkton or the overbearing Coach Lawrence. But they didn't know Professor Lempke. Quite possibly the most arrogant man in all of Southern California, he clearly believed himself to be the rightful heir to the secretary of the Smithsonian and was just polishing up his résumé before he got the call. He ruled the San Bernardino Historical Society Museum with a dictator's fist, and though that was probably why it was a such an esteemed institution, it was also why kids avoided it. The guy expected everyone to stand before art as one would stand before God, silent and penitent. If you were a little kid and squealed with delight, he'd ask you to leave. If you were elderly and coughed too much, he'd make the same demand.

He was our nemesis and we were his.

Lempke whipped off his horn-rimmed glasses.

"For the last time, boys, this is not your playpen! Nor is this your playground shortcut!" He stuffed the glasses into the pocket of his tweed jacket and began stamping his way down the stairs. Each step revealed argyle socks so scrupulously arranged that the diamond patterns on either ankle were in dizzying alignment.

Tub affected a contrite posture. I followed suit, hanging my head.

"This is a vaunted institution," Lempke continued, "filled with works beyond your conceptions of value. Should your horseplay knock a bust from its pedestal or a canvas from its frame, your parents would be in so much debt you'd be in the poorhouse before you could—"

"The poorhouse," that was our cue. Tub jerked from his apologetic pose and went scrambling down the stairs. I was right behind him, beating at his shoulders, panicked and giddy all at once. Lempke knew he'd never catch us in his stiff jacket and argyle socks, but he bent himself over the railing and raised his clipboard as if it were a throwing spear.

"By my count, you each owe me over nine-hundred dollars in admission fees! Don't think I won't collect! As soon as I get a free minute, there's a call coming to your mothers and fathers, mark my words!"

He had no idea that Tub lived with his grandmother and I only had one parent. Depressing thoughts usually, but for the moment the joke was on Lempke. We burst from a service entrance onto a loading dock, laughing like mad, and we didn't stop running until we were back on the road. We hung on to each other for a few minutes until we got to the first intersection, reliving the escape through gasped sentence fragments.

We gathered our breath and grinned at each other. Our wounds from the long day no longer looked so pathetic. They looked like tattoos shared by warriors of the same tribe. I felt great. Then I noticed the sky. It was dark, almost full night. We must have spent more time in that parking lot than I had thought.

Tub grabbed me around the neck and expelled an affectionate sigh.

"I know your pop's uptight," he said. "But, seriously, how worried could he be?"

A siren squelched. We looked down the perpendicular road and were bathed in swirling red-and-blue light.

9.

Word on the street was that Sergeant Ben Gulager had been born with that lush mustache, and many a playground bounty had been placed on photographic evidence. It was just Gulager's third most notable physical feature. His hairpiece was also awe-inspiring, though only in its ineptitude, a black bowl-cut mop that always looked as if he had put it on sideways.

Yet no one dared laugh at Sergeant Gulager. The hairpiece existed to conceal his most defining characteristic, a gruesome, puckered scar on his right temple. Ten years before he had been the first responder to a domestic disturbance on the south side of the city, a garden-variety case of plate-throwing between husband and wife. But after Gulager arrived, things turned ugly, and the father whipped out a gun and started waving it at the triplets huddled behind the sofa. Gulager had not hesitated to throw himself in front of the girls, taking a bullet to the skull at nearly point-blank range.

His survival had been one of those miracles of physics at which doctors shrug. Surgeons judged it too risky to remove the nine-millimeter bullet from its position halfway between skull plate and brain matter, and six months later Gulager was back on the force, no different except for a relentless stutter. The hair around the wound never grew back.

The mustache, though, that was pure style.

I can tell you from experience that one thing worse than being handed to your dad by a cop is being handed to your dad by a cop who is a local hero, a man who has never, as far as anyone can tell, done anything wrong in his entire life, and would certainly never come home late enough to make his family worry.

"You realize, Mr. St-St-Sturges, that this can't go on muh-muh-muh-much longer."

Released from Gulager's grip, I slunk across the kitchen and leaned against the refrigerator. Through the open front door, I could see Tub slumped in the back of the police cruiser, looking despondent behind the fiberglass.

Dad threw me a baleful glance before giving Gulager his most chastened look.

"Sergeant, you have my word. Jim Jr.'s a good boy, but in this matter I'm at a loss, same as you. I have told him, again and again, *emphasized* to him, *stressed* to him the importance of getting home on time. Nighttime is dangerous for everyone, but especially boys of Jim's age—"

Gulager cleared his throat.

"Sir, it's not J-J-Jim that I'm talking about."

Dad adjusted his glasses by the Band-Aid and squinted.

Gulager drew a report book from his back pocket and flipped it open.

"May the twenty-sixth, seven-oh-five p.m. We picked him up a bluh-bluh-bluh-bluh-block away—"

"Well, that's two blocks, really, if you count Oak Street—"

"June the fifth, seven-ten p.m., two huh-huh-hundred feet away—"

"It was raining that night. Anything can happen in the rain—"

"July the ninth. August the tenth. September the th-th-th-th-third."

"Sergeant. I'd like to stop calling you. I would. But the world is a dangerous place. Surely, you of all people . . ."

Gulager raised an eyebrow and a portion of his gnarled scar dipped beneath the edge of the shaggy toupee. For a few seconds Dad looked obstinate before his shoulders sagged.

"I know," he whispered. "I apologize."

While he wasn't being looked at, Gulager's eyes flitted about the room, taking in the steel shutters, the three control panels' worth of blinking lights, the front porch security camera buzzing above his head. Lastly his eyes landed on me and I read his sympathy. I felt both grateful and offended. I stuck out my chin and Gulager sighed.

"Luh-luh-look, Mr. Sturges." He crooked a thumb at his cruiser. "I need to drop off the portly one. I'm not going to raise any k-k-k-k-kind of official stink about this. But I want to explain something, and I wuh-wuh-want you to pay attention. There *are* dangerous things out there. And those dangerous things n-n-n-n-n-need our attention. That's why you are not to call us again. Not for something like th-th-this. We cannot spare the manpower. Am I muh-muh-making myself perfectly clear?"

"Of course." Dad's voice was soft. "Thank you."

Gulager held our eyes for a moment longer as if showing his willingness to listen if there was something else we wanted to say. But one thing we Sturgeses were good at was keeping our mouths shut. Gulager nodded briskly enough that his boyish wig shimmied, snapped shut his report book, and turned away, donning his hat. The security camera tracked him on his way to the cruiser.

Dad closed the door and began the safety song of the ten different locks, though this rendition was more maudlin than I'd ever heard it: *Click. Rattle. Zing. Rattle. Clack-clack-clack. Thunk. Crunch. Whisk. Rattle-rattle.* I held my breath for the final note, the conclusive *thud*. But Dad's hand had quit working. His thumb slid off the deadbolt and dangled at his side.

When he faced me, his lips were quivering.

"I have my reasons, Jimmy. I know it seems unfair. All I'm asking is that you honor my request. Be home before dark. Son? Please? Be home before dark?"

I felt anger. I felt frustration. I felt pity. All were emotions I didn't like feeling about my dad. He was losing it. Year by year, day by day, he was getting worse, and it reminded me too much of myself in the school parking lot that afternoon, jumping at shadows and hallucinating monsters.

"I don't get it," I said. "I just don't get why."

He leaned in, so close I could smell the salt of his welling tears.

"Because it is not safe." His jaw shook; the teeth rattled. "I've lost too much already, and I promised myself it wouldn't happen again. And it won't, not on my watch."

I don't know what he saw when he looked at me. It wasn't the cheekbone bruise from my trash compacting or the blisters on my hands from the gymnasium rope or the scuffed knees from the parking lot chase. As always he was distracted by his own murky memories of the older brother who once

"You know the deal, Tubby. Five bucks a day. I regret if this wasn't clear."

called him "Jimbo." He turned, punched complicated codes into all three control panels and waited for the varied automated responses: *Residence Secured. Total Lockdown Achieved. Safety Mode 3-A Initiated.* He flicked a switch and nighttime floodlights bathed the front and back yards. Neighbor dogs to both sides of our house howled their nightly disapproval.

Dad moved down the hall in his slippers, not making a sound. He entered his bedroom, closed the door, and after thirty seconds I heard the soft sounds of a familiar song playing from his old speakers, a syrupy tune I'd been hearing all of my life, some song by an oldies group called Don and Juan.

"I stood on this corner, / Waiting for you to come along, / So my heart could feel satisfi-i-i-ied. . . ."

10.

When midnight came, I learned it from pop-up warnings on my phone and laptop. I had set the alarms to make sure I got some sleep after the long day, but I dismissed both of them in disgust. All the lights in my room were off and my eyes were straining at the screen, yet sleep wasn't going to happen, not anytime soon.

I wasn't making it any easier on myself with the subject of my surfing. Instead of studying math, I'd been scouring the most popular video sites, and some lesser-known ones, too, on a hunt for anyone else who'd seen what I'd seen. My initial searches, limited to subjects like "sewer drains" and "locker rooms," came up empty, but after ninety minutes of tweaking I'd found a second layer of content, videos so unpopular and poorly indexed that you had to learn a new language of misspelling to have a shot at uncovering them. Most of these were blurred snippets of absolutely nothing, while drunken voices hollered off-camera, "Look at that! Look at that right there!"

It was when I began noticing location tags that I started to sweat. I found no less than six videos posted within the past six years uploaded from right here in Saint B. To call these videos amateur would be putting it nicely, but that doesn't mean there wasn't something moving through those dimly lit alleys and behind those distant dumpsters. The videos were marked with only one or two "likes" and underscored with comments along the lines of *omg so fake*. But to someone who'd seen hands and feet and shoulders of unimaginable dimension, the shapes looked eerily familiar.

It got so I couldn't take any more. I tore out my earbuds. Right away I wished I hadn't done it. The stillness in the house was unnatural. I can't put it better than that. It was as if there were new mouths in the house sucking up our supply of air. I could hear things I normally couldn't: the buzzing from the front porch security camera, Dad's breathing from his bedroom.

The idea that someone could be inside, though, was insane. The place was a fortress. You couldn't get through our doors without a chainsaw and blowtorch, not to mention the screaming of multiple alarms and the arrival of three different security company vans. Through the crack in my door, I could see the proof on the other side of the living room: two red lights signifying that the various security systems were armed. I had been watching those two lights from bed all my life. So why did they seem wrong to me?

The two lights blinked.

Yes, that's what was bothering me.

They weren't console lights at all. They were *eyes*.

I lay there, unable to breathe, as the red eyes shifted about. Floorboards moaned beneath a great weight. I heard an exhale like the nickering snort of a horse. And then the red eyes moved from the far edge of the living room, revealing the much smaller security console bulbs behind it. Whatever it was, it was coming toward the bedrooms. It was about the worst thing I could possibly imagine. Until the next thing happened.

More eyes opened: three, four, five, six, seven, eight. Each of them swam in the same space of air as if connected to the same head, though each operated independently, some snaking to the left, some to the right, some glancing backward, and the rest straining right at me. Whatever this thing—or things—was, it filled the entire hall. I looked over the edge of my bed for some kind of weapon, but all I could see was kids' stuff: half-built models, unfinished homework, and random other evidence of a guy trying to figure out what he was good at. None of it had helped me before, and it wasn't going to help me now.

The first door it reached was Dad's. Like me, Dad kept it cracked open and all I could do was hope that he was already crouched for attack. A few of the red eyes disappeared from view as they entered his room. I heard a jangling, as if the thing were reaching into pockets filled with change, and then an unpleasant, moist noise that continued for a good minute: *Sluuuurp. Sluuuurp. Sluuuurp. Sluuuurp.*

My shoulders shook so violently I grabbed the laptop to steady them. Yes—the laptop! The screen had gone to sleep but all I needed to do was jog the touch pad and it would fill the room with white light. I reached for it but hesitated. Something warned me that what I might see would haunt me forever. I might end up like my dad. If I was too afraid to do it, though, wasn't that just as bad?

A shadow fell over me. I know that seems strange, as the house was completely dark, but this dark had weight: I could feel it cover my body like a layer of mud. It had texture, too:

scaly, cold, slithering across my skin. And it most definitely had a smell: a brackish funk like a dead animal rotting at the bottom of a well. Though the slurping noise was still emitting from my father's bedroom, several of the eight eyes had squirmed their way through the crack of my bedroom door and orbited the foot of my bed like slow, radioactive bugs.

Faces filed through my mind: Tub, Claire Fontaine, Dad. It was a good-bye, I think, because, in a way, I was doing this for them. I spun the laptop around and swiped the touch pad.

There was no moment of adjustment; light was everywhere. My eyes, so wide and frightened, instinctively shut, and I had to blink and blink and blink before the spots swam away and I could see beyond the foot of my bed. I saw the closet at the other end of my room, the door, the hallway outside, the living room.

Nothing was there.

Here is the truth. I didn't feel relief. I didn't feel joy. I shoved the computer off my lap and sunk my head into my hands, clawing my fingernails into my scalp. This was it, then. My sanity was bidding me adieu. Impulsively I threw back the covers. I would get out of bed, turn on all the lights, and scour the rest of house. I had to. Maybe there would be some evidence that absolved me from my derangement. I swung my legs around and was about to stand when my eye caught the closet.

Like I'd told Tub, it had been my closet that had scared me the most when I was little. Still, it was awful small for the thing I had seen drifting through the house—though with all those eyes moving around it had been impossible to accurately gauge its size.

My heart was hammering as I put one foot down. The

floorboards creaked. I winced at the noise but kept my eyes on the closet, trying to catch any motion behind the slats. Then, carefully, I put my other foot down. Again, the floor creaked. Still no movement inside the closet. All the fears of my childhood came rushing back. I had no choice but to go up to it, fling it open, and take whatever came next.

I stood and craned my neck for a better look.

The computer's light revealed that the closet was empty.

Then two massive furred paws shot out from under my bed and locked around my ankles, sinewy palms greased with hot sweat, jagged yellow claws cold as a river. After the paws yanked but before my head struck the floor, I had but a single, rueful thought:

Tub was right. Under beds, that's where the monsters live.

PART II

The Killaheed Cometh

11.

Water dripped into my eye. It was acidic and stung. I rubbed at it and became aware of stiff needles of straw poking at my skin. More drops of liquid splashed down, and I sat up, wiping at my face with an elbow. I saw that I still wore my bedtime sweatpants and T-shirt. A pile of dirty straw, though, had replaced my bed, and a cave had replaced my room.

On unsteady legs I rose, brushing off the straw. The room looked to be carved from rock, though what I could see of the ceiling was threaded with the bottommost layer of the real world: gurgling, ancient water pipes; openings of moss-coated sewer canals; and scorched electrical grids covered with soot. Orange rust water dripped steadily from a dozen outmoded joints. A single passageway led out of the room into a hallway. A claustrophobic instinct told me to take it.

My sight adjusted as I walked, and I began to make out piles of junk all around me. Had it been random trash, I would have been less frightened. Instead, it was painstakingly organized. To my left was a hill of typewriters, old-timey ones with manual return carriages as well as models from the 1980s featuring miniature display screens. The whole pile reeked of ink. To my right was a wall of microwave ovens stacked like brickwork—black ones, white ones, brown ones, red ones—some of them old and dusty, others newer and still spattered with the remains of their last meals. All of them were unmistakably broken.

I moved into the hall. To my surprise it was illuminated by oil sconces hung higher than I could reach. Lamps didn't light themselves—I reminded myself to walk softly, though it didn't much matter. The place was loud with the hissing of the lamps, the babbling of water through the overhead pipes, and a subterranean rumble that must have been the foul-smelling air churning through the underground passages. This was worse than any Trophy Cave I'd ever imagined.

The hall branched off into several rooms, each stocked with other detritus of human life. One room contained a quicksand of watches: digital, analogue, calculator; men's, women's, kids'; and so many of them that you'd have to wade waist-deep through the glittering moat. Another room was filled with fans: dust-coated ceiling fans, plastic desk fans, big industrial fans that stood on thick metal poles. Cords from a few wreathed up into the tracery of pipes and wires, and those fans were on, the blades clanging and the gears grinding with every oscillation. The last room I dared look inside was the worst: refrigerators, maybe fifty of them in every condition, standing like headstones in a grassless graveyard.

The end of the hall opened into a spacious cavern lit by a bright fire, though I struggled to make out any details through the rain of fetid water dripping from the towering entryway—a stone arch that looked as if it had been grafted from a sixteenth-century church. I began to pass through but paused in astonishment, the oily water weighing down my hair.

It was a cathedral of junk. Everywhere I looked, piles were gathered against grimy brick walls, these artifacts even more frightening because they were the stuff of kids. There was a mountain of cheap toy weapons. Jumbled in a corner were a thousand mismatched roller skates, one or two of which were squeaking as they rolled across the uneven floor. There were two dueling towers of lunchboxes emblazoned with happy cartoon faces. Most disturbing of all was the gigantic pyramid that dominated the room: bicycles, hundreds of them dissolving into rust, tangled together and reaching twenty feet into the air.

Clusters of flickering fluorescent lights were bundled together with wire and rigged into some source of stolen power. But their sick blue glow paled next to the hot white fire that burned from an oven at the far side of the room, crackling as if recently fed. I could not resist walking toward it as humans had done since the dawn of time.

A butte of discarded dolls blocked my view of the oven's mouth. I began to circle my way around the dolls when the flames revealed a large stone mural carved into the wall. It was rough-hewn but of jagged complexity. On the right it seemed to depict a series of beasts exiting from beneath a series of bridges to board a large sailing ship. This same ship was present on the left of the mural, with more beasts departing and ducking beneath new bridges.

Spanning across the entire ocean was a rendering of what seemed to be the most important bridge of all. Carvings of grasping hands, paws, tentacles, and claws all reached up toward the central stone, which depicted a horrid lording figure with six arms. Its eyes were uneven: one was a sparkling ruby embedded in the stone, the other a gaping abscess.

Those details were lurid, but what was carved beneath them was worse. It seemed to suggest a war between beasts and humans so tumultuous that you could not tell where one raised club melded into another firing gun, or where one biting mouth blended into another swinging axe. I averted my gaze to the border of the mural, which was made up of portraits of individuals I could only assume were important figures. All of them were hideous. One had a dog's snout and fangs. The next had practically no head at all, its beady eyes centered upon its smooth chest. The third had scarlet eyes, eight of them on long stems.

The eyes swayed.

They were not part of the mural.

The thing from my house glided toward me with surprising grace for something with an indeterminate number of legs, all of which were hidden behind a patchwork kilt scaled with layers of medals, prizes, trophies, and award ribbons. An incalculable tangle of tentacles twined around one another as if dying to squeeze something to death. As it passed the oven, the firelight revealed the thing's olive-green coloring, reptilian texture, and lacquer of slime lubricating its undulating appendages. Its mouth, a horizontal gash, opened and released a strangled bleat:

"Grrruuuuglemmmurrrrrph."

My feet caught in a knot of doll hair and I fell.

The thing came faster, nattering with nonsensical grunts. I was on my back and covered with grinning, poseable plastic. I could feel the heat of the stove and wondered if it might house a poker or some other sort of weapon. But there was no time. The thing was stomping dolls flat and leaning right over me. Tentacles threaded the air. Eight eyes hovered over my field of vision. I braced for destruction.

But a few of the eyes behaved as if uncertain that I was there. Like an idiot, I passed a hand back and forth in front of one of them. It did not react. I considered running. Was I fast enough to bolt before feeling one of those tentacles tighten around my neck?

"He can't see you," a voice said. "He's nearly blind."

The horrid thing straightened up and turned toward the oven. It gibbered a few more indescribable syllables. I looked in that direction, too, and saw, rising from a squatting position by the mouth of the oven, a man made of metal. Rising with him were two long, glimmering swords. The blades of both were stained with blood. He flicked them to expel the excess carnage and then, in a single expert movement, sheathed the weapons in twin scabbards bolted to his back.

"His name's Blinky," he said. "Trolls have a sense of humor about their names."

He paused.

"Not about much else, though."

The man's voice squawked with feedback, as if forced through a ramshackle stereo speaker. In fact, that looked to be the case: covering his mouth was the metal grill of an antiquated boom box. He was not, I saw, a robot, but rather a human-sized being equipped in specialized gear. Like everything down here, the suit was constructed of junk. The mask was dominated by an oversize pair of aviator goggles, but also featured part of an old football helmet, ear protectors made out of industrial headphones, and a chinstrap fashioned from a child's slingshot.

All of the junk had once belonged to children.

The missing children.

The Milk Carton Epidemic.

I found that I couldn't move.

His armor, if that's what it was, was just as incredible. His fingers flexed within mismatched winter gloves coated with sharp tacks. His forearms were studded with soda caps, each one of them dimpled from bottle openers. His biceps were protected with the wire from a hundred spiral-bound school notebooks. His chest was plated with relics from a little girl's baking set, miniature pans in the shapes of hearts and stars and horses. All down his stomach were die-cast cars and trucks, their little chrome parts shining in the firelight. Both of his legs were wrapped over and over in bike chains. Some were red with rust, but a few still glimmered with oil.

When he moved, it sounded like a bowlful of nails being stirred.

I rolled away from both him and the troll—Blinky, if that was to be believed—and leapt to my feet. The man stopped advancing. The handles of his swords jutted up behind his head like horns. I had not forgotten that they dripped with blood.

The metal man held up a hand. The tacks glinted in the firelight.

"You need to listen to me."

"Why?" I asked. "Who are you? Where am I?"

"We don't have much time."

"Why not? What are you going to do to me?"

"You overslept. It's almost dawn."

"What happens at dawn?"

"You go home."

"I don't believe you."

"There's no time to explain."

"Talk fast, then."

He sliced a hand through the air. Metal chimed against metal.

"We do *not* have *time!*"

From a distant chamber came a growl of something large awakening.

"Now you've done it," he said. "You've woken ARRRGH!!!."

The battle cry slammed around the cavern. When it was gone, the only sounds were the man's quick breaths and the toy cars attached to his chest, spinning their tiny wheels.

Then even those sounds were overtaken. Massive footsteps began crashing from inside a tunnel next to the stone mural. Everything in the cave reacted to the vibration: roller skates escaped, plastic guns tumbled and made electronic shooting noises, bikes spun their flat tires.

I backed away.

"Arrrgh?"

"You're not listening. I told you to listen." The metal man took a deep breath. "ARRRGH!!!."

I backed away some more.

"Three *R*s, three exclamation points. Take my advice and don't mispronounce it."

"I won't mispronounce it, I swear."

The goliath emerged from the tunnel as comfortably as a dog from a doghouse, coarse black fur pouring into the chamber before I could make out any actual arms or legs. It rose to its full height after passing beneath the archway and stretched its arms as if working out the kinks of a nap. Even beneath the fur I could see huge loops of muscles flexing. The same clawed paws I recognized from the manhole, as well as from under my bed, tightened into fists.

ARRRGH!!! was built like a gorilla but three times larger: two arms, two legs, and, thankfully, just two eyes. Horns, curled like those of a ram, nicked across low-hanging pipes. One of the pipes sprung a leak and gray water spilled across greasy fur. The thing's orange eyes cast about with animal perceptiveness, and it raised its snout and sniffed. Its mouth fell open to reveal a purple, slavering mouth armed with haphazard daggers of teeth.

It had smelled me.

I retreated until I was backed against a pile of bedsprings. ARRRGH!!! crossed the room in four colossal lopes that shook rust from overhead pipes like falling snow. The beast loomed over me, then bent at the waist so that its wet nose was inches from my face. It sniffed once, then exhaled. The blast blew the hair back from my face. Viscous drops of saliva fell from a chipped tooth and pooled warmly on my stomach. Its avid eyes, each the size of a softball, catalogued my details.

It snarled and the bedsprings sang.

The metal man slipped a gloved hand between two cake pans of his chest plate, scrounged for a moment, and then withdrew a bronze medallion swinging upon a dirty chain. The symbols were clear even from a distance: a long-sword, an unrecognizable language, and the howling mug of a troll.

"Put this on," he said.

ARRRGH!!! took one look at the medallion, turned its awful face to the ceiling, and let loose with a tyrannosaurus roar. Its horns struck a patch of fluorescents, and sparks spilled upon the metal man like molten rain. Whether ARRRGH!!!'s cry was one of rage or elation, I couldn't tell. What I could tell was that both characters were distracted.

I bolted for the nearest corridor, passing the metal man so closely I could have swiped the medallion had I wanted to, which I did not. They all noticed: I heard a jangle of bike chains, an apelike snort, and the moist slurp of multitudinous feet scrambling across the cave.

"Prrrruuummffffflllarrrrggg!"

Blinky's cry rattled my bones as I dove into the passageway. I collided against a cold wall. There were no lamps. I pressed one hand to the wall and kept moving. The tunnel crooked left; I managed not to flatten my face. It crooked right; I lost contact with the wall and spent a few seconds floundering in the eclipse. Drifting from behind were ominous sounds of pursuit.

Instantly, I was lost.

"Stop! Don't go any farther!"

The man of metal was closing in. I took the darkness at a suicidal sprint. Then I noticed a light. It was dim, but I picked up my pace until I found myself hurtling through a hall so narrow that I could feel the walls press at both of my shoulders. There was a glow here just bright enough to allow me to avoid crashing into the tunnel's dead end. What a sad, dark place this was to die.

Something wet ran down my cheek, and I looked up to see that the light came through a drain pipe just wide enough for me to crawl through. The idea of wedging my body inside was the worst thing I'd ever considered, but at least ARRRGH!!! and Blinky, both of whom were getting closer, would be too large to follow. I gripped the edge of the pipe and hauled myself into it.

Sewage filled the bottom few inches, and the fecal stink had me gagging. The metal man would hear; the only option was to crawl farther. Using my elbows and knees I inched through the morass. My head bumped along the pipe's ridges and sewage soaked through my clothes, but I kept moving—the light was growing brighter.

The end of the pipe took a dramatic downward slant. I peered over the edge and could see nothing but mud. But there were light sources down there, potentially hundreds, flickering in restless patterns. There was noise, too, not the industrial drone of the sewers but voices, shouts, laughter, the clunking of wood, the ringing of metal, the rattle of what sounded like coins.

I had no other choice. I wiggled myself forward. For a terrible second I thought I was stuck and entertained a fantasy of being drowned in sewage over a period of weeks, but then I pushed off with my feet and shot out the end of the pipe.

For two seconds I was airborne. Then I landed in a soft pile that, given its placement beneath a sewer pipe, I shouldn't have been surprised to learn was not, in fact, mud. I sat up and glopped the muck from my face in handfuls. Finally I gave up and sat there, panting and reeking. It took a minute for me to appreciate that I could see quite well by the torchlight. It took even longer to appreciate the sound of a bustling marketplace. I had not looked up from my lap yet. I wondered if I should. The lights and the sounds seemed so familiar, so *ordinary*, until I remembered that I was somewhere deep underground and nothing down here was ordinary.

I looked.

12.

It was an entire city of trolls. The landscape of narrow pathways and askew structures stretched for a good mile before dropping into darkness. Sloppy, mud-packed dwellings were everywhere but largely empty, having voided their troll contents so that they might take part in the clamorous bazaar. Smoke rose from food stands, where small skinned corpses of what I hoped were squirrel and rabbit roasted on spits. Other lean-tos offered up strange works of art: foreboding crests printed on rawhide, stones polished so that they glowed as if lit from within, bizarre periscopes and outlandish metronomes and other devices. Steam billowed from shop fronts where glowing metal rods were hammered into shape. Cauldrons of mysterious goo were stirred and poured into crude wooden bowls. And everywhere there was bartering: misshapen coins going from tentacle to paw, satchels of croaking frogs traded for jars of lightning bugs, and seemingly indistinguishable rocks scrutinized through a magnifying glass and set upon scales before their cautious exchange.

Crawling, stomping, and slinking through this demented metropolis was a pageant of beasts of indescribable variety. The first to notice me was a trio of ten-foot behemoths pulling behind them the remains of a car frame with every square inch wrapped in Christmas lights. The three trolls were of alarming complexion, sported gray beards down to their knees, and were identical aside from the pattern of their scars. Actually, there was one more difference: only one of them had an eye, a bulging sphere that flicked around with birdlike sensitivity. The cyclops saw me and held up an arm to halt his companions, each of whom had a single empty eye socket. When the eyeless ones began to yammer unhappily, he removed the eye, which looked wrinkled and dry, and handed it to the left one, who stuffed it into his own socket. In this slow fashion, they each took a turn staring.

I stood up, dripping sewage. I could dash past them, but was I safer right here?

From somewhere nearby came the earsplitting answer. It was ARRRGH!!!.

I raced at the left troll, currently eyeless, and though he swiped an arm in my direction, I ducked beneath it and found myself barreling down a main avenue. Suddenly there were trolls on every side of me, their bizarre anatomies brushing across my skin. Some were gargantuan, and I dove between their legs. Others were less than a foot high and scurried about like vermin, clambering over one another and rattling tiny shields and sabers. Some wore threadbare capes and tattered gowns complete with frayed insignias. Others wore makeshift tunics of thistledown and thornbush. Most, though, were naked, and I saw them as a blur of colors: jet black, burnished bronze, pink as tongue, red as blood.

Bursting from the crowd, I found myself inches from a butcher counter. I collided with it. Carcasses swung wildly. A noseless, cross-eyed troll wearing a dirty apron and holding a rusty butcher knife bellowed in outrage. I backpedaled into a mass of hungry customers, who at last had time to notice the human invader in their midst. Deafening foghorn bellows were joined by high-pitched snarls and resounding grumbles. Answering their call, from two aisles over, was ARRRGH!!!.

Pelted arms and scaled hands and chilly tentacles tried to hold me in place, but I wriggled free, rolled beneath the butcher counter, and shot out into a side alley, cutting through a family of pudgy blue trolls with skeleton wings that flapped in agitation. A six-foot mass of yellow hair—which, oddly, was topped with a pair of lit candles—slumped down the alley toting a pig's head on a stick, which I assumed was a kind of scepter before I saw him nibble on it. It was a snack. I veered away and came upon a line of crude wheelbarrows filled with goods. I skittered aside and butted into a troll so withered his ribs poked out from his flesh, each one adorned with bejeweled rings that jangled like a tambourine as he squabbled his dissatisfaction to a troll resembling a giant, armless worm. There was a gash in the worm's stomach, and I thought it was a stab wound until four smaller worms poked their heads out of the marsupial pocket.

Both trolls halted their argument and looked at me.

"Sorry to interrupt," I said. "It looks good. Really. I wish I had my wallet."

It did *not* look good. The wheelbarrow was stacked with jars of a granola-like substance, except instead of oats, nuts, and raisins, it was roaches, hair, and teeth. I turned to reverse my direction when I saw a familiar black-furred giant poke its snout into the alley. Its orange eyes lasered in on me.

ARRRGH!!! huffed with such force that two smaller trolls were taken down by the spray of snot.

I jumped over the wheelbarrow. My toe caught a jar and it shattered on the ground, white teeth bouncing across brick and roaches racing away into crevices. From behind came the pound of my pursuer's feet. Up ahead, a troll with a leathery baby face mischievously tied together the ponytails of two spotted trolls locked in separate disputes. I ducked beneath the knot, leapt over a smolder pit, and kicked through a low wire fence surrounding two little green creatures with long, furry tails facing off in battle. I spun around and found myself surrounded by gambling trolls clutching coins and howling at the disruption of the fight. I shouted apologies and hurtled over the opposite fence, the furry green gremlins snapping at my heels.

Vice was all around me. Intertwining strains of music cranked out of a busted accordion and a warped Victrola. Neon beer signs, flashing crosswalk signals, and whirling bits of carnival machinery, all stolen from the human world, lent a hallucinatory, strobe-lit feel to this red-light district. I whirled around like a drunkard until I bounced off a large-breasted female troll who had proudly modified her body with the contents of a human sewing kit. Her toes had been replaced with thimbles, several of her fingers with pinking shears, her nipples with mismatched buttons, her hair with unraveling spools of yarn. She smiled at me luridly. Her toothless gums had been fitted with hundreds of sewing needles.

I stumbled down another alley. Groups of trolls hunched over strange war games built of stone, and all of them were cheating—I could see extra playing pieces stuffed into their fur. Other gangs tossed hubcaps at a weathered old tetherball pole while one troll kept score by making claw slashes on a board. Everywhere I looked, fights broke out. These scuffles were sudden, savage, and generally short-lived; after a few blows, the disgruntled beasts returned to their games and their stone steins of foamy mead.

Strangest of all were the TVs. In this district they were everywhere. Oversize cabinet models from the '70s, portable black-and-white sets from the '80s, sleek monitors from the '90s, and the occasional high-definition brands of the modern day. Some were piled on the ground and others lashed to wooden poles with barbed wire, but all of them were jerry-rigged with makeshift antennae and attached to dozens of extension cords that snaked into the overhead power grid. Not a single program played on these sets. Instead, they broadcast different patterns of static. Trolls handed over money (or small rodents) for the privilege of standing slack-jawed and glassy-eyed in front of the bad signals.

ARRRGH!!! was less impressed. The troll bounded through sawhorses and fences. TVs were destroyed, board games scattered, and mead cups overturned. Countless trolls bayed their chagrin. Heart pounding, I wove through the smallest thoroughfares I could find, sliding between tightly packed shacks so the troll couldn't follow.

It didn't work. ARRRGH!!! began tearing these shacks to pieces. It was like trying to outrun a tornado. I fled with my arms above my head to protect myself from the hailstorm of wood and metal siding, and kept jagging around every bend I could find. The lights of the gambling district faded, and I became aware of a dramatic decrease in population. The slap of my feet against brick was replaced by squirts of mud. Each landing of ARRRGH!!!'s feet sounded like the dropping of a boulder into a thick mire.

Right away I identified the sparkle of water. Buildings were growing sparse, so I had no option except to sprint for it. With ARRRGH!!!'s hot breath burning my neck, I made it in thirty seconds. It was not the cool, rippling brook I had imagined but a sweltering ditch of excrement that twined through the underworld. Four or five trolls with ornate tusks were scattered along the bank using nets to capture junk that tumbled along in the current. This looked to be the main point of entry for much of the trash with which the troll city was built. Hills of it, yet to be categorized, towered behind each fisherman.

I sprung across the creek at its narrowest point and clawed my way up the bank. This was the edge of the city. Sporadic campfires lit by solitary trolls revealed the wooden braces that kept the cliffs from collapsing. The light was dim as I raced past and I was grateful, because the body parts I glimpsed were hideous—ancient, powerful beings whose quietude suggested that they wanted only to die in peace. Their flesh was covered in lichen and toadstools from decades of inactivity.

A figure swung down from an overhead pipe and landed on two legs in front of me. Firelight reflected from his aviator goggles and soda-cap forearms. For an instant I felt the notebook spirals around his biceps before pushing away, but there behind me, emerging from the gloom, were the eight red eyes of Blinky. I spun on my heel and started in a third direction but was met by ARRRGH!!!, whose cemetery teeth gleamed from the darkness.

"You've wasted so much time." The metal man's voice crunched from his stereo speaker between blasts of static. He raised a spiked glove. Dangling there was the bronze medallion. "Don't make me say it again, Jim Sturges. Put this on before it's too late."

It took a few seconds before I recognized my own name. This had been no random abduction, which meant Dad had been right: there had been things in the night trying to get me. I thought of the ten locks on our front door and for the first time ever longed to hear their protective rhythm.

The man of metal read my mind.

"Your father refused this once," he said. "Don't make the same mistake."

My muscles trembled with overdue exhaustion, and my mind gave out beneath the madness of all that had happened. I wanted to cry but didn't have the energy. I slumped and hung my head, defeated by the stink of troll breath and the icy realization of a terrible truth. I covered my face with my hands.

"You're the ones," I said, "who took Uncle Jack."

"Yes."

"Who ruined Dad's life."

"Yes."

"And now you want to ruin mine."

"Take this." The medallion jangled. "Take this and you'll see."

A piercing ululation tore through the air. I dropped my hands. Bells rang throughout the city and shepherds' horns were blown. I turned to look and saw the snuffing of a hundred fires at once, the lowering of flags and the folding of scaffolds, the silhouette of carts and wheelbarrows pushed from the center of town to the edges. The ground began to shake as every single troll hurried to clear the streets. Many were headed in our direction. The stampede was coming.

That's when I saw the ray of sunshine.

It broke through a crack somewhere overhead, firing like a lightning bolt into the mud near the sewage creek. The ray of light widened, and I heard the strangled yelp of one of the fishermen as he went down. That began the panic. Shrieks rose up, one after another. A second ray of light struck a leaning tower in the center of the city.

"You!" The man of metal thrust the medallion at me. "Take this! Now!"

"But they're coming—"

"Happens every morning," he snapped. "Put it on!"

Sunlight stabbed through dozens of cracks then, turning the cavern into a quilt of light and dark through which threaded the scattering forms of a thousand unbelievable ogres. A large blade of sun shot down just ten feet away. I couldn't help it—I took a step toward it and the warmth it offered.

ARRRGH!!! and Blinky recoiled from the beam.

Hadn't the metal man said I would go home at dawn? I tore my eyes from the advancing surge of monsters and looked at him. He was strangling the medallion chain, unafraid of the sun that had his two companions edging away. Droves of trolls began teeming past us, dancing around the light with multifarious legs and screeching at such volume that the cave sounded like a steel tower being crushed in a giant fist. Larger trolls dove into tunnels while smaller ones scrambled up vertical walls like lizards.

I took another step toward the sunlight.

"If you don't take it now," raved the metal man, "we'll come back for you tomorrow night. And the night after that. And the night after that. And that will be your life, Jim Sturges, until you do what we say."

It was an excellent threat. I teetered between the options. There was no more stone or concrete or mud that I could see, just a writhing mass of grotesque bodies that devoured the world like a plague.

The man of metal ran out of patience. He withdrew both swords in a way that communicated some sort of signal. ARRRGH!!! charged, a great paw falling at me like a bulldozer shovel, and Blinky sailed in as well, tentacles reaching, eye stems tightening into a single, tortured braid. I felt stiff fur and the powerful suckers of an octopus, but I was already diving for the sunlight, watching my hands turn white as they entered its beam, and then going blind when the ray hit me dead on. My skin hurt, my sinuses filled with the smell of cinder, the back of my throat clotted with the taste of my own fear, and then I was on my back with all of my bones aching as if they had been bent to the breaking point. My head was on a soft, sweaty pillow.

Dad paused by the crack in my bedroom door. He was wearing his weekend mowing gear and was fussing with the button on his left sleeve.

"Morning, son," he said.

He moved along down the hallway.

Something dropped to the mattress beside me. I held in a scream.

It was the medallion.

13.

I spent less than twenty minutes at home before I left, and every one of them was upsetting. I stashed the medallion beneath my pillow to get it out of my sight, and a few seconds later, the sweat on my body began to cool as I convinced myself that it had all been a nightmare brought on by a monumentally crappy day. Relieved, I threw aside my covers only to find legs crusted with dry sewage and feet blackened with mud.

I scrubbed the crud in the shower as if it were a flesh-eating disease. The gray water swirled down the drain, and I watched it until I remembered where drains led. I fled from the bathroom, threw on clothes, and after some deliberation brought out the medallion. Menacing though it was, it felt no different in my hand than any earth-built piece of jewelry. There was no more magic in this thing than there was in a class ring, and there was one way to prove that to myself.

I put it on.

Nothing happened. Absolutely nothing.

I exhaled in relief—a small victory for common sense. I tucked the medallion beneath my shirt. After a full day of wearing it, maybe the rest of the suffocating fear would go away, too.

My plan was to dart into the kitchen to grab my sweatshirt and be out of the house in seconds. But as I was throwing it over my head, I smelled the strangest thing. I poked my head from the top of the sweatshirt to find my dad putting strips of crispy bacon upon a plate and transferring that plate to the table, where a steaming stack of pancakes awaited. I couldn't believe my eyes. I hadn't seen such a feast since before Mom left. Dad sat down and took a satisfied pull of his coffee.

"Great timing, Jimmy. Pull up a chair."

Dad was whistling. Sure, it was Don and Juan's "What's Your Name?" but still—whistling? It was so unprecedented that for a moment I forgot everything else.

"You okay, Dad?"

"Better than okay. Had the best sleep of my life last night. Jimmy, I tell you, I haven't slept that well since I was little, back when I shared a room with my brother, Jack. Never thought I'd sleep that well again."

He absently touched his Excalibur Calculator Pocket, as if fantasizing about how he might even find the courage to stand up for himself at work. His fingers moved to the Band-Aid on his glasses, and he nodded as if deciding to fix those frames once and for all. I'd never seen him so happy. I couldn't help it; I smiled back. He reached across the table for the syrup.

That's when I saw the little trail of sores leading from the corner of his lip, across his jaw, and down his neck, and remembered that terrible sound coming from his bedroom the night before: *Sluuuurp. Sluuuurp. Sluuuurp. Sluuuurp.*

He beamed at me and a scab from one of the sores flaked onto his pancakes.

"Have a seat," he said. "I think things are finally turning up Sturges."

The tableful of food was left behind. I was out the door and on my bike in seconds. It was the first day of the Festival of the Fallen Leaves, and all sorts of roads were blocked off. I made the mistake of heading straight toward the Kids' Jubilee on Main Street, but managed to cut across the town square before having to dodge three hundred costumed kids. Ignoring every honked horn and middle finger offered by affronted motorists, I swerved down side roads like my life depended on it, which, at this point, I was pretty sure it did.

At last I reached Papadopoulos Dental Solutions, threw my bike into the bushes, rocketed through the front door, and crashed into the front desk. The receptionist flinched. I gasped for air. The smooth jazz piping from the speakers mocked my frantic state.

"Mlookinfortub."

"Slow down, dear. What now?"

I gulped a quick lungful of air.

"I'm looking for Tub."

"I still don't understand—"

"Toby D."

"I don't know who that—"

"Tobias F. Dershowitz."

The receptionist adjusted her glasses and consulted her ledger. Her gaze ticked down the list of names.

"Dershowitz . . . Dershowitz . . . oh!" Her smile quickly faded as she examined her notes more closely. *"Oh."*

The sound of a drill sliced through the walls.

Moments later I ducked into the third, and most serious, patient room to find Tub alone and strapped into a chair with his lips stretched wide in four directions courtesy of a spiderlike metal contraption. His new braces made the old ones look debonair. Big chrome nodules were attached to every tooth, while steel wire twisted about in dizzying patterns. An acrid cloud of smoke hung above his head, the manifestation of his mood.

Tub couldn't move his head from the grips, but he managed to raise an eyebrow.

I rushed to the side of the chair.

"It came back," I gasped. "The thing from the parking lot."

He raised his other eyebrow.

"They took me! The thing from the parking—I didn't tell you, but there was a thing—when I was under—it had claws—Tub, no one's gonna believe me! I was in this place—there was all this stuff, and I think it was from when all those kids—there were three of them, one with all these eyes—Tub, you wouldn't believe it, all these eyes flying around all crazy—and a guy wearing all this junk and he was smaller but really scary—but the worst was the one with the claws—Tub, it was huge! Arms like a mile long! Teeth—a million teeth! Huge as, like, traffic cones—"

"Teeth that big I'd like to see!"

Dr. Papadopoulos came striding in holding a fistful of X-rays. I stepped back from the chair. Tub had always said that Papadopoulos was a hairy guy—when he wanted to gross me out, Tub would pretend to find curly pieces of Papadopoulos's arm hair stuck in his braces. It was no exaggeration. Papadopoulos's black mane began about an inch above his unibrow, and each of his four gigantic rings was lost in knuckle hair. He grinned at me. Perfect teeth, of course.

"What are we talking about? Some movie you saw?"

I felt myself nodding.

"Don't get a chance to see many movies myself. What can I say? Teeth are my life. Tobias here will be with you in just a couple minutes. He just needs a wee bit of tightening." He tossed the X-rays onto the counter, peered into Tub's open mouth, nodded to himself, and headed out of the room again.

I swept back to Tub's side.

"Tub. *Tub*. What am I gonna tell Dad? I can't tell him, can I? He'll go mental. He'll lock me up with chains. We need to do something. You and me. Maybe we can set up a trap. Oh, man, Tub—they said they'd come back. Tonight. Tonight! We don't have time—"

"Always time for proper dental care," Papadopoulos said, cruising back in.

He had in his hands a tray of the most horrifying medical devices I'd ever seen: misshapen hooks so sharp they glinted, a scalpel with form-fitting plastic grips, a thing that looked like tongs except much sharper, and a svelte handheld rotary blade. Each tool was constructed of lustrous silver. I'd consider them pretty awesome if they didn't exist for the sole purpose of torturing Tub.

Papadopoulos bent over the instruments, fingers wiggling.

"Tobias's case has been an inspiration to me. These tools here I invented in my personal lab. Forged and soldered them myself. It would not surprise me if I received an invitation to this year's Dental Association Conference in Anaheim. No, it would not surprise me one bit."

Papadopoulos took up a wrench and leaned over Tub with the look of a man eyeing a succulent turkey and deciding where to make the first cut.

Something warned me that what I might see would haunt me forever.

"Ah, yes," he purred. Metal squealed and popping noises came from teeth being driven tightly into sockets. The dentist's body blocked the specifics of the attack, though I saw plenty of flailing from Tub's limbs. Papadopoulos proceeded, unconcerned. "Aha. Yes. Yes. My, my, my!"

An unbearable five minutes later, the mad scientist straightened and exhaled with a great amount of pride. He released the prongs holding the four sides of Tub's mouth and began to remove his rubber gloves.

"Rinse and spit. I'll see you next week."

Papadopoulos's eyes caught mine as he passed. Rather, it was my agape mouth that caught his attention. He frowned and leaned in, inspecting my unbrushed rows.

"Mmm-hmm. There are things I could help you with. Make an appointment. It'll change your life, son."

He winked. I shuddered. He strode out the door with a clipboard containing the details of his next victim. He paused in the hallway, sniffing the air. He scowled, sniffed some more. He pressed an intercom button on the wall.

"Betty, I distinctly smell sewage. Could you get a plumber out here ASAP?"

Several curly hairs fluttered in the air after he was gone.

I clutched at the arm of the dentist chair.

"This isn't a joke, Tub! I'm in trouble. We're all in trouble, the whole town, the whole world! You have no clue. You have no idea what kind of things we're dealing with here. There's a whole land of—"

Tub held up a single finger. He sat tall, carefully picked up the paper cup of water, sipped it daintily, swished it around his cheeks, and then spit into the basin. He repeated the routine

with fastidious care: sip, swish, spit. Then he took up the end
of his paper bib and dabbed at his mouth until he was all
clean and sat back in the chair. He sighed and turned to look
at me. He parted his lips to speak and I squinted as the fluorescents shone off his mouthful of new metal.

"Are you *nuts*?!"

14.

Tub shouldered open the door. A knitted cat above the peep-hole rang its belled tail.

"Grandma! I'm home!"

Somewhere between fifteen and twenty cats, live ones, coordinated their assaults from ground and aerial positions. As always, I flinched from their overenthusiastic claws and desperate mewling. Tub, though, had mastered the art of harmlessly toeing aside felines without even looking. They hissed with annoyance and leapt to the plastic-coated sofa and the coffee table that no one was allowed to put coffee on. The whole place was decked out in the gewgaws of classic Americana: framed cross-stitches imploring God to bless this house, shelves containing ceramic miniatures of angelic cats, and endless baubles of wicker and crystal, none of which, under any circumstance, were you to touch. Adding unity to the hodgepodge was a fine layer of cat hair and the delicate bouquet of cat urine.

"Tub," I pressed. "What are we going to do?"

"Do? We? Well, I'm going to go lock myself in my room until I can come up with some way to hide these deal-breakers on my teeth. I think Grandma's got some thread, maybe I can just sew my lips shut. Leave a little gap for a straw. Live on liquid meals. I mean, what girl is going to be seen within ten feet of me now? These things on my teeth look like bullets. Bullets, Jim. Girls hate bullets!"

"Tobias, you took off your shoes?" The voice came from the kitchen.

"Yes, Grandma!" Tub shouted. With two practiced kicks, both shoes rocketed down the hall. I bent down to untie mine. I hated this part. Shoe removal was mandatory in the Dershowitz household, which was a real shame, considering how the shag carpet was soggy with hairballs. Also, possibly, dung.

"Hey," Tub said. "You about to lay down some dope rhymes?"

"What?"

He indicated his braces. "Bling don't impress me, J-Fresh."

I looked down at my chest. While I'd been working on my second shoe, the medallion had slipped from under my shirt. I caught it in my fist.

"Yes! Look! This is proof, right here! One of them gave this to me."

"Which one? King Kong? The Incredible Squid? Or Mr. Roboto?"

"Mr. Roboto," I said, then shook my head in irritation. "You have to listen to me!"

He continued into the kitchen, so I followed, ignoring the cat surprises beneath my socks.

Grandma Dershowitz was a short, hunched woman with thick glasses strung upon a beaded chain and gray hair colored an unconvincing magenta. I had never seen her without her frilled, polka-dotted apron, and that day was no exception. She was baking cookies, which she was always doing,

bowls and bowls of them that Tub devoured for no other reason than to clear the counters for the next wave. Tub reached
for a blob of cookie dough and Grandma slapped his wrist.

"You'll get worms."

"That makes no sense, Grandma."

"You want to help, wash some of those dishes."

Tub shrugged his shoulders at me.

"I washed last time," he said, nabbing the dishtowel.

I rolled my eyes and took up my usual station.

"Oh, Jim Sturges!" Grandma cried. "Welcome, welcome.
There will be cookies for all."

"Thanks, Mrs. Dershowitz."

"It's so nice to have a man around the house."

"Grandma!" Tub raised his palms in disbelief. "What the
heck? I'm a man."

"Yes, but Jim is older."

"By three weeks, Grandma!"

To say the least, we'd been through this before. I plunged
my hands into the suds. With one hand I withdrew a dirty
measuring glass. With the other, I withdrew a small head with
pointy ears and fangs. It hissed at me and I almost screamed.

"In the *sink*, Tub?"

The cat jumped from the water and landed on the counter
next to me, shaking suds from its body. It was Cat #23. Tub
had long since given up trying to remember the names of
the fifty or so felines that had come and gone, and had therefore instituted a streamlined numerical system. Somewhere in
his room was a highly valuable laminated list of their actual
names in case of emergency, but Tub hadn't seen it in a while.

"Cats aren't supposed to be hiding in sinks," I said. "They
hate water."

Tub shrugged. "One in a million doesn't. And we have a million."

He shooed Cat #37 from where it was curled up asleep in the drying rack.

I snatched the sponge from the faucet and began scrubbing the measuring glass.

"If you don't help me, I'm going to have to tell my dad."

Tub glanced at his grandmother, who was facing the opposite counter. With the stealth of a secret agent, Tub tiptoed across the linoleum, extended an arm toward Grandma's ear, and succeeded in cranking down her hearing aid. He relaxed and sighed, then returned to the sink with exasperated slowness.

"Fine, tell your dad. You two can bond over it. No hugging, though, since you'll both be in straightjackets."

I held the medallion away from my chest. Tub took it and leaned in to give it a hard look.

"Looks fake. That language even looks fake. What's it supposed to be, Chinese?"

"No." I girded myself for mockery. "It's Troll."

Tub let the medallion drop to my chest.

"It was nice knowing you, pal."

"Tub!"

He threw down his towel.

"I'm serious, Jim. You need to put this crap *away*. You walk into school on Monday talking to me, or anyone else, about the city's pesky troll problem, and you're not exactly going to get a lot of people saying, 'Gee, thanks for the warning.' It'll spread faster than mono. You think things are tough for us now? Jim, this will be the end. I'm sorry if you had a crazy nightmare. I really am. But I can't let you ruin our lives."

Cat #31 sidled up to his leg and he shook it off.

"Butterscotch chips make cookies extra special," Grandma said from another time zone.

In frustration, I reached for another dirty dish and ended up pulling the plug on the sink. The water gurgled and the bubbles started sliding away. Not having to worry about Grandma overhearing, I cursed my best curse and leaned against the sink.

"All right," I said. "I've got a proposal. Indulge me for one night. Just one night. You've still got that archery set, right?"

"Yeah, I got it, but—"

"And I know you have the nanny cam, right?"

"Well, sure. That thing wasn't cheap. Grandma really thought she'd catch the babysitter stealing cookies. Didn't have the heart to tell her it was me."

"Okay, you find that stuff and bring it with you to the play tryouts at noon."

"The play tryouts? Wait, Jim, no. I'm not doing any of this."

"I'll give you Dino-Mountain."

That shut him up. Every kid dreams of unattainable gifts—expansive race-car sets, towering doll houses, futuristic clubhouses that cost more than your parent's car—and one year I received exactly such a holy grail: Dino-Mountain, a plastic play set as high as my chest, complete with caves and tunnels from which one of ten different dino-troops could attack.

"I . . ." Tub started. The offer had caught him by surprise. "Come on. I'm too old for Dino-Mountain." He did not sound entirely convinced of that.

"And a bag of sour worms. No, a case. A full case. Tub, that's like eight bags."

"Jim . . ."

"Anything you want. Just name it. It's yours. I just want one night of help and then, tomorrow, I swear I'll never mention it again."

Tub looked at the floor, where Cat #40 and Cat #17 were swiping at each other's tails. He knocked them aside with his ankle, though his heart was not in it. His cheeks were pink beneath the freckles. My offers had embarrassed him.

"A fiver," he murmured. "Just a fiver. You know. For Steve."

I reached out and gripped his shoulder.

"You got it, Tub. Noon at the school, okay?"

"Fine, whatever."

I tossed the sponge onto the counter and wiped my hands on my jeans.

"I have to go dig out some sports equipment from my attic."

"Sports? No one said anything about sports. This deal's getting worse by the second."

"I'll explain later."

I approached Grandma Dershowitz to crank up her hearing aid and say good-bye, but was distracted by the slurping noise of the final suds being sucked down the drain. I cradled my hands to my chest, wondering how I had made such a stupid mistake as plunging them into a sink with a drain the perfect size for an extending tentacle.

15.

Because *Shakespeare on the Fifty-Yard Line* was an outdoor production, the auditions were held on a knoll just to the side of Harry G. Bleeker Memorial Field, where the football team was packing in an extra weekend practice beneath the jumbotron installers. Two doomed lines of would-be headliners, girls and boys, paired off to read for *RoJu*'s title roles while Mrs. Leach, the drama coach of the exhausted hair, frowsy hairbands, and floppy sweaters, took notes.

Opposite of where the team was scrimmaging, at the north end of the field, Dad rode his industrial lawn mower around the end zone. The thing had cost a bundle when he'd bought it five years before, but I had to hand it to him—it had already paid for itself. The monstrosity was twice as big as a regular mower and painted a garish gold. The back wheels had been lifted from a defunct monster truck called the Destruckshunator and the huge, eight-wheeled mowing deck stuck out like the wings of a 747. The sixteen-inch discharge chute shot out grass with machine-gun force. Seriously: I'd stood too close before and been *bruised* by the flying grass.

Thankfully, Dad hadn't noticed me when I'd arrived for the auditions. In his goggles, work gloves, steel-toed safety boots, allergy mask, and hair net, he looked like a frantic alien nerd piloting a gigantic moon rover, hell-bent on destroying our grassy planet one blade at a time.

I'd been last in line, but now it was one o'clock and I was just one actor away. Studying the pages in my sweaty hands was difficult; Tub had yet to show and I kept visualizing him arriving with Sergeant Gulager, who would haul me off to the nuthouse for my own safety. Just as distracting was the current Romeo's butchering of the Bard.

"It is my soul that calls upon my name?" Shakespeare's unfamiliar rhythms had the kid doubting the most fundamental precepts of English. "How silver-sweet sound? Lovers' tongues by night? Like softest music? To attending ears?"

"Romeo!" his Juliet responded. An easy line, for sure.

"My . . . niece? Nice? Nessie?"

"Niesse," Mrs. Leach said for the thirtieth time that day. "It means young hawk."

A conflagration of footballs converging on the same target drew my attention to a rotund figure slumping through the end zone. It was Tub, on foot, as his previous nine bicycles had been stolen from school bicycle racks over the past nine years. He was carrying a duffel bag and grimacing against the half-dozen balls thumping down around him from shoulder-padded bullies. Only the last one struck him, on the shoulder.

"Enough monkey business, men!" Coach Lawrence hollered. "Though that *was* a real bull's-eye, Jorgensen-Warner!"

Tub threw his duffel bag down beside a table. On it were the tattered scraps of the free donuts promised by the flyers. Tub lifted a thin sheet of deli paper spotted with powdered sugar with the same delicacy one might handle a war-torn American flag. He set it down, wobbled backward a few steps, and plopped down on the grass, grinding his jaw like he always did after a tightening. He looked to the grassy stage and gave me a morose nod.

"Sleep well upon thine eyes?" the boy continued. "Peace in thy . . . breast? Breast? Can I say that?"

Mrs. Leach rubbed at her eyes and the kid skulked away in surrender. She consulted her sign-up sheet while Dad's mower droned on in the distance.

"Jim Sturges Jr." She peered through her glasses at the makeshift stage. "We're out of Juliets. Claire, can you read with Jim?"

My heart sunk. Of course Claire Fontaine was to get front-row seats to my degradation. I took a deep breath while she set aside her pink backpack, uncrossed her legs from the grass, and brushed off. It was no secret that Claire had Juliet locked. Sure, she read with impressive poise, and her swings between melancholy and ecstasy were convincing enough to have every boy pledging his nonexistent sword to her defense. But it was the authentic accent that sealed the deal. Next to that, everyone else sounded like the absolute worst: a regular high school kid.

Claire took her place next to me, knocked the mud from her boots, and gave me a kind, if brief, smile. The wind was doing wonderful, wild things to the hair outside of her beret.

"Act two, scene two, page two," Mrs. Leach said. "Let's do this."

Tub gawped at me, the donut scandal forgotten. I cleared my throat, looked at the spinning letters upon the page, and dove in.

"Oh, are you going to leave me so unsatisfied?"

One line in and I was blushing.

"What satisfaction could you possibly have tonight?" Claire asked.

"I would be satisfied," I said, "if we made each other true promises of love."

No doubt these lines were masterpieces of meter and meaning, but for all the feeling coming out of my mouth, they might as well have been ingredients from a cereal box. Claire, of course, turned Juliet's lines into things as natural as breath, one word as full as rainwater gathering on the tip of a petal, the next dry and windswept as the desert outside of town.

I looked at her in wonder and saw that she was reciting by heart and that her eyes were focused on the football field. There at the nearest corner was a helmetless Steve Jorgensen-Warner running drills. Just drills, and yet he executed them with supernatural grace, vaulting over lesser humans and grinning like he'd just as soon keep going until he conquered the world. Claire was rapt and I couldn't blame her. That sort of movement was a kind of poetry, too.

"Oh, blessed, blessed night," I whispered from a script I hadn't realized that I'd memorized, too. "Because it's dark out, I'm afraid all this is just a dream."

Was it, in fact, a dream? I lowered my eyes and regarded the chewed, dirty fingernails holding my script, the scuffed shoes on my feet, and realized that these were the symbols of my pitiful little life: worn-out, insignificant, ready to be thrown beneath Dad's industrial mower. With one hand I touched the medallion beneath my shirt, a different symbol entirely, and thought of that dark world beneath the surface. Which dream was preferable, the wild danger down there or the slow suffocation happening up here?

Mrs. Leach took her glasses by the frame, lips parted to

demand an end to this pitiful farce. But my voice continued, louder now, my despair as real as anything Romeo could come up with.

"A thousand times the worse for me, to want your light! / A lover goes toward love as schoolboys from their books. / But love goes from love, like boys toward school with heavy looks."

Mrs. Leach released her glasses.

Claire turned away from the football field and gave me a curious look.

"It is my soul that calls upon my name," I continued. Until then, anguish was something I'd felt in my heart and head. Now it had a voice and I let it flow. "How silver-sweet sound lovers' tongues by night, like softest music to attending ears."

Claire smiled with not just a corner of her lips but her whole mouth.

"I shall forget," she said softly, "to have thee still stand there, remembering how I love thy company. Romeo!"

"Romeo, indeed," Mrs. Leach said.

The drama coach was standing and clutching her hands to her bosom. Like any good teacher, she knew that keeping decorum was priority one. But her flashing eyes revealed that she was rapturous. I expanded my gaze. The other auditioners sat there with stunned looks upon their faces. Even Tub's face was void of sarcasm. Two water boys on their way to the football field had paused with their bag of thermoses and were staring at us, enraptured. Mrs. Leach turned to a wardrobe parent, who was clapping her hands with tears in her eyes.

"Mrs. Dunton, take some measurements. I think our Romeo might just wake up this town of football fans."

"Yes, I think so," Mrs. Dunton replied. She tilted her head a little. "If we can make him taller, that is."

The wardrobe lady approached, unspooling her measuring tape and running it from foot to inseam and waist to armpit, making disappointed *tsks* at every step. I had learned in math class just how much taller Claire was than me, but Claire herself didn't seem to care. She crossed her arms over her frayed jacket and a dozen bracelets slid down her wrists. Her dark hair blew and caught on her lips, and she spoke just loudly enough to be heard over the gridiron warriors and the roaring mower.

"Very interesting, Mr. Sturges."

16.

"I'll never figure out how that nut sack made a living writing," Tub said.

"Flames," I groaned. "I'm going to go down in big fiery flames of fire."

"I'll show Mr. Shakespeare a renaissance. A renaissance of my *fist*."

"Nobody can say those sentences without sounding like a jerk. Right?"

"Generally you're right," Tub said. "It's definitely an elite club of superstars who can wrap their tongues around that baroque bullcrap. Sir Lawrence Olivier, Sir Kenneth Branagh. We'd be remiss, of course, to leave out that legend of stage and screen, that matinee idol of the ages, Sir Jim Sturges Jr."

Tub slapped me on the back. He had a big hand; I stumbled. I heard chuckles from the direction of the football field. I kept my head down and picked up the pace. We were heading home, but the talk of the audition would not die. I looked at the *RoJu* script in my hand. Only forty-five pages, but it felt a whole lot heavier.

"How am I going to memorize all this?" I asked.

"Here's a tip," Tub said. "You forget a line, just shout 'Saint

B. Battle Beasts rule!' and those morons in the stands will go crazy." He winked at me. "That one's a freebie. Next one costs."

By now we were passing the San Bernardino Historical Society Museum, a lure too great for Tub not to bite at. He gave me his usual impish grin.

"Not today," I pleaded. "I don't have the required speed."

"Speed? You? You're not the one schlepping this bag, Sir Jim."

What could I say to that? He was doing me a favor. So we made our way down the walkway, passing beneath a new vinyl banner. It didn't make a lot of sense, though the heavy block letters were nonetheless imposing.

KILLAHEED

THE COMPLETE STRUCTURE

WESTERN HEMISPHERE DEBUT

It snapped in the breeze as if preparing to swoop down on bat wings.

Neither of us was encouraged by what we found inside. Carol was absent from the ticket booth. We peeked around the corner. No one was manning the coat check. We perked up our ears. There were sounds, dim vibrations of voices, but there was no telling from which direction they came. Tub shrugged, hitched up his duffel, and pushed his bulk through the turnstiles. I followed and we proceeded, more carefully than usual, up the stairs and beneath the bison. Tub didn't touch the chin hairs this time.

The Sal K. Silverman Atrium looked no different from the outside. But when we pushed through the smoked-glass doors we were greeted by a hive of activity. Museum staff, everyone from Carol to docents to board members, were buzzing about with frowns, while men with hardhats and work gloves called back and forth to one another from behind packing crates and the seats of small forklifts. Tub and I were dumbstruck. When we approached not a single person paid us notice.

Spanning the entire length of the room was a stone walking bridge. Had it been stretched across a country stream somewhere, it might have looked harmless enough. But indoors it pushed against the room's paltry boundaries with a formidable, primordial force. It was ancient, its every notch and outcropping scoured with the nicks and discolorations of centuries. Fiberglass cushioning hid much of the detail work, though a dozen workers were preparing to remove it. Clearly the bridge had been delivered in sections; both ends had been reconstructed, but a center monument connecting the halves was missing.

Tub and I wandered closer. If not for the laborers, we could have passed beneath the bridge without ducking. Cobwebs swayed from spires at either end and moss grew in moist patches around many of the intricate carvings. The bridge was practically a living thing—you expected rats to come pouring out of the innumerable small chasms. The air was unaccountably cold and I shivered as I tried to see over a man in a houndstooth coat.

He whirled around, nose raised as if he'd sniffed me out. It was Professor Lempke. His left hand clutched a clipboard but the right hand shot out, somehow snaring both of our collars in a single fist.

"Aha!" he cried. "My perennial trespassers! My shadow skulkers! Young masters Sturges and Dershowitz, reporting for duty!"

We squirmed but his grip was iron.

Lempke's hyena grin widened. The effect was troubling. His teeth were caked with crud and his breath was sour. In fact, everything about him suggested lack of sleep, if not some worse affliction. His bloodshot eyes rolled within a pudding of violet flesh, and his jaundiced cheeks were dusted with gray stubble. A tide of pimples swept out from his hairline and there was a pink rash extending from his shirt collar.

"No bounding about like wildebeests, not today, not whilst such a delicate artifact rests in proximity. You intrude on an auspicious afternoon! What you see before you is the grandest achievement of my career. Eighteen years I've worked with Scottish historians to protect this edifice from destruction, a destruction that simpletons of the Scottish Highlands insisted upon because of primitive, archaic superstition. Can you believe it, my boy busybodies? Those ignoramuses wished to destroy quite possibly the most important piece of architecture in all of Europe. I saved it. I did that. And now it's right here in the Golden Valley."

His fevered eyes began to swim with tears. Both Tub and I recoiled, hoping to evade contaminated spatter.

"Do you undereducated brats have the slightest idea what you're looking upon?"

Tub dared to shrug.

"A bridge?"

Lempke's cheeks slackened in mortification. Two hard tears rolled like ball bearings, one from each swollen eye, though he did not seem to notice. His horrified expression slowly screwed into one of mordant amusement.

"A bridge," he mused. "Amusing. Not yet, my pubescent

meddlers. You see, the head stone that connects the two halves . . . alas, it has yet to arrive."

The assistant who cleared his throat had been standing there for some time. Lempke's fingers loosened enough for Tub and I to extricate ourselves and massage our throats. Sweat dropped from the assistant's face onto a stack of paperwork. He clicked a pen nervously.

"The head stone," he said. "I've got news."

"Out with it," Lempke barked.

The assistant consulted a scrawled note. "Okay. The cargo was shipped to San Sebastián by mistake."

"San Sebastián, Puerto Rico?" Lempke seethed.

The assistant gulped down his nervousness.

"San Sebastián, Spain." While Lempke's jaw fell open, releasing a stink, the assistant hurried on. "It should arrive there within a day and the historical society has been given instructions to reroute it to us immediately."

Lempke's whole face had gone the color of his rash. He raked jagged fingernails across his whitehead pimples.

"*Explicit* instructions?" he raged. "Were *explicit* instructions given? I know those boobs in San Sebastián. They'll want a look. They'll crack open the casing and say it happened during transport, just to get a peek, without even thinking about the lighting conditions under which they're exposing the stone, the moisture in the air, anything! They'll take photos. *Flash* photos!"

"Yes, explicit," said the assistant. "I was very explicit—"

"Call them again. Underscore the sobriety, the gravity of our instructions. Those thickheaded dunderheads are to wait outside nibbling their *pinxchos* until the shipment arrives. I don't care if they stand there all night. I did, and I was proud to do it. You cannot trust some adolescent dropout minimum-wage Spaniard with a shipment of this caliber."

"Yes, sir, day and night. Sir . . . you're . . . bleeding. Are you all right?"

Lempke was itching the back of his right hand. He'd dug bloody furrows.

"This wool coat," he muttered. "It bothers me."

For a quick moment, he pushed up the sleeve of his jacket to itch beneath it. We all saw it: the rash had devoured Lempke's entire forearm. A yellow glaze of hardened mucus glistened in the sunshine pouring from the skylight. The sleeve fell back into place and the assistant forced himself to stare at his notes.

"Ah, the, uh, head stone should be here Friday. Just in time for the final day of the festival—"

Lempke flapped his ruined right hand. Skin, loosened from scratching, floated in the air. Tub and I dodged it.

"Trifles! What's happening in this museum dwarfs some measly street fair! Mark my words, the halfwits who populate this town will regret squandering so much of their limited energy on street processions and athletic events and teenage theatrics, when they could have been studying up on their Scottish history. They will self-castigate. Wait and see. Apologies will be made to me personally."

A foreman shouted out to his workers: "People, step back! Okay, men, on three!"

Lempke's head shot up and he gasped like a man spotting his long-lost beloved. A second later, his hands—those hot, suppurating pincers of disease—clamped down on our necks. He steered us past the assistant, who skittered aside, so that we faced the great stone structure at the moment of unveiling.

"One . . ." the foreman yelled.

Lempke's chapped lips moved in silent recitation.

"Two . . ."

Lempke's razored nails sunk into my neck flesh.

"Three!"

With that, the workers pulled downward on the panels that protected the sides and underside of the bridge. Beneath was a thick layer of industrial carpet and beneath that a layer of straw, both of which fell to the floor with a loud *whump*. A cloud of dust flew upward and a thousand pieces of straw were tossed into the air. Workers squinted behind their goggles and museum personnel shielded their faces with their elbows. Only Lempke did nothing, beaming at eighteen years' worth of his most fervent dreams. Black dust rolled into his open mouth. A piece of straw nicked his eyeball and he didn't flinch.

"The Killaheed Bridge," he whispered.

Tub coughed and turned away. But I couldn't.

I'd seen this bridge before.

The central image of the stone mural in the troll cave had been a reproduction of this very bridge, though the depiction hadn't been able to replicate the real thing's impregnable power. Each twisted tentacle and gnarled claw was so deeply etched that your eyes got lost inside the voids, and each one grasped toward the missing head stone. I could not forget the central character as depicted by the mural: a towering troll with six arms, one empty eye socket, and another of sparkling ruby.

Clouds interrupted the sun, throwing the atrium into unexpected gloom.

"My, my, my, yes," tittered Lempke. "Scotland reborn. Looks

so much more commanding bathed in gray, don't you think, my juvenile jesters?"

A cry of pain slashed the silence. Lempke leaned toward the source of the sound with too much eagerness. A worker retracted his hand from where he had been feeling around inside one of the bridge's clefts. I saw only a smear of blood before he shoved the injured hand beneath his opposite arm.

"It bit me!" he shrieked. "Damn thing bit me!"

Concerned others swarmed around the man to help. Lempke placed his rash-covered hands on his hips. Tub motioned his chin at our usual escape door, and we crept away from the scene. The stairwell was unguarded and we were thankful. But we didn't move fast enough to escape Lempke's final words.

"Stop your whining. It doesn't hurt that bad. It's an honor, in fact. Be proud."

17.

By eleven o'clock that night the two of us were squeezed inside the cramped confines of my closet. Tub snored from behind a hockey mask, the hockey stick across his chest rising and falling with every lion purr. The previous hour had been spent griping—"My legs are asleep because you're sitting on them," "Can you remove your knee from my ear?" and so forth. Finally, though, Tub snoozed, the string of the archery bow digging a temporary scar into his cheek. Easy for him. He still didn't believe a word of what I'd said. Me, I'd be up all night. I leaned back into a pile of clothes and distracted myself by thinking through our attempts at preparation.

The first thing we'd done after returning from the museum was give my room a thorough examination. For a guy who had a tough time putting on his own socks, Tub didn't hesitate to get down on his stomach and squeeze beneath the bed, flashlight in hand. I stood as far away as I could, heart pounding.

Finally he pulled himself out. His frizzy hair was clotted with dust bunnies and his face was drawn and serious.

"There's something terrible under there," he whispered.

"Ha! Now do you believe me?"

"I do. And it's worse than I thought. I've never encountered a sock of such stink. We should arm ourselves, my liege, before it's too late, and see if we can best it in battle. Alas, we may not survive but history shall treat us well."

The bedsprings giggled as Tub took a seat.

"Sorry, Jim. No monsters. No trap door. There's not even a crawl space in this joint. This is your basic, boring mid-'80s suburban house plan, same as fifty more down the street, same as my place. It's like I said: there's nothing special about our homes, nothing special about us. Get that through your dumb head."

The following hour was nonetheless spent setting up the nanny cam. To the untrained eye it looked like a teddy bear, but its mouth held a wide-angle camera and its butt housed various cables for connecting to a TV. The quality was worse than the camera on my phone but the stuffed bear had better stamina: it could record for up to twelve hours. I posed it on the dresser facing the door, and it grinned at me like an imbecile. I sure felt like one.

Next we built a fake me that we named Jim Sturges Jr. 2: The Decoy. We fashioned JSJ2's body out of a sweatshirt and sweatpants and stuffed it with dirty laundry. For a head we appropriated a bowl that had last seen use five years before, during my unintentional slaying of five innocent goldfish. After Tub got done threatening, again, to report me to a local animal rights organization, we covered JSJ2 with a blanket and grunted our satisfaction. Now all we needed was for something to take the bait.

We waited for Dad to go to bed. Tub killed time browsing for naked celebrities on my laptop while I studied *RoJu*, and after the late news we heard Dad going through his nightly triple-check of the doors and windows. The chimes of the armed security systems made me feel even lamer. How was what Dad was doing out there any different from what I was doing in here?

Dad poked his head into the room to say good night—Tub knew how to conceal computer-screen boobs faster than anyone I knew—and afterward we withdrew the archery set from the duffel bag. Tub thumbed the single arrowhead and pronounced it nice and deadly. I brought out the athletic equipment that I'd collected in a hamper, and Tub claimed the hockey gear, leaving me with the less-impressive whiffle ball bat. The last thing I did was spread marbles all across the floor. Finally, we opened the closet, realized how closely we'd have to squish together, and made each other swear we'd never mention this to anyone else. Ever, ever, ever.

For two hours, the only sound was the soft whirring of the nanny cam.

It was midnight when I heard a creaking noise through the wall.

I elbowed Tub.

"I don't *want* dentures, Grandma."

"Tub!" I hissed. "Wake up!"

He snorted, looked around, and pulled the hockey mask to the top of his head. I pressed a finger to my lips and pointed to my ear. He nodded.

Nothing for several minutes. Tub's eyes began to droop.

Again: a creak, this one long and tortured.

"Tub. Tub. This is it."

"Just your dad, Jim."

"Dad would be checking all of the locks. We'd hear him."

Tub opened his mouth to protest before his sleepy brain realized that I was right. A third floorboard creaked, then a fourth. Whatever it was out there was getting closer. I looked through the closet slats at the crack beneath the bedroom door. A moment of unbearable tension passed. Then a shadow daggered the moonlight. My breath caught in my throat. I wanted to tell Tub to get the arrow into position but couldn't utter a word.

Then the shadow slipped away.

Tub was oblivious. He raised the head of the stick to his nose.

"This thing smells weird."

"Shhh!"

"Not like sweat. It smells, I don't know. Brand-new."

"Never got used. Shhh!"

"Oh. Well, don't feel bad. It's not your fault you lack muscle tone. It's glandular."

I pressed my sweaty forehead against his and hissed. "Dad took this stuff away because sports are dangerous. Too many late nights and away games. So he took it all away. Never even let me try."

Something metallic crashed to the kitchen floor.

Tub and I jumped. Our foreheads peeled apart and our eyes widened.

His knuckles went white around the hockey stick.

"You want to try now, Jim? Give this stuff a spin?"

There's no telling how long we stared at each other in the darkness of the closet, ratcheting up our bravery through a sequence of manly nods and the throttling of our athletic gear. Fifteen minutes might have gone by before we were properly psyched up to go exploding from the closet like a sports team, albeit one that wasn't sure what sport it was playing.

Right away my foot hit the marbles. I grabbed for Tub, but

he was skidding on marbles, too. While he went face-first into the artificial crotch of JSJ2, I went sprawling backward into the dresser. A slew of forgotten objects fell upon me in succession: a broken kite, a bottle of foul-smelling cologne, a plate of half-eaten scrambled eggs, and, of course, the nanny cam.

Even in this shameful state, I recognized momentum as the only thing we had going for us. I raced from the dresser. The teddy bear bounced along behind me, tangled up in kite string caught around my foot. Tub was throwing open the bedroom door, the bow slung across his back, the hockey stick and arrow in either fist, and a few delirious seconds later we were charging down the hall with weapons raised. Distantly I realized that Dad would not be waking up to join us. From his bedroom came that awful noise again: *Sluuuurp. Sluuuurp. Sluuuurp. Sluuuurp.*

We hesitated at the edge of the kitchen. The lights were off but sounds poured out: the clanging of tin, the crinkling of plastic, the rustle of paper, the crude slamming of ceramic to Formica. Substances, some hard, some soft, were dropping to the linoleum floor in irregular patterns. Blurting between each noise were inhuman snorts.

"Tub," I hissed. "What do we do?"

He bared his shiny steel teeth and lowered his hockey mask.

"We do not. Negotiate. With terrorists."

He lifted the brand-new hockey stick and bounded into the kitchen. With the tangled nanny cam trailing after me, I secured my baseball helmet and followed, rearing back with a bat that had waited all its life to swing.

18.

The first thing I noticed was that the ceiling fan was shoved into the corner, smashed to pieces. All in all, it was an odd thing to notice first, given that there were two enormous trolls contorted inside my humble little kitchen. I hated to admit that I was on a first-name basis with terrifying monsters of any sort, but these two I knew all too well. Blinky's eight eyes were weaving in and out of the cabinets, down the sink drain, through the nooks of the dishwasher. ARRRGH!!! was grasping, and inadvertently crushing, various human-sized items upon the counter. The beast growled and its hunched back scraped against the dangling guts of the ceiling fan.

For some reason, the microwave was on, the plate inside empty and spinning.

With my free hand I gripped the back of Tub's shirt.

"What . . . what are they . . . doing?" I managed.

Tub's voice gurgled back with feeble horror.

"Sandwiches, Jim. They're making sandwiches."

Two of Blinky's tentacles took turns diving into a jar of peanut butter, emerging each time with a beige glob that he smeared across an array of white bread scattered across the counter. Far too much force was used, and the bread tore into puffs that flew about the kitchen like scraps from a wood chipper. Some of it made its way into the gash of Blinky's mouth, and through his scaled skin I could see the chunks as they made their way down two separate throats before landing in one of several quivering stomachs.

ARRRGH!!! was even less artful. It snatched whatever scraps it could from the air and shoved them at its slobbering jaw. Not all of it hit the mark: pieces of white bread were adhered via peanut butter all across the troll's fur. There was no doubt it was enjoying itself; with every mighty swallow, its horns gored enthusiastically at the cabinet and its gargantuan feet stamped the dropped bread and peanut butter into a brown paste.

Neither paid us any attention. They were focused on the task, blurting incomprehensible remarks around mouthfuls of mashed food.

Tub pushed his hockey stick into my hands and unslung his bow. His eyes were glazed but determined and I felt a surge of pride. Dad was in some kind of irretrievable slumber. This was up to the two of us and Tub knew it.

"I'll take the smaller one," he whispered.

"That's your plan?" I hissed.

"What? The smaller one looks tricky."

"Tricky? He's almost blind!"

"Oh, yeah? Well, I bet he's got perfect hearing."

With trembling hands, he fit the arrow into the string and began to pull it back.

"Aim for the heart," I urged.

At least five different spots on Blinky's chest beat in spasmodic rhythm.

"Which one?" Tub demanded.

"Any of them!"

"Fine, fine!" Tub winced as he pulled the bowstring as far back as he could. The arrowhead dodged around like crazy—up, down, left, right. I took a step back, uninterested in falling victim to a spectacular misfire. Tub squinted and aimed. "You get ready to go apeshit on the furry one."

I raised the puny baseball bat and insignificant hockey stick. They felt about as lethal as a couple of pretzel rods. The only optimistic thought I could conjure was that ARRRGH!!! filled the entire room. No matter where I struck, no matter how sorry the attack, it would be impossible to miss.

Tobias F. Dershowitz had spent his entire youth as the target of ridicule. The Trophy Cave was only the latest in a long series of treacherous locations, Steve Jorgensen-Warner only the most infamous of those who'd dedicated their lives to his debasement. But on that night, in that kitchen, against the most daunting of foes and armed with the flimsiest of weapons, Tub's aim was true. The bowstring fired with a melodic *bing* and the arrow cut through the air, hard and fast, right at the center of the multi-tentacled monster. It was entirely possible that Tub might have felled the troll had not the man of metal leapt in from the living room and deflected the arrow with his leg of bicycle chains.

The microwave beeped, its nonexistent meal done cooking.

The metal man came for us.

I backed against the wall and hit the lights. ARRRGH!!! flinched from the brightness and Blinky's eight eyes dove for dimmer cover. Rude fluorescents shone off the man's armor but we were the only ones fazed. He withdrew both swords from his back with such force that a sugar bowl was sliced cleanly in two. The sugar itself seemed to suspend midair before scattering.

Tub wailed and threw the bow at him, but the metal man flicked a sword and the wood split in half. I let loose with a strangled cry and swung the bat. The metal man stepped easily to the left, caught the head of the bat with his spiked glove, and used the forward momentum to send me flying against the stove. The hockey stick clattered to the ground, but Tub picked it up and with a girlish yelp swung a spastic uppercut. The man of metal brought both swords together in X formation, catching the stick in the crux before giving another shove and chopping the blade of it clean off. Tub dropped the rest of it like it was hot.

The kitchen was a maelstrom of noise. Tub was screaming. I was screaming. ARRRGH!!! and Blinky were doing the troll version of screaming. The man of metal spun his swords in either hand, cutting the air with swooping sounds until both weapons faced skyward. The bottle caps on his arms jangled and the die-cast cars on his torso spun their wheels. He roared.

"QUIET!"

With simultaneous swipes, he sliced the hockey mask free from Tub's face with one sword while splitting the bill of my baseball helmet with the other. Tub reached to his temple and I did the same to my forehead, but neither of us found so much as a scrape. We had stopped screaming, though, and so had the trolls. Tub and I blinked at each other, unarmed and unmasked.

The man of metal sheathed his swords and put both gloved hands behind his head. The aviator goggles of his eyes wiggled out of place and the boom box grill of his mouth pulled to one side. He next unlatched the slingshot band that served as his chinstrap and lifted off the headphone ears, along with the football-helmet exterior. I braced myself for the kind of scarred, gnarled visage a lifetime of sci-fi films had prepared me for.

The smooth, healthy face I saw was a less welcome surprise.

I knew that face.

It was my Uncle Jack.

Not Uncle Jack if he had lived and matured to be fifty-eight years old. This Uncle Jack was the same kid who stared at me every day from the milk carton photo on our living room shelf: tall for his age, loose blond hair flopping over his forehead, eyes flashing with intelligence and courage. The difference was that this boy was not freshly scrubbed and smirking with confidence. Instead, his frowning face was scored with mud and grime, and he sniffed at the air as if uncomfortable with the smells of dish soap, pine air freshener, and peanut butter.

"Uncle Jack?" I managed.

His eyes were guarded.

He nodded once.

"Get a grip, Jim." Tub's voice was shaky. "That's nobody's uncle. That's some kid. Some crazy kid. Some crazy kid with swords who broke into your house and . . ." Tub leaned forward and the recognition hit him. "Oh, wow. Oh, geez. Jim, you know who that is? That's Uncle freaking Jack."

The trolls moved into positions behind Jack. ARRRGH!!! lowered its boulder-sized head so that the straggly hairs of its chin tickled Jack's ear. Blinky's tentacles twisted around Jack's arm while two of the long-stemmed eyes hovered about Jack's head as if lending him doubled sight. Both trolls made noises

It was an entire city of trolls.

back and forth. Jack nodded as if he understood. I gripped the oven door and brought myself to my feet.

Jack stepped toward me, his metal parts jangling, and reached for my neck with one of his tack-edged gloves. I held my breath and wondered if this was it—the premature, and quite weird, death of Jim Sturges Jr. Instead of squeezing, though, Jack looped his finger around my chain and pulled the bronze medallion out from where it hid under my shirt. Jack flashed me an impatient look, then took hold of the sword on the face of the medallion and twisted it. It went from horizontal to vertical.

My ears popped. Suddenly I was hearing Blinky in midrant.

"—a doltish look about the face, doesn't he? And that slackness of jaw? That hunch of back? Ignominious breeding, I'm afraid. Ignominious! I ask you, what are we to assume from that outrageously bland ceremonial garb? Where is the roguish *joie de vivre*? The vainglorious family crest? And no battle scarf? *No battle scarf?* That's an affront! A direct affront! But hark! I see a spark of intelligence! Why, it's rather adorable. The little fellow is . . . Is he . . . ? Oh dear. Oh dear, indeed. He can understand me now, can't he?"

Though mostly blind, Blinky had extended one of his eyes so that it hovered and squinted from a foot away. His peanut butter–covered appendages dithered a bit at the faux pas. In short order all eight of the eyes were turned in my general direction and blinking rapidly. His bigger companion licked the inside of its cheeks thoughtfully before lowering its head to look at me.

"Hullo." Peanut butter slime dripped from ARRRGH!!!'s fangs. "Boy. Human."

"They talk," I mumbled. "Tub, they talk."

"Don't go crazy on me, Jim," Tub said.

"Of course we talk," Blinky said. His English accent was impeccable. "We are hardly *cattle*. We are, by the best estimates of troll intelligentsia, the most advanced of all existing species." His haughty tone collapsed into a remorseful sigh. "We can also be the rudest. Do accept my apology. We regret that we do not have a second translator for your noble man-at-arms."

"They're apologizing, Tub," I said. "Because you can't understand them."

"Tell them apology accepted. No! Tell them I'm sorry about trying to shoot them. Tell them that first. That's important."

"They can understand you just fine, Tub."

"Oh. Sorry." Then, louder, to them: "Sorry! I mean it! Please don't kill me!"

"Kill? You?" Blinky looked baffled. "Such savagery is not the providence of the elite! Heed this: if you are to irk me, boy, *irk cautiously*. You are fortunate that my patience is renowned— I can out-wait anyone, anywhere, anytime. Why, my waiting contest with Prothnurd the Persistent is legend. Three years I sat opposite old Prothnurd, happy as you'd like, and I would've sat for three more had the old boy not died. So I wish you well in your irking. My hirsute colleague, though—patience is not her strong suit."

"Her?" I looked doubtfully up at ARRRGH!!!.

"Her?" Tub parroted. "It's a her? I mean, she's a her?"

"But of course," Blinky said. "Most of the great troll warriors are female. To be a warrior worthy of song, brute strength alone will not suffice. Not nearly! You must possess cunning as well as compassion, and neither quality is the male's forte.

Traditionally, we males are more proficient at whipping up imposing smells and choreographing the ceremonial disembowelment waltzes. Besides, isn't the color of her coat a dead giveaway? It's *ink black*."

"Ink black," I said, nodding.

"Exactly," Blinky said. "How you could mistake that for the *coal black* of males is entirely beyond my understanding."

Jack glanced at the clock on the wall. It was spattered with peanut butter. He gripped the mask in his hands as if dying to put it back on. He was, at least, human, and I turned to him in desperation.

"Uncle Jack," I said. "Where have you been?"

"With us," Blinky said. "For forty-five years, your uncle has been our equal, deserving of the respect and praise so often tossed at our collective feet. There are kneeling rituals I can suggest to you if you'd like. Beautiful, sightly rituals! Ah, if only we had the time. For now, forgive your uncle's taciturnity. If you'll permit me an opinion, I believe he might be overwhelmed at being in the house of his older brother. Your father's scent is everywhere here, you understand."

"You want me to get Dad?" I asked. "I can wake him up."

Jack's eyes blazed.

"You cannot, actually." Blinky's voice was apologetic. "He will not wake until first light."

"Why? What did you do to him?"

Blinky fluttered various tentacles. "Posh! Details are unimportant—"

"Tell me."

"I predict you will find it unappetizing. But as you wish. We have introduced into his digestive system a schmoof. A schmoof is, oh, how shall I put this? I shall just come out with it. It is a fetus. We have a few on generous loan from the Schmooffingers. Seeking a womblike warmth, the young schmoof crawls in through the mouth and down the esophagus and burrows into the stomach lining, where its enzymes release a powerful sedative effect upon its host. Schmooffingers are renowned for their sleeping. They have sixty-six different words for *snoring*. To catalogue every possible permutation of slumber is their *raison d'être*. To that end, they sleep for eleven hours a day. The twelfth hour—well, it's best not to be around then, I'll leave it at that. Now, do not fret. Being extremely sensitive to sunlight, the schmoof will crawl back up the esophagus at dawn, la-dee-dah, and find its way home through a drain, at which point your father will wake up feeling refreshed and—"

"*You put a troll fetus into my dad's mouth?*"

"Jim!" Tub shouted. "What the hell?!"

"Schmoof," ARRRGH!!! grunted. "Is friend. Good for ache of head."

She gestured at what looked like a large boulder halfway embedded in her skull.

"We have aspirin for that!" I cried. "Aspirin! Not fetuses!"

"Oh dear," Blinky said. "I suspected that this was a bad topic with which to begin a friendship."

"*Enough.*"

Jack's young face was twisted into a snarl. The single word, only his second, seemed to have taken a deal of energy. His chest rose and fell beneath his armor of junk. He glared at Tub and I, then glanced at the trolls before jabbing an impatient thumb toward my bedroom.

Blinky's tentacles spread out in a way that somehow communicated apology. He then explained to me, in sentences that were, for him, remarkably concise, that we all had to go, right now, and then he told me why. I was more afraid of Uncle Jack than these two walking nightmares and found myself nodding agreement to whatever came out of Blinky's strange mouth.

"What's it saying, Jim?" Tub pressed. "What's going on?"

Even before I replied, I could not believe my response.

"We're going hunting."

PART III

The Trollhunters

19.

The floorboards beneath my bed telescoped downward, a whirlpool of wood, the boards cracking and popping as they locked themselves into a new alignment: a spiral staircase of treacherous, uneven steps. The stinky sock Tub had mocked earlier went tumbling down the stairs until it was swallowed by darkness. A few rogue marbles followed suit and we did not hear them land.

Jack bounded downward. He was almost out of view before realizing we hadn't moved.

"Let's go," he snapped.

Tub and I stared at each other, then at the bed being held over our heads by ARRRGH!!! as if it weighed no more than a sheet. She nodded us on, her horns ripping through my posters and helpfully rearranging my models.

I descended with baby steps. Soon my eyes adjusted to the dim orange glow radiating from underground electrical grids. But this remained a staircase without a railing, and I moved with a caution that frustrated Jack. He sighed and took steps by threes and fours. It made me feel lousy—this thirteen-year-old kid was making me look bad—but what else was I going to do? I inhaled the briny funk of troll, tried to ignore the slither and thump of their weird appendages, and focused on maintaining my slow and steady pace. Tub, meanwhile, kept two handfuls of my shirt.

Ten minutes were spent passing through freezing air. Then we dipped into a lower stratum that was warmer, then hot, then sweltering. Light now came from oil lamps, the same as I'd seen on my previous adventure, and at last I could see the walls around me. The staircase ran out of steps and my foot landed badly. Tub's full weight slammed me from behind and we started to topple, but warm, rippling tentacles curled beneath our armpits and brought us back to standing position. *Look thankful,* I thought as I shivered in disgust.

Jack chose one of three stone archways and charged into the lamplit tunnel. I didn't cherish the idea of being left alone with two trolls, no matter how nice they were being, so I took off at a sprint. Nearly a full, harrowing minute was spent alone in the shadowed tunnel before I caught up.

"Uncle Jack, wait," I called. "You have to explain all this. At least some of it? Or just a tiny little bit of it? I don't know why you brought us. You said you want us to hunt. Look, that's fine, that's great, Grandpa took me mushroom hunting once. I was pretty good at it, found like twenty of those things. I don't mind helping, really. But Tub and I are pretty freaked, so maybe you could just—"

Jack turned around. Though I was two years older (or forty-three years younger, depending on how you looked at it), he and I were the same height.

"Grandpa?" he asked.

"Yeah. Grandpa. One time we—"

Jack's eyes were shining.

Several seconds passed before I realized that the man I

called "Grandpa" was Jack's dad. This made me feel rotten because I knew what he'd ask next.

"Is he . . . ?" Jack let the question trail off.

I swallowed.

"He died five years ago."

Jack blinked hard for a few seconds, then nodded. This left his face pointing downward, and he seemed to notice his wire-covered right arm for the first time. He turned it this way and that, examining the makeshift armor as if it were a colony of leeches that had attached itself to his arm.

"I've missed," he whispered, "so much."

"Come up with me," I urged. "Dad will be so happy. He never really stopped looking for you."

Jack examined me as if looking for proof that we were related.

"You're a Sturges," he said.

"I guess."

"You know what the name means? Did Jimbo—your dad, I mean—did he ever tell you?"

"No."

"And Dad—I mean, your grandpa—he never told you, either?"

"Sorry."

Jack pressed his lips together in disappointment.

"Comes from the ancient word *styrgar.* Means spearhead or battle spear. It's the name of a warrior."

"Great," I said.

Jack leaned in with a snarl.

"No," he said. "It is not great. It is the worst kind of burden. Before we're through, you'll wish you had been born with a different name. You'll wish you could wake up a different *person.* Because warriors? They go to war. And war is not fun. War is bloody. Things that were alive end up dead and sometimes you're the one who has to burn what's left over. And when they go, Jim, they don't go quietly. They make sounds. For the rest of your life, when you try to sleep, those are the sounds that will keep you awake."

Back a few bends in the tunnel, I heard the crushing footfall, serpentine slither, and tennis-shoe stumble of the absent characters.

"Hey, look," I said. "You've convinced me. I don't want in your club or whatever."

"Got no choice," he grunted. "Every few generations, the Sturges clan produces a warrior of consequence, a paladin. It might be you, Jim. It might not. Either way, we have to find out. I can't do this by myself anymore. Something's happening. And we're going to need every paladin we can round up."

"There's more? Why can't you get them instead? Where are they?"

Jack shrugged. "Sure, there's more. From other families. Probably. Somewhere. If they didn't die out. But the lines have been lost. For now it's just you and me." He gave my skinny body another dubious perusal. "You and me and the battle of our lives."

Tub came around the bend with a ghastly pasted-on grin. Behind him loped and slunk the two mismatched trolls, leaving in their wake tumbleweeds of hair and a trail of sludge. Jack turned on his boot heel and recommenced his stomping.

Tub grabbed me by the shoulder. He kept his voice cheery.

"Gee, *Jim.* Thanks for leaving me all alone with the troll patrol."

"Sorry, Tub."

He pushed me in the direction of Jack and lowered his voice.

"They jabbered at me so crazy I thought I'd puke. I don't know if they were asking if I wanted a juice box or if they were planning my dissection. *I can't understand them, Jim.* Please try to remember that. It was like being trapped in a preschool. Except where the toddlers could eat you."

Blinky sidled up next to me with those mysterious legs, his kilt of medals creating wind-chime music.

"Do not sodden your battle scarf with tears," he said. "I fear your uncle was, shall we say, *coarse* when addressing your concerns? Understand that this rushed introduction is far from ideal. The ideal way, incidentally, according to customs in which I am fully literate, is through cuneiform tablet invitation to a midmorning tea complete with the competitive gobbling of succulent goat pudding and the call-and-response recitation of the ode to amity, 'The Epic of Greinhart the Grinning,' in which both you and your man-at-arms, and we, as well, would recite alternating stanzas in the voices of the Old World Elders. O-ho! How I would savor lending full vociferation to Stugnarb the Affectionate while you responded in the agreeable tones of Funkletta the Affable. Alas, we live in a time ill-suited for long-form poetry. For this reason and more, I beg that you forgive your uncle's brusqueness. Since the very hour we brought him into our realm, his life has been hardship."

"You're the ones who stole him?"

"Technically, it was ARRRGH!!! who did the stealing."

"Boy stole," said ARRRGH!!!. "Boy sad. Sad boy."

So it was all true. The legendary monster that had taken Uncle Jack in 1969 was not a figment of my father's screwed-up imagination. That monster was real and she was right here, communicating with me, walking on all fours so as to fit through the tunnel, her long red tongue licking stray globs of peanut butter from her fur. Unexpectedly I felt anger rather than fear.

"You two have no idea what you did. To my Dad. To his whole family. To me, too—my life has gotten ruined right along with everyone else's, you know."

Several of Blinky's eyes drooped so low they touched the stone floor.

"Many a long day have I spent undulating in regret rather than sleeping. Shall I admit to you a shameful truth? Indeed, I shall! The night we took Jack we were uncertain that we had claimed the correct child. In fact, we'd tried to take both brothers and failed in spectacular fashion. But Jack, frightened though he was at being taken from your remedial world and plunged into our advanced kingdom, would not permit us to go back and exchange him for your father. He said—and this I shall never forget, for it fills my seven cold bellies with warmth—'Keep me. I'll do what you ask. Just leave my little brother alone.'"

I tried to imagine my dad, uncredited inventor of the Excalibur Calculator Pocket and lawn-mower-for-hire, down here among the trolls. But I could only imagine him rolled into a ball in the corner. Nonetheless, Dad had been right about one thing: Uncle Jack might be the bravest kid who ever lived.

"Translate, Jim, translate," Tub hissed.

"No time," I murmured. "This one talks a ton."

"Oh, okay. I'll just keep on being completely terrified, then."

"Nothing so drowns me in melancholic murk as does Jack's uneasy fate," Blinky continued. "Yet I rouse myself from that lachrymose lugubriosity by recalling the forty-five years of peace that followed. The hundreds of human children whose lives were saved. Your uncle is responsible for that, with the humble assistance of present company. Jack Sturges brought an end to what you call the Milk Carton Epidemic."

"Why did it happen? Who took all those kids?"

Blinky's eyes grew redder. Half blind though they were, every one of them found me.

"Gunmar the Black."

ARRRGH!!! howled. Lamps flickered. Stones spilled from the sides of the tunnel.

"An apropos reaction from my shaggy sidekick! Jack helped us vanquish Gunmar the Black—alias the Hungry One, alias He Who Sups of Blood, alias the Untangler of Entrails—thereby draining Gunmar of his considerable power. Now, for reasons we do not yet understand, Gunmar is once more growing stronger. It has always been his goal to invade the human world and feast at will, and that is precisely what will happen if we do not locate him soon."

The tunnel darkened as we passed through a stone portico opening into a spacious cavern. Once my eyes adjusted to the brighter light I recognized it as the place I'd been before. There was the steaming stove and the mountain of old bicycles lording over the various other foothills of junk. Above, the packets of hot-wired fluorescent lights spat irritably and radiated sickly glows.

"Oh, neat," Tub said. "Can I have one of these bikes?"

He reached out and I slapped his wrist.

"Dead kid bikes!" I hissed.

Tub scrubbed at his hand as if he'd plunged it into a bowl of spiders.

Across the cave, Jack was standing before a large, flat stone and sifting through a pile of sharp metal that glinted in the firelight. I found that I didn't especially want to know what he was doing. Instead, I turned back to the trolls.

"This Gunmar guy," I said. "How do you know for sure he's getting stronger?"

Four of Blinky's eyes performed a nodding gesture at ARRRGH!!!. The hairy beast squirreled a massive paw into her thick pelt and after some rustling around emerged with a battered old cardboard box. Gently she lowered it to our level. The box itself seemed irrelevant: it bore the stamps and stickers of a shipping company and it was addressed to a San Bernardino address. The top flap, though, was moving as if nudged by something inside. My feet felt cemented to the ground.

"Fine," Tub sighed. "Tell Grandma I love her. Make up something nice about the cats, too."

He psyched himself up with a few quick breaths, then threw open the flap and looked in.

"Oh, Jim." His voice was monotone. "Jim, oh. Oh, oh, oh. Jim, Jim, Jim."

I gritted my teeth and bent over the open flap.

Inside the box was a giant eyeball. The iris was the mixed colors of pea green and cantaloupe orange, the vitreous humor was a sickly yellow, and laced throughout was a grasping network of desperate red blood vessels. Not only was it the same size as Steve Jorgensen-Warner's ill-famed basketball, but it made that infamous threat seem downright benign.

"The Eye of Malevolence," Blinky said. "ARRRGH!!! ripped it from Gunmar the Black during the final confrontation in 1969. Let me assure you that the Eye is a bad thing that ought to be destroyed, in the off chance that is not self-evident. But pray give pause to your urges to squash it! The Eye serves a dark purpose. As owner of the accursed orb, ARRRGH!!! has the ability to use it to see what Gunmar sees. For decades, it was darkness, obscurity, despair. In recent weeks, however, the view has changed. And ARRRGH!!!—dear dutiful, selfless ARRRGH!!!—has been tasked with looking through the Eye far more frequently than advisable."

"*Glurrrgrrummmfahfrummmph*, eh?" Tub said. "Fascinating!"

I apologized to Tub before giving him a quick recap.

"Okay, that's actually pretty interesting," Tub said. "Can we see it? Can you put on the eye right now?"

It was strange to see a being as large as ARRRGH!!! cower. Blinky's eight eyes arranged themselves in sympathetic formation. But the hairy troll rolled her massive jaw and found the courage to throw back her shoulders until they were as big as the sails of a ship.

"Boy human. Favor ask. I do. For friend."

We bent over the cardboard box in anticipation of the Eye's removal. The pupil was blacker than black, an abyss so absolute that I felt my body tipping toward its promised oblivion. It had a salty seaside odor, strong enough to make me dizzy. Yet I wanted to inhale its pungent gases until I'd absorbed all of its sick power. I leaned closer, just inches away, fantasizing about what the Eye of Malevolence might feel like against my skin. Hot? Cool? Silky? Rubbery? I had to know.

The Eye contracted like a bicep. The vessels thickened as if pumped full of paint. One of the vessels popped, spilling greasy orange blood that fizzed as if carbonated. The black pupil yawned like a mouth and the iris shattered into triangular daggers of teeth, which gnashed at my eyelashes before someone yanked me back to safety.

"Bad idea."

Jack slapped the box flap shut, wrapped ARRRGH!!!'s fingers around it, and shoved the hand away with all of his might. The towering beast snorted as if awakening from a daydream and discovering with honest surprise that the wilted box was resting in her great gray palm. Ducking her gigantic head like a chastened child, the troll tucked the box into her draperies of fur. Jack glared at Blinky, whose guilty eyes found eight different things to look at. Then Jack found someone else to glare at: me.

"You connect too often with the Eye, you start seeing things like Gunmar. Start acting like him, too. Not good. Believe me."

Given that I was doubled over coughing the Eye's invasive stink from my lungs, I believed him. If this was the effect of one small piece of Gunmar the Black, I had little interest in meeting the rest.

Jack hitched up a loaded burlap sack.

"Come on. Long night. Let's get to it."

Eager to return to Jack's good graces, ARRRGH!!! and Blinky hurried by on either side of me. I took a personal moment to expectorate the rest of the Eye's residue from my mouth. While bent with hands on knees, I glanced at the stone mural and remembered how the bridge depicted as stretching across the Atlantic Ocean was identical to the one procured by Professor Lempke.

"Hey," I said. "What does the Killaheed Bridge have to do with all of this?"

The cellar dwellers halted in unison. First, Blinky's wide red eyes oscillated in my direction. ARRRGH!!! moved next, turning her slobbering snout over her goliath shoulder. Jack

was the last to look at me, his face unreadable in the chiar-
oscuro light.

I wiped the spit from my lips and cleared my throat.

"Did I say that wrong? Killa-hide-y? Killa-hoo-dee?"

Nobody moved.

"I just noticed it on your wall there. Tub and I saw the real
one at the museum. It opens to the public on Friday. Tub and I
could probably sneak you in free if you—"

Jack dropped his sack with a metallic crunch, stalked
across the room, leapt over the pile of dolls, and collided with
me straight on. He snared my collar with both gloves, his pin-
studded knuckles ripping through the fabric.

"Here? How? What the hell are you talking about?"

Tub, my hero, patted ineffectually at Jack's shoulder.

"Let up, man! It's just part of a stupid exhibit!"

Jack threw me to the floor and charged Tub, who fell to his
butt against the hill of bicycles.

"The Killaheed Bridge?" Jack shouted. "In San Bernardino?"

"Yes!" Tub pleaded.

"And Friday? What happens on Friday?"

"I don't know, man! Something about the head stone? It
shows up on Friday or something?"

Jack's shoulders raged up and down. He forced himself to
back away, as if afraid he might accidentally tear us to pieces,
and in a swift motion pulled his mask back over his face. With
those emotionless glass eyes in place, he withdrew both swords
from their scabbards, twirled them once, and held them with
trembling fists. Then he leaned back and bayed like a coyote
through the metallic filter of the mask. The pipes overhead
buzzed and shed filaments of rust. Tub and I held our ears.

Before the shout finished echoing, Jack whirled around and decapitated a doll with his left sword and sliced the handlebars off a bike with his right. Both items toppled into the mouth of the oven. Jack did not pause to bask in this impressive feat but instead stomped across the cave, sheathed his swords, picked up the burlap sack, and marched into a side tunnel. He vanished into the darkness.

I watched the doll's happy face melt into a disfigured blob. Tub helped me up.

"That uncle of yours is going to kill us."

"I know," I said.

Tentacles enveloped our shoulders, more than we could count, each quivering suction cup attaching to our flesh painfully and pushing us forward.

"There, there, nothing but a spot of dirt. Just some good-natured roughhousing between boys, eh?" His sigh was jittery. "Goodness, this is trickier than I expected. But worry not, dwarfish brave ones. We'll be at the training ground in three stones, no longer."

"Three stones?" I mumbled.

"Apologies, apologies." Blinky whisked us into the dark tunnel through which Jack had vanished. "Stones are a troll measurement of time. It's quite literal. Three stones being the amount of time it takes an average troll to eat three stones. In other words, not long at all."

"You eat rocks?"

"Not if it can be avoided. It's a bitter meal for the sophisticated palette. But culinary preferences are of little consequence right now. Hurry along."

Blinky's eyes emitted a pale red light, just enough for us to see by. Up ahead we heard the jangling of Jack's armor. He wasn't waiting for us to catch up, that was for sure. What's more, I no longer wanted to catch up. Maybe my uncle had been valiant in saving my father from a life beneath the world's surface, but the forty-five years spent down here had twisted his mind, turned him into a madman.

I put on the breaks and held back Tub with an arm.

"Feckless little leprechauns!" Blinky cried. "Your temerity shall be the death of me! Oh, why do I allow this life of conflict to interrupt the cozy solitude of the scholar? Favor me, runt animals, by continuing on?"

"Explain," I said. "That's all I ask."

At full volume Blinky's scornful tone was plenty intimidating.

"My emotional state is not to be trifled with!"

"The Killaheed Bridge, Gunmar the Black," I said. "We can't protect ourselves from that psycho up there if we don't know what you're even talking about."

Tub held onto my waist like a drowning man.

"Our Father," he mumbled, "who harks from heaven . . . shank us this day . . . some daily bread . . ."

"Tub!" I hissed. "You're Jewish!"

"I know," he hissed back, "that's why I don't know the damn words!"

ARRRGH!!! growled from behind us. Her hot breath dampened our necks.

"Explain!" I said, bracing myself against an outcropping of brick.

"And forgive us our bread," Tub continued, "as we forgive those who bread against us . . ."

Blinky recoiled his tentacles. With dry rustles, they twisted, untwisted, and laced into patterns the meaning of which I couldn't begin to guess. Ooze hung from his pores in beads; the effect was like that of a great inhale.

"Very well. You do, after all, have standing before you the foremost living authority on troll movement in America. But hark, young scamps! My explanations come with two conditions. Condition one! That I might save time by quoting liberally from my unfinished eleven-thousand-page, thirty-eight-volume dissertation, *Troll Migration from the Old World and Suggestions for Future Growth and Sustainable Materials; Featuring an Account of the Great Gumm-Gumm War in America and Appendices on Euro-American Troll Type, Size, Smell, and Hue.* Condition two! That we keep locomoting in *this* direction during the education. The night is not infinite in length. All agreed?"

"Sure. Fine. Start talking." I nudged Tub. "He's going to tell us stuff."

Tub sniffled from where he nuzzled my armpit.

"Amen," he concluded.

20.

Trolls have existed on this planet for as long as humans. This is what I was told and what I translated to Tub. The first mention of them in recorded history is from ninth-century Norway, when the nefarious creatures began showing up in song, verse, and bedtime stories to keep misbehaving children in line. According to Norse folklore, trolls are one of the Dark Beings, the purest embodiments of evil, and they scurried from between the toes of Ymir, the mythic six-headed Frost Giant whose murdered body became the universe in which we live: his bones became the mountains, his teeth boulders, and so forth.

This origin, Blinky said, is considered a fairy tale by modern trolls. Some even bristle at the very word *troll*, derived from an ancient Norse word meaning "one who walks clumsily." Regardless of what you call them, there is little doubt that human civilization after the Ice Age was frequently interrupted by the six varieties of troll: mountain, forest, sea, water, farm, and hulder-folk—all of whom held great hatred in their hearts for the humans who ruined the forests, fields, and rocks that had long been the trolls' domains. Thankfully, humans also built plenty of bridges, structures so laden with symbolism (the crossing from one place to another) that trolls were able to use them as shortcuts into the underworld.

("All bridges?" I asked Blinky. "Yes," he said. "Even foot bridges?" I asked. *"Yes,"* he said. "What if I just laid a plank over a hole, would that work?" I asked. "You need to let me finish this story," he replied rather sternly.)

Trolls also had the ability to come and go from beneath the beds of innocents. For all means and purposes this meant children, though these gateways were less practical than bridges for numerous reasons. If the child was deep in sleep, for example, trolls could become infected with their dreams, resulting in something like the flu, the severity of which would depend on what kind of dream it was. Though rare, human children, too, could use these doorways.

Despite these cunning entryways into our world, trolls had limited ways to fight. Sunlight turned them into stone, so their retaliation against humans was relegated to evening hours. Stories from the ninth century feature trolls protecting their habitats by any means necessary, often focusing their aggression on churches, which were, quite simply, convenient gathering spots for humans. One activity that brought trolls endless amusement was tossing boulders at these churches. This undying wrath, more than any inherent flavor, made human meat the most prized of all troll dishes.

But for as long as there have been human-eating trolls, there have been humans to fight them. The Sturgeon/Sturges family were the subjects of many a ballad, hymn, and shanty. Armed with sword and bow and shields painted with their crest (*Esse quam videre*: "Be—do not seem"), they defended their camps from troll attacks before adopting the more proactive stance of flushing trolls from their hiding spots. From this lineage rose several celebrated warriors. In 1533, Ragnar Sturgeon used his teeth to bite the head off a troll to save Wales from an invasion of Mugglewumps. In 1666, Rosalind Sturgeon was partly responsible for the Great Fire of London while fending off a horde of large Irish Batmuggs. Possibly the most controversial was Theobald Sturges, who rescued a battalion of English soldiers during the Battle of Mons from a pack of Gizcullders who attempted to burrow upward through the trenches.

("Damn," Tub said after translation. "Ragnar is a cool-ass name.")

Trolls spread like fire across the Eurasian continent. Iceland, Sweden, Finland, Germany, France, and Scotland were the locations of the most storied underworld kingdoms, though troll populations rose up as far away as China. However, as recently as the early seventeenth century—and seeing how trolls can live for up to a thousand years, that's pretty recent—there was not a single troll on American soil.

That changed when a ship called the *Mayflower* set off from Plymouth, England, on September 6, 1620, carrying an official list of one hundred thirty passengers. Human passengers, that is. As for the unaccounted trolls hiding in the cargo section, it is anyone's guess. Estimates range from two dozen to triple digits, especially if you count the green, furry-tailed gremlins, which could easily pack thirty to a barrel. Not that any serious scholar would bother counting gremlins, of course.

The *Mayflower* trolls were not just courageous explorers willing to risk life and limb on a perilous voyage across a sunlit ocean, but also staunch separatists. A philosophical argument had riven the troll communities of the British Isles into two factions. Most kept a traditional conservative view of troll/human relations. That is, humans would continue to spoil the natural resources the trolls held dear, and the trolls, in return, would eat the humans.

But a splinter group led by Ebenezer ARRRGH!!! of the Lincolnshire ARRRGH!!!s believed that this relationship was not only unsustainable but immoral, and promoted to his believers a program of better living through four-legged consumption. Abolished were the tender main courses of human children. Gone were the spicy after-dinner snacks of human sausage straight from the smokehouse. Forbidden were the breakfast treats of sugared old-person skin. These trolls favored rabbits, squirrels, raccoons, rats, certain varieties of bird, and the occasional seasonal cat.

("Are there any vegetarian trolls?" I asked. "In fact, for a time there was a sect called the Nilboggians," replied Blinky, "who believed that trolls could live on plant matter alone. 'Twas a most virtuous experiment, though after nineteen days every Nilboggian spontaneously dissolved into a puddle of green slime.")

No sooner had they landed in America than the separatist trolls fled the *Mayflower* by night and found bridges beneath which they could enter the underworld and begin to build livable homes. The Eastern seaboard flourished with fertile cave ground, and the trolls spread to new quarters in their characteristic fashion: slowly but steadily. No sooner would a new bridge be inaugurated than a troll and its family would take residence beneath it. Few trolls made the dangerous trek to the West and fewer made it alive, but many of those who did found themselves drawn to quiet San Bernardino, "The Cupped

Hand of God." At last trolls had found a temperate home that did not require the stocking of food for long winters.

The Sturges family arrived in the New World not fifty years after the trolls, settling first in Boston and Maine. The American Sturgeses, however, found themselves without reason to fight the peaceful Euro-American trolls, and over time their warrior lifestyle was overtaken by pursuits far more useful for a developing nation: the art of tannery, the brewing of ale, the growing of soybeans, and, much later, the perfection of the calculator pocket.

Three hundred and fifty years passed with little more kerfuffle than the occasional irate cat owner. Then something happened that changed the course of troll/human history forever. In 1967, the London Bridge, which ran across the River Thames and was the busiest hub of traffic in that great city, was disassembled and shipped in its entirety over five thousand miles away to Lake Havasu City, Arizona. Absurd though this may seem, it is true: a rich engineer purchased the London Bridge as a tourist attraction to bring people to his out-of-the-way real estate development.

The Arizona reconstruction took over three years to complete, but it took only an hour for the trolls who'd stowed away inside the bridge segments to escape. Upon landing in Arizona, the inhabitants of London Bridge tore apart their crates and fled into the night. By January of 1968, they had crossed the California border and set about doing what Old World trolls did best: eating children. This treacherous tribe, made up of all the worst elements of every troll family in Europe, was collectively known as the Gumm-Gumms.

("'Gumm-Gumms'?" Tub repeated. "That's pretty much the

least scary name I've ever heard." "Imagine what we think of 'Dershowitz,'" Blinky replied. This comment I didn't bother to translate.)

The Gumm-Gumms had terrorized the Eurasian continent for well over a thousand years. They were first mentioned in a parchment addressed to King Constantine II circa 920 A.D., wherein they were described as "horrid and of putrid breath and hoggish in their appetites." In the 1100s the Gumm-Gumms descended from the Scottish Highlands, and just one hundred years later were known to have taken possession of every single bridge in Londinium under the barbaric command of their ageless leader, Gunmar the Black. It is believed that Gunmar chose to center his clan in San Bernardino specifically to spite the self-satisfied pacifists who populated the local underworld.

Whatever the reason, he and his minions wasted no time stealing children. One per month for the first three months. Then one per week. By the time 1969 began, several children were disappearing every week in San Bernardino, each one of them dragged screaming to a hidden underground labyrinth and caged for weeks before being grilled over an open flame and eaten.

American trolls had lost their instinct for fighting and allowed the Gumm-Gumm blitz to continue for far too long. At last, the American tribes gathered for a "wapentake," an ancient Viking tradition whereupon the leaders of each clan, from the Bluzbumps to the Killtillians, turned over their weapons so that they might speak toward a common goal. Together, they admitted the consequences of not getting involved: a new war between trolls and humans on the continent they'd worked so hard to keep neutral.

Fortunately, they had strong numbers and a stronger leader. At the tender age of seventy-five, she was yet a child, but already possessed of a strong will, an optimistic outlook, and an aptitude for adventure. Her name was Johannah M. ARRRGH!!!.

("What's the M stand for?" I asked. "Mmmm," Blinky replied.)

Johannah M. ARRRGH!!! would lead an army of trolls on a hunt for the Gumm-Gumm lair. With great pomp and fanfare they dug up chests containing some of the most prized possessions in all trolldom: ancient astrolabes that, according to lore, had been gifted by the faerie folk of lower Scandinavia after a tribe of Snicksnuck trolls rescued a coterie of faeries from torture at the hooves of a deranged faun.

Guided by these mystical compasses, the trolls began searching for the Gumm-Gumms. At the same time, an up-and-coming scribe and record-keeper of the Lizzgump clan who went by the name of Blinky was tasked with the study of genealogical scrolls in hopes of locating a human paladin who could aid them in their oncoming battle. Day and night, Blinky scoured eight scrolls at once, devoting one eye per scroll, until the strain was so great that, one by one, the eyes went blind—but not before discovering a family of Sturgeses right there in San Bernardino.

("Sorry you lost your eyesight," I said. "Indeed it was a happenstance most disagreeable," Blinky replied, "seeing how I was but a lad of forty-four and four hundred years. I, of course, devote a full volume of my dissertation to this tragedy.")

The drafting of a paladin was considered a great risk. Living in peace beneath humans was one thing. But fighting alongside one? It had never been done. But with the Milk

Carton Epidemic in full swing, it was a necessary gamble. So it was that on September 21, 1969, Jack Sturges was taken against his will into Troll City, where he rapidly matured into a prominent warrior.

With Jack working in tandem with ARRRGH!!!, the troll army ransacked the Gumm-Gumm lair. While Jack single-handedly dispatched dozens of lesser trolls and commanded his legion of warriors with unflagging vigor, it was Johannah ARRRGH!!! who took on the Hungry One. It was a battle long in the making: eleven hundred years earlier, Gunmar had lost an arm to Remmarah ARRRGH!!!, Johannah's grandmother, in a fantastic midnight skirmish along the Austria/Hungary border. Since that night, Gunmar had not only sworn his revenge, but had also begun to notch each kill on the makeshift wooden arm he'd rammed into his still-bleeding stump.

The first wave of the onslaught was bleak. Gunmar, a beast so indescribably awful that he cannot, at this particular moment, be described, toyed with Johannah ARRRGH!!!. It was only when Gunmar embedded a boulder in the hairy troll's cranium that the tide began to change. Instead of killing Johannah ARRRGH!!!, the injury seemed to squash whatever small amount of hesitation existed in her brain. She became an uncontrollable, rampaging beast who came at Gunmar in a tornado of teeth, claws, and fur. One of Gunmar's eyes—the Eye of Malevolence—was torn out in the fray. Soon Gunmar fell, his minions were killed or captured, and it was left to Jack, the human hero, to deliver the killing blow to the Hungry One.

Exhausted of bloodshed, Jack instead banished Gunmar into isolation among the deepest of earth's caves. Gunmar slunk away, swearing revenge upon Jack, Johannah ARRRGH!!!, and all of their offspring. These curses were difficult to understand, for Gunmar was chewing upon his tongue in rage. Every sound he released hissed like a serpent: SSSSSSSS.

Jack's mercy was a success in one sense: the remaining Gumm-Gumms swore to switch to a four-legged diet and enlisted in several eleven-step programs to keep them on the non-human-eating wagon. Festivity reigned in the troll kingdom for months. As a sign of respect, trolls began referring to Johannah by her last name alone, and parent trolls would hold up their babies when ARRRGH!!! passed by so that the young ones could touch the boulder still sticking out of the back of her skull.

("That chunk of bedrock remains there to this day," Blinky said. "It is the reason for my friend's impaired speech." ARRRGH!!! agreed: "Rock make unhappy talk.")

What Jack realized too late was that he'd doomed himself to a subterrestrial life. His mercy had been a distinctly human thing—no troll would have hesitated to destroy Gunmar—and so he felt a responsibility to keep watch should Gunmar ever return. If Jack returned to the human world, he would grow older, and eventually the doorways to the troll world would be lost to him. He would need to stay young to defend against Gunmar, and the only way to do that was to remain underground.

Jack, forever thirteen, trained every day, every year, ever watchful, ever paranoid. He was the only one not surprised several months before when the Eye of Malevolence showed them Gunmar's slow trek back from the bowels of the earth. Jack had made speeches in Troll City, but nobody listened. The trolls there had become fat, complacent, consumed with their food and trinkets, and certain that nothing like the Gumm-Gumm War could happen again.

So defensive efforts were up to Jack, Blinky, and ARRRGH!!!. As Gunmar's power grew, Jack decided with great regret that Jim would have to be tested for paladin potential. But Jack had figured on having months, even years, to properly train his nephew. Now with the news of a bridge being reconstructed in the San Bernardino Historical Society Museum, those months and years had been shaved down to mere days.

The Killaheed Bridge had been the ancestral home of Gunmar the Black in the far northern region of Scotland known in Gaelic as *A' Ghàidhealtachd*. It is where he murdered every blood relative, erasing his surname in favor of "the Black," and began the Gumm-Gumm cult with himself as the principal deity. The bridge was the nexus of his ancient power, and its shipment from across the ocean toward California must be what was powering his quick regeneration and drawing weak-minded trolls, a new army of Gumm-Gumms, back under his influence.

For months, trolls had been infiltrating San Bernardino at night and creating havoc. Nothing so far as abduction, not yet, but Jack, Blinky, and ARRRGH!!! had been kept busy enough that they'd had little chance to search out Gunmar himself. It had been a gamble revealing themselves to Jim, and, inadvertently, Tub. But in war, such wagers were necessary. This was the lot of the trollhunters.

(*Trollhunters*. I couldn't help smiling a little. I liked the sound of it.)

Each twisted tentacle and gnarled claw was so deeply etched that your eyes got lost inside the voids, and each one grasped toward the missing head stone.

21.

Jack waited for us in an unlit clearing with the burlap sack over his shoulder. The clay wall before him was cracked to reveal patches of intricate tile mosaics and begrimed frescoes created by troll artists of yesteryear. Entering this clearing from the tunnel was like traveling from throat to stomach; the rumble of motor vehicles, somewhere far above us, completed the illusion.

He seemed smaller inside that scrap-metal armor than he had before, more the dimensions of an adolescent boy than an inscrutable devil. Surely he had heard our approach, yet he did not react. I was about to say something when I noticed a group of trolls off to the right. Tub and I skittered aside, but Blinky and ARRRGH!!! showed no alarm. In fact, in their strange faces I saw pity.

It was the same routine I'd seen in the red-light district. These trolls stood in a trance before a leaning tower of flickering, half-busted TVs, their faces pressed to the sets, their long tongues lapping at the screens.

"Do not stare," Blinky said. "It is a lamentable sight."

"What's with you guys and TVs?" I asked.

Blinky spoke in a hush. "Do not be quick to judge, small-brained one. There is no sun in the life of a troll, indeed scarce little light at all. Is it any wonder that we cherish your televisions, that some of us even worship them like primitive man worshipped his sun gods—Ra, Helios, Apollo, Sol Invictus, Huitzilopochtli?" His tentacles rippled haughtily. "There is not a troll alive who possesses fewer than two sets."

"What shows do you guys like?"

"What you would consider lacking in entertainment value, we prefer. Commercials, in fact, are prized among us for their accelerated pace and bright colorings. Nothing, though, satisfies like pure static. Should you find time to study this liquid weave, you will discover beauty, divinity. So many sifting layers, so many patterns of meaning, so many whispered secrets."

Drool poured from the slack mouths of at least two of the mesmerized trolls.

"So it's like a drug?" I asked.

"It is precisely a drug. The calming effect is unlike anything else, and it is perfectly healthy in moderation. Today's troll experiences almost daily televisual contact. Nurses use them to ease the dementia of the elderly. Mothers use them to quiet their brood. I myself once spent a period of years riveted by an extraordinary signal from a faraway place called the BBC. I like to think that it contributed to the melodious harmonics of my voice."

"It did," I said. "Trust me."

"But I am one of the fortunate. Like any drug taken in excess, it can ruin a mind. Those poor souls there will give every coin they have to try new signals, better signals, any signal at all, and while doing so will forget to eat, forget to drink, forget to excrete their waste. It is no coincidence that many cemeteries are located near Static Dens."

"Why doesn't it affect people that way?"

"Doesn't it, dear boy?"

"All right. I see what you're saying. But why—"

Jack slapped the brick with his right hand and snarled without turning around.

"You ask too many questions. Why this? Why that? How does it all work? What does it all mean? Down here things are what they are. You better get used to it. Or better yet, stop caring. Because there will never be enough answers to satisfy you, and even if there were, we don't have the time."

From within his suit of metal he withdrew yet more metal—the intersecting discs and dials of an astrolabe. I knew from school that astrolabes were used in the Middle Ages to identify stars. But none that I'd seen in textbooks measured up to this clockwork contraption. It was no larger than a teacup saucer but intricate beyond imagination. At least four rings, each pitted within the other, rolled about on sharp bronze teeth, while two hands notched with indecipherable measurements struck collision points. The whole thing was encased in a lattice of gold and decorated around the circumference with a forest silhouette so detailed that I could make out the etchings of individual leaves. Craftsmanship notwithstanding, the gold was burnished, the bronze stained, the various components bent and chipped.

Jack held the weathered astrolabe in the air, spun the wheels, and swept it across an increasingly small stretch of wall until he was able to touch one single brick with a finger. This was ARRRGH!!!'s signal. She shouldered her way closer, footfalls disrupting the TV signals. Several trolls broke from their trances and threw us spiteful looks.

ARRRGH!!! placed both paws to the wall. The muscled carpet of her back rippled and the wall opened along the irregular pattern of the brick. I covered my face against the specks of stone sent swirling by the churning cloud of dust. Tub and I shooed away the grit and watched as Jack and the two trolls made their way into a place that looked oddly familiar. We, too, passed through the door and were so amazed by what we saw that we weren't startled by the sound of the wall sealing shut behind us.

A road sign. That's what we were looking at. Not in troll language, not featuring some multiheaded beast, just a regular yellow road sign warning truck drivers that the bridge had a low clearance. Yes, that's right—we were under a bridge. More specifically, a highway underpass in a darkened, industrial corridor in what looked like an anonymous suburb. We looked around and found worthless crap that now was the most welcome sight in the whole world: obscene graffiti on the concrete, six-pack rings collecting against a chain-link fence, and the red-and-yellow lights of a fast-food joint just over the next rise in the road. There were street signs, too, and Tub was excitedly pointing them out.

"De La Rosa! We're in De La Rosa! We could walk home from here!" He addressed Jack. "Is it cool if we walk home from here?"

Jack was still consulting his astrolabe. Cars crossed overhead, oblivious of the creatures that lurked below. After an interminable silence, he snapped shut the golden device and pointed.

"Nullhullers. Two blocks away. They're converging. We need to make this quick."

He threw down the sack. I flinched at the violent clashing noise. Jack jabbed his chin at it.

"Go ahead."

Accepting the bag's contents seemed like it would solidify my position in this bizarre brigade. I hesitated. The thirteen-year-old unsheathed a sword and drove it into the pavement. Alarmed ants scrambled out of the fresh fissure. Jack's voice crackled from the boom box speaker.

"Gunmar the Black gets stronger every day. More and more trolls, dangerous ones, are disappearing because they're drawn to do his bidding. Every night minions like these Nullhullers stray farther. They're in De La Rosa tonight. You want them to be at your house tomorrow? You want kids on your block to start disappearing? You want to know what that's like?"

Tub made an impatient gesture at the bag. I took a breath, leaned over, and opened it. Inside were two weapons: a dull, pockmarked long-sword and a short, curved cutlass. I held them in either hand, so thrown off by the uneven weight that I wondered if I'd be able to take two steps without pitching over.

"What about me? I don't get any weapons?" Tub asked.

"No," Jack replied. "You want to walk home? Walk."

Tub's shoulders slumped. He looked hurt.

If Jack cared, you couldn't tell through that mask. He pulled his sword from the cement and swirled it through the air with such speed that it seemed to become liquid mercury. It caught the yellow streetlights and drew upon the nighttime canvas like holiday sparklers.

"Three rules," Jack said. "Rule number one: be afraid."

"No problem," Tub said. "We're going to nail that one."

"Being afraid means being aware. Think of the rabbit."

The sword drew a simple sketch of a rabbit. It was so graceful and unexpected that I gasped. Then it was gone so quickly that I was left wondering if I had imagined it.

"The rabbit is nothing but vulnerable parts and good meat: throat, belly, thigh. Yet it is hard to catch. It watches and listens, all of the time, because it is afraid. Trolls smell fear and charge it. You can use this to your advantage."

Again the sword swirled through the sky. This time the golden outline of a bull burned into my retinas long after it had dissipated from the air.

"Just like a toreador in a bullfight. Use their weight or velocity or anger against them. When you do strike, do it hard and do it fast."

Jack squiggled the blade across the sky and I saw an elegant sketch of a python with a forked tongue and a long tail. I tried to follow the tail to its end but I blinked and the delicate artwork was lost.

"Imagine you're injecting poison. Attack and retract. Attack and retract."

Rabbit. Bull. Python. My imagination assembled a mythological beast with parts of all three. How this amalgamated monster related to my own theoretical fighting tactics should have been entirely unclear. And yet it wasn't. A strange clarity swept over me regarding how these three animals made the perfectly lethal mix.

Jack swung the sword like a golf club, shooting two stones—one that hit my knee, breaking me from my fantasies, and one that struck Tub in the stomach. I hopped up and down in pain and Tub grunted, clutching his tummy. He had our attention, all right.

"Rule number two: there are three vulnerable spots on a troll."

Jack pointed his weapon at ARRRGH!!! and she shuffled over and leaned down, an eager model. Jack swung his sword at her body. I held my breath as the sword halted just short of her chest fur. ARRRGH!!! wiggled like it tickled.

"The heart," Jack said.

He spun around, weaving reflected light around him so that he was ribboned in temporary golden lace. The tip of the sword swooped toward ARRRGH!!!'s lower belly.

"The gallbladder."

The sword cut downward and Jack hopped over it as easily as skipping rope. It passed behind his back, from one hand to the other, before Jack extended his limbs and the tip of the blade rested at the side of ARRRGH!!!'s neck. There, I noticed, a small growth bulged beneath the fur.

"The softies."

ARRRGH!!! yawned—a ghastly sight.

"Softies," Tub repeated. "I must've missed that day in biology. What's a softie?"

Jack whirled around. Yellow light burned off his lenses.

"It's a part that kills trolls when you stick it," he snapped. "This is what we'll be doing this week—*all* we'll be doing this week. If you're right about the Killaheed, we have seven nights, counting tonight, before the bridge reaches completion. We have to eliminate the Gumm-Gumm minions before then and be ready to take on Gunmar. Heart, softies—that's how you kill a troll. The gallbladder—that's how you make sure he stays dead. That fire in our cave? That's where we burn them.

Collect and burn. Got it? A gallbladder left behind can sprout the troll back to life like a seed."

I felt nauseated. The frog dissection in seventh grade had been difficult enough.

"You know, this week's not so good," I said. "It's the Festival of the Fallen Leaves. Wouldn't surprise me if Dad needs help mowing some of the parks. And I'm in this play? We've only got this week to rehearse it. And math! There's a huge math test on Friday, too, and Ms. Pinkton says if I don't get eighty-eight percent I'm going to flunk. So I've really got to study—"

"You will study. With me. Out here. Every night." He swung his blade so that the tip rang across both of my own swords, causing them to twirl in my hands. I had to grip them more tightly so they wouldn't clatter to the pavement; I wondered if that had been the point.

"Name them. Quick."

My palms were still stinging.

"Name what?"

"Your swords. A trollhunter must name his sword before he draws first blood."

I looked blankly at the long-sword and cutlass.

"Now," Jack seethed. "The Nullhullers are gathering."

"I . . ."

"Something that's important to you. Just say it. Whatever comes out is the right answer."

"Claire," I blurted, holding up the long-sword.

Tub gave me a sidelong smirk.

"Claire?" he repeated.

I hoped that the darkness covered the flush of my cheeks.

"Claire . . . blade. Claireblade."

Tub covered his laugh with his hand. "Whatever, man."

"Quick," Jack urged. "The cutlass."

"Uh . . ." I stared at the sharp, pocked metal. The dull, stubborn surface revealed nothing. I turned to Tub. "What was the name of that cat you had?"

"*That* cat? We've had sixty or seventy."

"The cat! You know, the one that liked me."

"Oh, right. Cat #6."

It would have to do. I held up the cutlass and flashed a desperate grin.

"Cat #6!" I shouted.

Jack stared at me. Even through his armor I could feel the chill of his disappointment. Behind me, I could hear Tub's muffled snickers and the tut-tutting of Blinky. Even ARRRGH!!!'s shoulders quaked in a manner that suggested laughter. I squeezed the handles of Claireblade and Cat #6 and glared at Uncle Jack.

"What are yours named? If you're so great at naming inanimate objects."

Blinky and ARRRGH!!! went silent. Tub, too, sensed the change in mood and stifled his laughter. Even the vehicles on the bridge above seemed to sense the weight of the moment—there was no traffic for the longest time. Jack contemplated the long-sword he held in his right hand. After a time, he reached back and withdrew a shorter blade. He held both with tenderness, as if they were not weapons but monuments to the dead.

He indicated the long-sword.

"Victor Power."

He raised the scimitar.

"Doctor X."

All of us could feel in our guts the significance the words held for Jack.

He rolled his shoulders to rouse his body from contemplation. His stance broadened and the bike chains wrapped around his legs crackled. He lifted both swords, one high and one low, in a threatening attack formation; the die-cast trucks on his chest spun their wheels and the notebook spirals around his biceps clicked like barbed wire.

"Pay attention," he said. "This is going to be fast."

He wasn't kidding. Over the next ten minutes, he swung, thrust, parried, feinted, and jabbed with dazzling agility and coordination, Doctor X barely finishing one breathtaking stroke before Victor Power blurred by with the speed of the next. The lessons were furious: attack formations, defense positions; footwork for advance and retreat; techniques for battling those taller than you, as well as those far smaller; jarring changes in tempo to bewilder your foe; the combination of both blades to redirect an onslaught; fighting one-on-one as well as taking on an entire group; the calculations of speed versus brute strength that determined a one-handed versus two-handed grip.

Each technique, drawn from renaissance and medieval schools of combat, had a name and he barked them out: Boar's Tooth, *botta secreta*, double rownde, *durchführen*, false edge, *imbrocata*, kissing-the-button, on-the-pass, *scandiaglio*, *volté*. Then he added a few techniques from the Jack Sturges school—showier moves with names more befitting a thirteen-year-old boy: the Drunken Chicken, Blah-de-blah-de-blah, the Blue Jean Surprise, Idiot Gets a Face Full, and his magnum opus, Fling the Poop.

Right away it was clear that I was expected to memorize this menu of mayhem.

The reason I can repeat them to you in alphabetical order is because I *did*.

I didn't mean to. If I couldn't memorize the banal bits of information hurled at me by Ms. Pinkton, and if I couldn't muster the minimal athletic ability demanded by Coach Lawrence, how was I expected to combine the two, and do so under the duress of a swashbuckling, back-from-the-dead uncle, two hideous trolls, and the promise of hunting down something called a Nullhuller? Yet I felt the information file into never-before-used compartments of my brain, as if the cerebral space had been waiting all this time, absorbent and hungry, for the right kind of facts to fill it.

ARRRGH!!! sniffed the air. Her orange eyes blazed and she drove the points of her horns into the underside of the bridge. Crumbles of cement colored a patch of her hair gray. Jack understood and reached for the astrolabe. But ARRRGH!!! was already loping away from the bridge, nose lifted, drool hanging down in eight-foot strands. Jack made a hand motion to Blinky. Instantly, tentacles curled around my and Tub's shoulders.

"Courage can ebb when the moment of confrontation is nigh. But worry not, diminutive pixies. Fate would not allow a troll of my character to be struck down upon such an undistinguished field of battle. Not before my greatest wish is fulfilled. I speak, of course, of my unfinished historical dissertation."

That wasn't enough to put me at ease. I pointed at ARRRGH!!!.

"What's her greatest wish?" I asked.

"Better dental hygiene," Blinky answered without hesitation.

ARRRGH!!!, crooked, crud-covered teeth and all, was quickly leaving us behind. We exited the velvet darkness of the bridge and entered the menacing coolness of an autumn evening. ARRRGH!!! avoided streetlights by adopting a low, four-legged trot and keeping beneath an overhang of trees alongside the road. I was the last to pass Jack, who was sheathing his swords, waiting to bring up the rear.

His gloved hand shot out and nabbed my arm.

"Don't be nervous." His voice was a low rasp. "You'll *love* it."

It did not sound like a promise. More like a curse.

22.

Suburbia looked vulnerable to me now. The houses were built of flimsy walls instead of solid stone; the picket fences were laughable in their meager attempts at claiming a piece of land; the ornamental mailboxes and flower lattices cried out for indifferent destruction. Each identical row of houses looked like a line of eggs waiting to be stomped on.

We rested on our elbows among the bushes in a backyard. ARRRGH!!! concealed herself in the opposite fashion, standing straight enough to be mistaken for another tree. Fifty feet away was a house painted a pale pink, and I strained for signs of trolls in the flower bed, the scatterings of garden tools, the swinging porch bench, the coils of water hose.

"There," Jack said. "There. There. There. There."

It took me several minutes before I could see the Nullhullers. Concealed in shadow by scruffy gray coats, they were the size of monkeys and had noodly arms and legs unequal to the task of carting around their obese bodies. Their eyes were large and completely black and their noses dark and runny. Most notable were mouths so wide that the corners almost met at the back of the head. As they crawled, the top halves of their heads popped up and down like garbage can lids.

"Dammit," Jack whispered. "There's number six."

"Why, is that one worse?" I asked.

"Nullhullers, the odious cretins," Blinky replied. "They travel in packs of five."

Indeed, four more fat, long-limbed creatures wobbled onto the scene, and then there were ten giggling and snorting Nullhullers. Eight of them were gesturing at a second-floor window, though I could not imagine how creatures so fat would scale the wall. Meanwhile, the remaining two began scribbling across the side of the house with what looked like red chalk. They made a circle, then within that circle drew an upside-down star. I recognized it as the sign of Satan cherished by all the heavy-metal kids at school.

"Nullhullers are Satanists?!" I hissed.

"Don't be silly," Blinky scolded. "They're Irish. More to the point, the Nullhullers are such a disorderly bunch that they are attracted to order wherever they can find it. Hence the traveling in fives; hence the attraction to drawing symbols of perfect symmetry. It was only by accident that they discovered that this particular symbol struck fear into the hearts of suburban adults, who would blame attacks on humans with impure beliefs. An ingenious cover, I must admit."

There was a nattering among the Nullhullers indicating that they were ready to act. The ten of them drew together in a loose circle, quivering in excitement, their mouths lifting open to reveal sparse, square teeth that looked like chunks of granite.

"How lucky you are," Blinky said. "You are about to witness possibly the most vile ritual in all of trolldom."

The Nullhullers' squat bodies began to hitch and jiggle. Thick drool poured from their agape mouths, followed by a brown lard. A symphony of choking sounds emitted from their bodies as a plump, translucent sac began to emerge from each gaping throat. The sacs were nearly the size of a Nullhuller itself and crammed with soft objects of different shapes and colors. They squirted out of the Nullhullers' mouths and landed upon the grass with moist splats, where they palpitated and shivered.

"We're spending Saturday night watching trolls barf," Tub said. "Good times, Jim. *Legendary* times."

"The Nullhullers are nothing if not cunning," Blinky said with a measure of respect. "Knowing that their weight prevents swift movement, they eject their organs for a short time—all but their hearts—making them among the most nimble of all trolls."

Now as light and empty as pillowcases, the Nullhullers scrambled up the side of the house with the dexterity of squirrels. Beside me, Jack reached into the bramble of bike chains around his thighs and withdrew three corroded old horseshoes. He handed one to Blinky and one to ARRRGH!!!.

"I'll schmoof the parents," he said. "If there are siblings, grandparents, anything like that, use the horseshoes."

"Horseshoes," I repeated, trying to keep up. "Why horseshoes?"

"Didn't we mention?" Blinky asked. "Ye gods, there is so much ground to cover! Nullhullers are changelings. They are here to replace a human baby with one of their wretched own. It's an abominable practice. If left undetected, a troll changeling can grow to full adulthood under its human skin, terrorizing the world with ruinous behavior. A good deal of your world's top CEOs and politicians are Nullhullers, I'm sorry to say. Thus we must test the family members for trollhood.

The quickest way is by pressing a horseshoe to the forehead. Iron works best, but in a pinch, anything of horseshoe design will suffice."

"Well, give me one!" I cried.

"You're not coming in," Jack said. He shoved into my hands the burlap sack in which he had transported my swords. "You cut open those organ sacs, throw the gallbladders in the bag, and stand guard if any of those things start coming out the windows. If they do, remember your lessons."

"Hold on!" Tub cried. "What the hell am I supposed to do?"

Jack pointed at the satanic stars.

"Wash those stupid symbols off the wall. Use that hose." He scanned our faces. "Everybody ready?"

"No!" Tub and I cried in unison.

"Let's go!" Jack shouted.

ARRRGH!!! smacked her frothy lips and tore across the lawn. Jack ran at a full sprint at her side, the moonlight splashing across the metal edges of his armor. Blinky, too, raced along on his unknowable legs, though Tub and I were able to keep up with him.

"It was with unflagging dedication that I taught myself to move by touch and smell," Blinky narrated for our listening pleasure. "Tonight that is a mixed blessing."

Seconds later I knew what he meant. The organ sacs were rancid. Tub and I stopped short, gagging and coughing. Blinky continued without us, joining Jack at the back door he'd just jimmied open with Doctor X. Jack hurried inside the house, followed by Blinky. ARRRGH!!! was too large to fit inside, but mere physics didn't stop her. She popped both arms from their sockets and twisted her oversize simian body in startling ways, then, somehow, disappeared inside.

Tub and I stared at the back door as it shut. The house was dark and quiet. We peered up at the second-floor window, conjuring horrible fantasies of what might be happening just out of sight. At last there was nothing else to look at. We dragged our eyes down to the ten rippling organ sacs.

"That's all you," Tub said. "I'm on graffiti duty."

Tub held his nose and headed for the hose.

I forced myself to edge closer to the ten sacs. They throbbed upon the dark lawn like soft mutant embryos. I leaned over the nearest one. Purple lungs inflated against the translucent film; a slimy stomach surged against it like a red, blobby wave; pooled near the bottom was a white heap of squirming intestines. All of it floated within a snotty glop.

Slowly I withdrew Cat #6. I placed the tip of the cutlass against the sac and pushed gently.

It pierced the skin with a flatulent sound and liquid the color of mustard sprayed across my arm. It reeked of spoiled meat and my eyes began streaming tears. Briefly I considered just walking away, but then, before I knew what I was doing, I jammed the sword down so hard that it embedded in the dirt below.

The sac split down the center with the high-pitched whine of a perforated balloon and the organs spilled out in a multi-colored tangle. The second the translucent skin touched the grass, it melted into a foul gel. The bowels traveled the farthest, expanding around my shoes. I minced away in disgust. A tiny wave of movement caught my eye and I realized it was the escape of every ant, beetle, worm, and other insect that lived on that patch of soil. They wanted nothing to do with the sickness soaking into their world.

I surveyed the mess. That brown pouch was a stomach,

and that large green thing was probably a liver. But what on earth did a troll gallbladder look like?

From inside the house, a single clash of metal.

Tub and I looked at each other. His fear was broadcast by the sheer amount of his displayed braces. He began scrubbing frantically at the upside-down star with his wet shirt, turning both objects pink. I looked back at the spilled offal and tried to sift through the organs with Cat #6. More noises from the general direction of the second-floor window, this time a thumping and scuffling. There was no time to be delicate about this autopsy. I dropped to my knees and my jeans dampened in the coagulating mucus. I took a breath and plunged both hands into the warm viscera.

The entrails didn't like my touching them. They spat acidic juices that burned my skin. Ribcage blades scissored down on the tips of my fingers. A net of blood vessels twined up my forearm and gripped with painful ferocity. Each organ cried out in a tiny, angry voice. And still I dug with furious fingers, kneading each slick piece of meat for a hidden surprise.

I knew I had found the gallbladder as soon as I touched it. It was boiling hot. I pulled it from the muck with a loud slurp. The blood vessels around my hand snapped off and the rest of the innards went limp and moaned in tones of pipsqueak loss. I raised the gallbladder in a victorious fist. It was the size of a golf ball and the texture of wet spinach. It roiled in my hand as if it were filled with maggots. I reached for Jack's burlap sack and tossed the little orange bastard inside. Nine more to go.

From somewhere on the second floor came the sound of splintering wood. I flinched; Tub hit the deck as if under fire. A baby began crying from the upstairs window and I expected to see the parents' bedroom lights turn on before I remembered that everyone else in the house had been schmoofed. Victory here was up to the trollhunters.

With a battle cry more falsetto than intended, I exchanged Cat #6 for Claireblade and cut through the next sac. In seconds I had the gallbladder; seconds later, it was in Jack's bag. I hacked and scattered and splattered and grabbed: three gallbladders, four, five, six, seven, eight. Specks of guts sprayed against the house and I shouted for Tub to wipe those off, too. From the second-floor window came an agitated, bat-wing flapping—the loose flesh of the Nullhullers being disrupted from whatever they were doing to the baby. I sliced open the ninth sac with a swordsmanship that was darn near admirable. The gallbladder, as if surrendering, hopped right to the top of the gore, and I snatched it.

Chaos erupted. The trollhunters had breached the nursery. Lights turned on and the battle began to rage. I heard the panting of Jack, the growling of ARRRGH!!!, the sanctimonious snorts of Blinky. The Nullhullers made no other sound than the laundry-line snapping of their skin—after all, their throats had been left down with me on the lawn.

Some instinct, the same one with which I had memorized Jack's fighting techniques, told me that we were losing. There was a lack of finality to Jack's sword strikes and too many surprised yips coming from ARRRGH!!!. The Nullhullers grew louder as they flapped their skin in unison. But it was the absence of one noise that disturbed me most.

The baby had stopped crying.

I dropped the sack of gallbladders and hurtled toward the back door.

"Are you nuts?" Tub shouted.

I gave Cat #6 a backhand toss, and it impaled itself in the grass at Tub's feet.

"Use that if any come out," I yelled.

"*What?* Paint, Jim! I'm only authorized to scrub paint!"

Even at my speed the darkened rooms of the house gave off a mausoleum chill. The humming refrigerator, the empty easy chairs, and the random pattern of the scattered remote controls all took on deadly significance. These would be artifacts of the dead if I didn't hurry. I found the stairs, took the steps by threes, and was at the nursery in seconds, bashing through the doorway with Claireblade gripped in both hands.

The walls were painted a sunny yellow with a motif of pink panda bears. This detail I noticed despite the fact that I could see very little wall. Half of the room was matted, black fur: ARRRGH!!!, looking larger for being confined to such limited space. It had not occurred to me that, in the human world, her size could be a disadvantage, but that was the case: the cramped quarters slowed her down as the Nullhullers nipped at her like angry dogs.

Jack and Blinky were having better luck. I counted five dead Nullhullers, lying tattered on the floor like ripped rugs. The others waged active war, claws xylophoning across Jack's pinwheeling swords. Even with his face concealed behind a mask, I recognized the thrilled expenditure of energy unique to thirteen-year-olds. For the briefest of moments I saw a glimpse of the kid Jack could've been, if only he'd been gifted a life of snagging fly balls on the diamond instead of hacking at unspeakable hell-spawn.

With the flat side of his blade, Jack knocked a Nullhuller across the floor. Instantly one of Blinky's tentacles lashed out, squeezing the troll with enough force to tear right through the skin. Death was instant and bloodless. Six dead, four more to go.

Even without throats, the remaining Nullhullers could speak in a breathless wheeze, and with the medallion still around my neck I could understand them. These were not conversations. This was, instead, the ritualistic chant of a brainwashed cult, the same three chilling words repeated:

"*Change the baby.*"

"*Change the baby.*"

"*Change the baby.*"

The crib had been pushed away from the window so that it acted as a barrier to shield the Nullhuller duo hiding behind it. The crib itself was empty; these two trolls had the baby. I pressed myself flat against a wall and began skirting the room's perimeter, booting aside candy-colored toys. So far I was going unnoticed. I reached the edge of the crib and leaned over to have a look.

One of the Nullhullers had wrapped its empty skin completely around the baby. A pale nectar secreting from the troll's pores had covered the infant from head to foot. Before I could close my astonished mouth, the baby slid out of the ooze and landed supine and sleepy on the floor. But the nectar itself was stiffening, and I realized that the troll had essentially made a plaster cast of the baby. I leaned even farther over the revolting display and saw the baby-shaped space inside the hard nectar begin to weave with veins and nerves that started to grow organ clusters like hanging grapes. Already soft pink marrow was being fortified with white bone and covered with a pale elastic skin.

They were forging their own fake baby to leave behind.

The second of the Nullhullers reached out with its spindly

arms, took the real baby by her feet, and began to lower her into its open mouth. There were no organs left inside, which meant the troll intended to use its empty torso as a bag in which to carry the baby home.

I booted the crib aside and drove Claireblade through the second troll's softies, all the way out the other side. It uttered a death caw and dropped the baby. On instinct I let Claireblade clatter to the floor and dove to catch the child. She landed in my hands, smacking her lips through the daubs of secretion still covering her body. I held the baby to my chest, relieved not only to have saved her but also thrilled to have killed a troll. Jack had been right—I *did* love it.

The Nullhuller that had made the plaster cast flattened itself against the wall. I swiped Claireblade from the floor and swung it. The troll was too fast; it hopped, using the blade as a stair step, and bounded over the edge of the crib. The sword continued its movement—and cut the changeling baby in half.

It was the grisliest thing I'd ever seen. Feelers of skin tried in vain to cover the exposed innards. The chest cavity's organs, half human and half troll, clung to each other like blind kittens fresh from their amniotic sacs. Only the changeling baby's top jaw had been completed, and it gummed helplessly upon the air. The eyes, though, were pure troll—blinkless black orbs glowering at me in condemnation. The half-formed human skull exposed the troll brain hiding beneath, a glossy green thing nippled with twitching nodules.

I was crying when I killed it. It was an abomination; the job had to be done. But the changeling had already mastered a baby's voice, and it sobbed as I hacked it into smaller and smaller pieces while holding the real baby in my other arm.

By the end of it my entire body was shaking so badly that Claireblade fell from my grip.

The crib was thrown aside. Jack was in my face. I saw my numb, blood-spattered reflection in his goggles. He sheathed his sword and wrenched out his horseshoe, bringing it to the baby's face.

"She's not . . ." I said.

"Shut up," he said. He took a shuddering breath. I saw his fist tighten around his scimitar. Then he pressed the horseshoe against the infant's forehead. The baby scrunched up her face in annoyance. Jack sighed in relief and stuck the horseshoe back into his armor, then grabbed me by the front of the shirt.

"Where's the last one?" he demanded.

I blinked around the room and saw nine dead Nullhullers, including the one I had lanced. Vaguely I remembered the one who had dodged my sword and vaulted away.

"I think . . . it went . . ."

I gazed at the open window.

Jack cursed and bolted from the room. ARRRGH!!! spat hot foam and bounded after him, angling her massive shoulders to fit through the door; still, the tips of her horns drew squiggles through the sunny yellow paint. I felt a tugging in my arms and found two of Blinky's tentacles taking the baby. He did it with such gentle assurance that I did not object. Two other tentacles joined to shift the baby this way and that so that a fifth tentacle could daintily wipe the troll secretions from her body with a towel. The infant giggled and grabbed her feet with her chubby hands.

I retrieved Claireblade and began backing from the

nursery, astounded by the sight of a dozen other tentacles at work: pushing the crib back into place, gathering the scattered toys into a semblance of order, righting fallen lamps, reinserting pictures that had popped from their frames, and who knew what else. I'd have thought we'd never been there if not for the terrible feeling that I'd failed.

23.

The backyard stunned me with its normalcy. Studded gardening gloves draped drowsily across a deck chair. A clear sky pinpointed with stars hummed with the faraway progress of red-eye airplanes. Two dogs down the block had a conversation from their respective yards. Even the grass at my feet had reclaimed its territory: the piles of innards had dissolved, leaving ten patches of moisture no more threatening than dew.

The actors populating this easygoing stage looked as though they had wandered into the wrong play. ARRRGH!!! stood at the far edge of the lawn, her giant horned head swinging back and forth as she searched for the escaped Nullhuller. Streetlights glinted from Jack's twin scabbards as his upper body expanded and contracted with infuriated breaths. Even Tub looked out of place: a regular kid, sure, but with orange hair frizzed into a clown wig and a shirt slopped to his chest with pink paint. He gave me a helpless look.

"It happened so fast," he said.

"It's okay," I said. "It was just one."

"You know *nothing*," Jack snarled.

"Uncle Jack." I thought the formal title might help. "We killed nine of them."

"The bag of gallbladders? Did you forget that? We killed zero."

A sinking feeling overtook me. I looked to Tub, who shrugged.

"It flew down here, gobbled its own guts, and took the bag. What was I supposed to do?"

"This is not your friend's responsibility," Jack snapped. "He is *not* a trollhunter."

"It was just one," I pleaded.

"That 'just one' will go to Gunmar. It will tell him about us. About *you*."

"Look, I'm sorry—"

"I *told* you to stay out here. Why couldn't you listen?"

"But I thought you guys needed—"

Jack ripped the mask from his face and whirled around.

"Who asked you to think? Don't think. *Listen*. What, you believe it's just your precious little life at stake here? You're going to fail your math test? Screw up your stupid play? There could be another *war*. Dozens, hundreds, more than you'd believe could lose their lives. Trolls you might think are worth the dog crap on your shoe, but who just happen to be my *friends*. Humans, too, people you know—does that make it worse? We have a week, Jim. One *week*."

The ground shook. The three of us turned to see that ARRRGH!!! had fallen to her knees. Jack took off across the lawn. I followed but tripped on my own feet. Tub was there, though, to catch me by the bloody shoulder. Groaning in disgust, he placed Cat #6 in my hand so he could wipe the troll goo onto his jeans. We quickly came upon Jack, standing alongside his bowed friend. He had, for some reason, drawn both swords.

ARRRGH!!!'s posture was wracked. Her mighty back hiccupped with pain and her neck was so weak that her great horns weighed down her head. I took a step closer, hoping to comfort.

Jack halted me with the tip of Doctor X.

"No closer."

I'd made a few mistakes, but that hardly warranted an outright threat with a weapon. I was preparing to voice my grudge when I noticed a cardboard box discarded in the mown grass. Instantly I understood and my aching shoulders slumped farther. I began circling at a safe distance, Tub fighting me for every step.

The Eye of Malevolence was fastened to ARRRGH!!!'s face. The writhing stems had twined their way into the troll's orifices, streaming down her throat in red plaits, corkscrewing up both nostrils, and sliding beneath each eyelid. Pulling ever tighter at ARRRGH!!!'s brain, the Eye had flattened into a gelatinous oval that bubbled like pancake batter. ARRRGH!!!'s spine curled with agony beneath her lathered pelt.

"Get it off," I told Jack. "It's killing her."

Jack's muscles tensed, but he made no such move.

I clashed Cat #6 against Claireblade. Jack flinched, just a little.

"I'll do it!" I shouted. "Move!"

The tree-trunk legs pistoned and ARRRGH!!! sprung to her feet, paws curled upward as if holding two planets, head thrown back. Where I expected a howl came instead multi-octave laughter, cacophonous as a herd of trumpeting elephants. The curled horns struck a tree branch and it exploded into a hail of wood chips. Jack kept his swords ready as the spray dinged off his metal armor.

ARRRGH!!! swooped her head toward Tub and me. The Eye of Malevolence convulsed in delight, and the green-orange iris opened in a toothed yawn.

"SSSSSSSSSSSTURGESSSSSSSSSSS."

It was the soggy voice of one who'd spent decades gnawing on his tongue. Gunmar the Black, the Hungry One, saw me, smelled me, wished to eat me. From somewhere within the pupil's void I could hear the splintering whack of what I knew was his wooden arm. He was aching to add another few slash marks of conquer, and as much as he'd prefer to do it in person, he wasn't strong enough yet, so he'd just use this handy, four-ton puppet.

One of ARRRGH!!!'s clawed hands barreled at us, big as a school bus. The wind of it knocked us down before the paw itself arrived. Tub and I clung to each other in the grass, too scared to scream.

The paw never reached us. Gunmar bawled through ARRRGH!!!'s muzzle. Tub and I scrabbled away on all fours and saw Jack withdrawing his long-sword from ARRRGH!!!'s calf. Her hackles stiffened and she turned on my uncle, baring skewed teeth. But when she saw the boy bravely wielding his little blade, her shoulders fell. Both paws made fists and landed on the ground, and from there she eased her body to a seated position atop the broken tree branch. Tub and I were jostled by the impact.

The Eye of Malevolence fattened and wobbled like dough.

Dozens of veins retracted from ARRRGH!!!'s skull, each one unchaining her from bondage. The Eye quavered upon her muzzle for a few seconds before falling, bouncing once on the ground, and rolling to a halt amid the manicured grass. ARRRGH!!! dropped her weary face into her massive paws. Jack sheathed his swords, put his hands to his friend's neck, and whispered in her ear. The suburbs were quiet enough for me to hear.

"I'm sorry. I didn't cut deep. Just a scrape."

"Boy humans. Me want in belly. Ashamed."

"Shhh," Jack whispered. "I wouldn't let that happen."

"Not mean it!" ARRRGH!!! cried.

"Tell me what you saw." Jack pet the damp fur. "Before you forget."

"Nullhuller go to Gunmar. Gunmar send more. Gumm-Gumms find fuel. Fuel for Machine."

Even in the dim light I could see the paling of Jack's face.

"The Machine? We destroyed the Machine. I was there, I saw it."

"Gumm-Gumms work hard. Gumm-Gumms fix. Boy humans right. Killaheed make strong. Much sad. Much sad is ARRRGH!!!."

From my seat in the grass I forced out a question.

"What's the Machine?"

Jack's expression of dread unnerved me. He shrugged away my query.

"Nothing. Don't worry about it. What's important is that ARRRGH!!! confirmed everything. And none of it's good. Trolls like these tonight? That's nothing. Gunmar will keep send-ing them, every night, to occupy us while he waits for the

Killaheed to be finished. It's a perfect plan and we have to deal with it. If these Gumm-Gumms are out gathering fuel for the Machine—"

Jack cut himself off. He searched for solace in the lines of houses, the fences, the roads, all of the comforting right angles of the suburbs. But at last he drove both swords into the lawn with the red-faced frustration of a thirteen-year-old.

"Why does everything have to be so hard?"

The subsequent quiet would have been unbearable if Blinky hadn't chosen that moment to slither back to us. He used a single tentacle to lift Tub and I to standing positions as he passed. With curt movements, he plucked the Eye of Malevolence from the grass, gathered the cardboard box, and then put the former in the latter so as to save us from its blinkless stare. He tucked the box into ARRRGH!!!'s fur and began his jovial report.

"The nursery is as dandy as ever. Even dandier if you want the truth. I could not resist rearranging a few elements so that the room had a better flow. You wouldn't believe the wonders that can be achieved by a more cunning placement of a nightstand! I do believe I missed my calling."

Blinky waited for adulations. Instead he was met with a fatigued foursome rendered voiceless by a night of defeat. He sighed and looked to the east, where a line of orange razored the horizon.

"We've had worse days," he said softly. "Come, come. Let's take these boys home."

It was with some effort that Jack dislodged his swords from the dirt. Following this signal, ARRRGH!!! raised herself to her feet, favoring her left calf just a little. Blinky took the lead back toward the bridge, and the other warriors began shambling after. I lagged behind just enough so that I could grab Jack's arm. The web of notebook spirals swallowed my fingers.

Jack looked at me with bloodshot eyes.

"Why?" I asked. "Why are you dragging me into this?"

Jack's reply was as hushed as branches blowing in the night breeze.

"It's a terrible thing, isn't it? To be dragged under?"

24.

I awoke before Tub. Leaving him spread-eagled on my bed alongside Jim Sturges Jr. 2: The Decoy, I stashed my ruined clothes in a gym bag and tiptoed to the shower. The medallion tapped against my chest as I soaped; I tried to ignore it. The water swirled at my feet in currents of mud black and blood orange, and I watched it slip through the drain on its way to another world.

The thought of cereal made me sick. Instead of flakes growing soggy with milk at the bottom of a bowl, I visualized coiled white Nullhuller intestines. I avoided the kitchen altogether, undid the ten door locks, and dove into the daylight, gulping down fresh air in the hopes that it would calm my stomach. My arms hung at my sides as if they each clutched an iron horseshoe. I sunk to the steps beneath the security camera, folded my arms across my knees, and wondered how long I could sit here before I ran back inside and double-checked each lock.

Dad came around the corner, surprising me. He was dressed for mowing in his work gloves, stained shirt, old pants, and steel-toed boots. Thankfully, the most ridiculous parts of his wardrobe—the goggles, face mask, and hair net—were still

"Your father refused this once," he said. "Don't make the same mistake."

stashed, allowing me a rare opportunity to take him seriously. He hesitated as though equally surprised to see me, then took off his work gloves, stuck them in his back pocket, and took a seat next to me on the stairs.

His brother, I thought. *His brother is alive.*

It was something I couldn't say, because how could it really be true? How could that lean and fearless kid from the underworld be related to this man of the hairless pate, collection of worry lines, and Band-Aid glasses?

"A bit late today," he said.

"Sorry."

"Not you. Me. My trimmer was clogged. Just spent two hours hacking at it with a screwdriver. But we're good to go. You want to come along? I'm doing Joseph A. Kearney Park. Good chance to put in some time piloting the big guy."

"I don't know. I'm pretty tired."

He nodded. "Yeah, I figured."

We sat in silence for a minute. I kept an eye on his profile as he watched life going on as usual. Little girls on bikes rode by ringing their bells. A teenager washed his car a few driveways down. Across the block, there was hammering—a new deck, maybe a tree house if some kids were lucky.

"I suppose we should have a talk," Dad said.

Such a sentence would have terrified me had I not been wrung dry.

"About what?"

"Jimmy." He gestured over his shoulder. "The kitchen."

It was a lifetime ago that Tub and I had come upon the trolls in the kitchen. I tried to recall the damage, but there was too much: the obliterated ceiling fan, the scorched microwave, the piles of broken dishes.

"Dad," I said. "I . . ."

"It was bound to happen. How long could I expect you to run around like a trapped rat before you tried to break out? You know, I originally wanted more kids. Four was the number I decided on. Two girls, two boys, so nobody ever had to be lonely. Even when things got bad at the end there, I kept making my case to your mother. Can't blame her for saying no, I guess. Having more kids is no way to save a marriage. I suppose at that point I wasn't trying to save the marriage, I was trying to save you. I've had it both ways, you know? I had a brother. And then I was an only child. I know the difference between the two. And I kind of feel like I robbed you of that. Having someone for when I can't be there. Which is often. I know that."

"Dad." I knew no other words beyond that.

"With a brother? Hell, there'd be messes worse than that kitchen. You can't have two boys and not have things break. Catch fire. Explode, even." He turned his glasses to the clouds and laughed. "You wouldn't believe the trouble Jack and I used to get into. You honestly wouldn't believe it. They had these chemistry sets marketed to kids back then, rockets that you ignited with fire. They should have been sold with tourniquets and directions to the nearest hospital. There weren't bicycle helmets back then. Or locks on doors." His smile died out. "I don't know. Maybe there should've been."

"I'll clean it up." This promise came out with startling ferocity. I *would* clean it up, cleaner than it'd ever been, and I'd ride my bike to the store, get replacement dishes, a new mop, some cleaning products, and a new ceiling fan, which I'd buy on layaway along with a serviceman to install it, and when Dad got back from mowing, soppy with perspiration and dotted with grass shrapnel, he'd light up with renewed energy when he saw what a success his son could be when he set his mind to it.

Dad brushed it all away with a shrug.

"Already cleaned," he said. "Don't give it another thought. It's festival week. I want you to enjoy yourself. I ran into Mrs. Leach at the hardware store this morning. Why didn't you tell me you'd gotten the lead in the play? I mean, I know why. Late-night rehearsals. You were afraid I wouldn't let you do it. Well, I *am* letting you do it. I'm not going to lie, it makes me nervous. Practically sliced my hand off in the trimmer this morning thinking about it. But that's *my* hand. Yours is yours."

For the first time that morning he faced me. A fresh dotted line of scabs trailed down from the left corner of his lips, the tracks of the schmoof that had spent the previous night snoozing inside his stomach: *Sluuuurp. Sluuuurp. Sluuuurp. Sluuuurp.* It was my fault that Dad had been subjected to that. I felt on my back the full weight of what I knew.

"I want you to be great in that play, Jimmy. I want you to be great at something. Or, heck, if that's too much pressure, I just want you to have fun." His smile faltered, but he tried to make it work. "Don't stay out too late. I mean, no later than you need to. I won't give you grief about it. Not this week. Maybe not next. What I'm saying, Jimmy, is that I'm trying. All right? I am beginning to try."

I looked into the sun, hoping my fresh tears would tip back into my eyes rather than streak down my cheeks. Posed in that way, I managed a nod. From my peripheral vision, I saw Dad's hand raise as though he was going to pat my back. Part of me prayed that he wouldn't—the tears would roll from my eyes as easily as marbles. Part of me wished that he would.

He stood, taking the gloves from his back pocket and slapping them across his thighs to knock free the adhered grass. He adjusted his glasses and I thought, in its own way, the Band-Aid around the temple had a sort of courage—it clung to the glasses with the same tenacity that Dad clung to his responsibilities in the face of a lifetime of fear.

A minute later he was pulling out of the driveway in the San Bernardino Electronics van. He gave me a toot of the horn as he backed into the street. It was only as he pulled away, observing the posted speed limit, of course, that the screen door behind me opened with a crow squawk.

Tub clomped down the steps as if he had been sewn together from corpse parts. He staggered past me, stood in a wide stance upon the lawn, and stretched his arms in a yawn. The pink-smeared shirt pulled taut across his wide back.

"You—ow. You have a nice—ow. A nice talk with your—so sore! Talk with your dad?"

I shrugged. He looked from me to the step I sat on, but seemed dubious that his leg muscles could take the pressure of lowering his bulk. Instead he just stood in place like an overstuffed scarecrow, teetering in the mild breeze. I waited for the spill of expletives that would mirror my own feelings: we needed to screw irons bars to the floor beneath my bed, whatever it took to stop the trollhunters from returning.

Instead, his puffy, pillow-scarred face cracked into a lopsided grin.

"Crazy night, huh? I mean, no girls were involved, but still, I've been waiting fifteen years to be able to use that phrase and mean it. *Crazy night*, am I right?"

I shook my head miserably.

"I can't do this, Tub."

"Yes, you can. You *did*. We both did. Sure, we didn't ace it, but how could we? I mean, graduating from a baseball bat and hockey stick to a couple of gnarly swords is going to take more than one night. You think they'd give me one if I practiced? You know, showed them what I could do?"

"What's wrong with you?"

"Huh? Nothing's wrong with me. You're the one who looks all freaked out."

"Tub. Wake up. We can't do what they asked us to do."

"Jim." He smiled, but it died when he saw my cold expression. "Jim, don't do this to me."

"To you? I'm doing something to you?"

"They're coming back tonight. They said. And we're going to help them."

"It's not your decision."

"It's not?"

"You heard them. You're not a trollhunter."

Tub's metal mouth snapped shut. A red color began to creep up his neck.

"That's crappy of you, Jim. To treat me like that."

"What do you want me to say? 'Yahoo, let's go get ourselves killed'? Didn't I translate enough for you last night? They're talking about war. Real war. Something called the Machine. You and me weren't meant to do this, Tub. We're in way over our heads."

"Our heads? Who's *ever* cared about our heads before this? Jim, you're wrong. We *were* meant to do this. This is exactly what we've been waiting for. They've chosen *us*. Of all people! Us!"

"Not us. Me."

"This means that all those times I told you we weren't worth anything—"

"I never said that. Don't include me in that."

"Fine!" His face was scarlet now. "Then just me! I'm the one who isn't worth anything! Jesus, Jim, take a look at my life! You know what I'm worth? To anyone? Zero! Nothing! I'm a fat loser and will always be a fat loser. Until this. This is like a present. Full of, man, I don't know. Hope? I know how cheesy that sounds, but I swear that's what it feels like."

"That's easy for you to say. I'm the one being asked to risk his neck."

Tub's voice cracked.

"They won't take me without you!"

Over his shoulder on the other side of the road, I saw a man with a stapler and a handful of flyers look up at the noise. He had been about to attach one of the flyers to a phone pole but instead started walking toward us. I groaned. A salesman was the last thing we needed right now. The idiot didn't even look for traffic before he crossed the pavement.

"Sorry to interrupt, boys," he said, "but—"

"Not a good time," Tub muttered.

"I'm sorry. I just wanted to ask if you've seen my little girl."

"We just got up," Tub said. "We haven't seen anyone."

"Last night, maybe. Maybe you were out last night and saw—"

"Listen, man—"

Tub whirled around to give the guy a mouthful, but it died on his tongue. The man was around forty, with a dyed black goatee and eyes that were red and exhausted. Dog poop was smeared on the side of his shoe and he didn't seem to care.

Every sign suggested he'd been out for hours canvassing the neighborhood.

The man held out a flyer with a trembling hand. On it was the color-photocopied face of an eight-year-old girl with purple glasses, a sweet face, and a grin missing at least three baby teeth. The seven block letters above her head must have been pure hell to type:

MISSING

"There's a reward." The rise in the man's voice conveyed that he didn't believe in the inherent goodness of kids, just their perennial need for cash.

Tub took the flyer.

"We'll let you know if we see her," he mumbled.

The man forced a rumpled smile and nodded. He backed away, still nodding, the pictures of his daughter crinkling in his grip. His shoulders relaxed when he returned to the telephone pole across the street. It was easier, it seemed, pinning his hopes on inanimate wood rather than on the whims of self-involved, shiftless teens.

Tub stared at his feet for a few seconds before lifting his eyes in a glare.

"Don't let us down, Jim. Don't you goddamn do it."

He shoved the little girl's face into my palm and charged away.

25.

The *Ğräçæjøïvõd'ñûý* were a race of trolls so nefarious that even their name was an assault, hard enough to write and impossible to say, an umpteen-letter monstrosity that would tie the most eloquent of troll scholars in such knots of quivering failure that they were slain before the first clash of battle had sounded. But the trait of which I'd been most warned during that night's journey through floorboards and sewers and bridges was their sense of smell, unparalleled in the history of the world. One sniff and they'd forever imprint your scent signature upon their temporal lobes. That was why *Ğräçæjøïvõd'ñûý*, more than any other troll, needed to be completely eradicated in battle. If a single specimen escaped, it would share your odor with others back at its hive, and your home would be overrun in hours.

Ğräçæjøïvõd'ñûý were attracted to areas of spoil, and that night we were meeting them upon the soon-to-be battlefield of Keavy's Junk Emporium. It wasn't just physical decay that attracted *Ğräçæjøïvõd'ñûý*. They sought out homeless shanties, orphanages, mental hospitals, old folks' homes, hospice care facilities, anywhere they could snuggle within the invigorating chill of discarded dreams.

Keavy's was a double whammy: not only was it the most sprawling concentration of decomposition in all of San Bernardino, it also bordered Sunny Smiles for Friends, a budget retirement home of infamous reputation. Ambulances made trips to Sunny Smiles multiple times per night, and it was widely believed to be a front for meth sales. Ğräçæjøïvõd'ñûý operated by infecting weak or elderly lungs with airborne poisons and couldn't be allowed to squat in any one location for long, lest everyone there become polluted.

Blinky completed these warnings as we made our way up the side of a dirt hill at the edge of the junkyard. It was after midnight, and the two of us lagged behind Jack and ARRRGH!!!. Tub was not with us. I had not heard from him since that morning, and as the day dwindled I had resisted calling or texting. He had no business with us. I felt terrible thinking it, but it was bad enough that I was being bullied into attendance.

Blinky and I joined Jack and ARRRGH!!! at the crest of the hill. Before us spread a labyrinth. Compacted vehicles, everything from motorcycles to trailer homes, made up the walls of the treacherous maze, while brambles of metal wire blocked easy exits.

"Behold," Blinky said, unspooling a tentacle over the vista. "The Ğräçæj . . . the Ğräçæjøïv . . ." He emitted a locust-flutter sound of irritation. If anyone was going to pronounce the unpronounceable, certainly it would be the self-proclaimed greatest living troll historian! But that achievement would have to wait for another day. The tentacle snapped with frustration.

"Behold the rust trolls," he mumbled.

Other trolls, I'd gathered, had tried to rob power from the

Ğräçæĵǒĭvǒd'ñǔŷ, pinning them with this simpler moniker. Right away I saw why it was fitting. They were the color of dried blood, equal parts orange, brown, and red. Each one was scaled with plates the exact shape and weight of rust flakes. Most chilling of all, the rust trolls were as flat as hammered tin, and they slithered across dilapidated car parts, barely distinguishable from corroded chrome detailing.

Jack sharpened Doctor X against a twist of metal lying in the grass. It was a nervous habit.

"All right. Rust trolls. Seven of them. Hard to kill. Hard as hell." Through the boom box speaker, his voice was emotionless. "Ever killed a tick? Same thing here. It's either fire or a sharp point. We're not going to set this joint on fire so sharp points it is. Jim, your sword. ARRRGH!!!, your claws. Blinky, you've got plenty of arms and there's plenty of scrap here, so find something pointy and get to it. We gotta pin these suckers to the ground till they stop twitching."

"How long do they twitch?" I whispered.

"Anywhere between ten seconds and forty-five minutes. Depends on age."

ARRRGH!!! was crouched over us to provide cover, and I found her gazing at me with what looked like affection. From deep in her throat came a low purr that somehow communicated that she would look after me. She bowed her head until the boulder embedded in her skull was within touching distance. I ran my fingertips across it for luck just as troll children had been doing for half a decade.

One of her orange eyes closed in a playful wink. I had no idea what to make of it until her mouth split open to reveal a hundred jagged teeth and she let loose with the kind of earsplitting roar that had me imagining nearby rats and raccoons falling dead from fright. Even Jack covered his ears and pressed his face in the dirt. I saw seven glints of light as the rust trolls perked up their rawboned heads.

With one incredible lunge, ARRRGH!!! leapt thirty feet through the air, and upon thunderous landing she stabbed a thick yellow claw through one of the Grǎçœjø*ïvõd'ñûȳ. Jack swung his face toward me, his dirty-blond hair flopping across eyes alight with excitement. He pushed himself to standing position and raised both swords over his head.

"Trollhunters!" he bellowed. "Attack!"

I was the kid who hung back when they picked sides in gym, the kid who hid behind his book while Pinkton searched for new blackboard victims. But at that moment I detected the rust trolls' poison. It was redolent with the rotten-fruit smell of a hospital that stored its dying people in rooms like separate stomachs; it smelled of the underarm sweat of bedraggled middle schoolers on the run from bullies; it carried the sharp stink of the pissed beds of children waking up in their latest foster homes. I coughed out these toxins before I heard the battle cry rumbling up my throat. There was evil in the world and I needed—I *wanted*—to stop it.

It was a battle both brutal and inspiring. Chaos was the rust trolls' chief defense. Just as we entered their acrid yellow mist, one tried to sever our feet by coiling itself into a sharp snare. Another writhed like a crackling live wire too dangerous to approach. Still others slingshotted themselves from car antennae. All the while they produced an asthmatic laughter that smelled of tar. But Jack proved himself with the tireless, inventive lancing of hearts and softies, while Blinky fended off several at once with shanks of scrap metal and ARRRGH!!! tore apart vehicles as if they were but *papier-mâché* nuisances.

Three hours later, the junkyard was a slapdash cemetery. Various serrated objects pinned rust trolls to the dirt as they sniggered their way through their drawn-out deaths. Only two remained. One was eight feet tall and so lean it disappeared when viewed from the side. Its cackle scratched at your brain like nails, and I'd seen ARRRGH!!! slap her ears to drive away encroaching madness. Jack and Blinky came to her aid, cornering the troll against the pulverized hull of a tow truck.

The other rust troll yet to be speared was the same rogue I'd been working on all night. There was nothing notable about the beady-eyed creature aside from a cross-shaped scar on its flat chin. It had drawn blood from me a dozen times, snapping its body like a whip, but for every hit I took I gave back two more, remembering my lessons: rabbit, bull, python. At last my opponent could take no more. With a sputter of laughter, it dove beneath a hill of tires.

Rust trolls, I'd discovered, left an oily black trail in their wake, and I followed it through the center of a tractor tire and over a pile of motorcycle wheels until I was deep inside the mountain of rubber. I spotted my foe pressed against an impermeable stack of tires, spit dripping down its cross-scarred chin. In the distance, I heard Jack's victorious cry—his battle was nearly won. I surged forward on my knees and brought up Cat #6, the perfect weapon for close quarters.

A quake knocked me off balance. I would've discounted it as a passing semitrailer if not for the reaction of the rust troll. Its gasping laughter heightened into a strangulated mewl, and its twiggy arms flapped in a state of blind ecstasy. Oil coated every one of its scales, and in seconds the troll was gleaming with black liquid.

The rumble grew stronger. The tires stacked around me began to jar apart. A section of the rubber cave collapsed. I put my chest to the ground and covered my head with both arms just in time—a tire landed on my back, knocking the wind out of me. While I heaved for oxygen, an orchestra of groaning metal struck up from the junkyard. Glass shattered, steel whined, and heavy objects avalanched from the car-part foothills. My rust troll gibbered with delight because he knew what we'd hear next.

Gunmar the Black's scream shot from a thousand different metal mouths at once. It howled through exhaust pipes, blasted from defunct car radios, gurgled through battery acid, and blared between truck antennae like the prongs of the devil's tuning fork. The entire junkyard was being played like a pipe organ.

Scrambling on my elbows, I shouldered aside each tire that battered me. I made it out into the open and flopped onto my back, only to see two tons of mangled vehicle parts sliding at me like snow from a roof. I shrieked and ran into a world that was raining scrap, burying all of us. Engine hoses slapped my cheeks; windshield wipers stabbed my ribs; edges of license plates sawed at me like teeth; and headlight lamps dropped and fractured, each of them glaring like an Eye of Malevolence.

The Hungry One's echo gave way to the sound of him chewing on his tongue, each moist squish piped up from the underworld, softer and softer, until there was silence and the dissipation of dust. What was revealed was a prison of tangled metal. Jack fought for the necessary leverage to cut himself free. Blinky's eyes bobbed above the surface of the rubble like eight periscopes. Trapped beneath several entire vehicles, ARRRGH!!! frothed with frustration, which at least told me that she was fine.

Rust trolls had none of these problems. Their slim forms easily snaked through the entanglements, and the two that had not yet died were on the move. I tried to make myself invisible, but the one with the cross-shaped scar sniffed me out, asphyxiating itself with hoarse laughter. A long vertical slit opened along its stringy torso, revealing teeth that circulated like a rusty chainsaw. I squeezed my eyes shut and waited for the first bite.

The jabber of a police siren interrupted my death. My eyes opened and I saw the slithering shadows of the fleeing rust trolls. Beyond the hill of dirt we had crossed earlier, I could make out the lazy oscillation of cop lights. A door slammed and I heard a familiar stutter.

"This is the p-p-p-p-p-police! Please disperse!"

Perhaps San Bernardino's top cop had been staking out the meth hub of Sunny Smiles when he'd heard the avalanche. After all, Sergeant Ben Gulager knew better than anyone the after-hours teen parties held at the junkyard. He looked pretty dang heroic atop that hill of dirt, his gun pointed at the ground in the standard double-hand grip, his mustache in full bloom, his cap covering the worst of his lopsided hairpiece. Even from a distance I could see the junkyard lights gleaming off the scar tissue at his temple.

His eyebrows knotted when he saw the fallen debris.

"K-k-kids? Hello? Everybody o-kuh-kuh-kuh-kay?"

I wanted to cry out but the flash of Jack's goggles beneath the ruin warned me to keep quiet. I grimaced beneath the weight of the trash and wondered how long I could hold out.

Gulager began moving down the side of the hill, sweeping the wreckage in search of trapped teenagers. He did not notice the rust trolls slithering away through the weeds a few feet to his right.

"Make a n-n-n-noise if you can hear me! Bang on something!" He pressed the radio button at his shoulder. "B-b-base, this is three hundred. I'm ten ninety-seven at K-K-K-Keavy's Junk Emporium on Grimes. I've got a code three st-st-st-structure collapse here, possible eleven forty-sevens. Request eleven eighty-nine and eleven forty-one as soon as p-p-p-p-p-p-p—"

The word went forever unfinished. His thumb slipped off the radio button, leaving the pygmy voice on the other end to repeat its follow-up questions. With a clatter like the biggest pieces of silverware in history sliding from the biggest plate, ARRRGH!!! rose from the rubble. Engine blocks, transmission systems, windshields, even entire vehicles tumbled off her back and shoulders. Slowly she rose to a full standing position and shook her head as if to clear it. A tire had been speared by one of her horns and held tight.

Emotion drained from Gulager's face and his jaw dropped. The gun, forgotten, hung at his side as he took in the full height of the monster with an expression of naked fear. But then his chin locked into the defiant position to which San Bernardino had become accustomed. His eyes narrowed and his hands curled around the gun. It flew upward, pointed in the neighborhood of the softies.

ARRRGH!!! crumpled a motor scooter in her fist and exhaled threateningly. In the foul-smelling gust, Gulager's cap sailed away and his hairpiece spun around so that the back was in the front, covering his eyes. He used a free hand to whip the thing into the weeds and looked even more heroic: bristled hair disrupted by a nasty scar, face folded into a resolute frown, gun barely shaking at all.

"Now," Jack hissed. "Follow me."

From beneath the tangle I saw him crawl on his stomach toward one of the still-standing hills of junk. I disengaged from the scrap and followed, wincing at the razor edges that drew long scratches across my skin. Blinky had already made it to the safety of the hill and was beckoning with a dozen appendages. My sinuous path took me right beside ARRRGH!!!, who remained locked in a standoff with Sergeant Gulager.

I reached the safety of the junk heap and collapsed against a knot of tentacles.

"You're bad luck," Jack said. "You know that?"

"Fault lies elsewhere," Blinky soothed. "The boy acquitted himself quite well."

"No gallbladders? Again? We're losing this war and it's barely begun."

"Let's go back to the cave," I panted. "We can come up with a better plan."

"The cave? Those were *rust trolls*. The cave belongs to them. They're following our scent there right now, and believe me, they'll bring friends. We wouldn't last five minutes if we went back." Jack's shoulders sunk in defeat. "We have no home."

"Volumes twenty-three and twenty-four of my dissertation were left on the credenza!" Blinky gasped. "Those vulgar blackguards shall tear my heartrending prose to confetti just to watch it fall. True, true, it should not take me more than eight or nine years to rewrite. Nevertheless I feel a loss—my calligraphy today is not what it once was."

"The weapons," Jack groaned. "So many weapons, all gone. And we're supposed to stop the Machine? Oh, this is bad."

From several blocks away came the blare of police sirens. Jack crawled to the edge of the junk heap and snapped his fingers at ARRRGH!!!. The tacks on his gloves made loud clicks.

ARRRGH!!! snorted her understanding and ballooned her chest. By now I knew enough to cover my ears. The roar detonated like a bomb. Dozens of windshields shattered at once, and I didn't have to look to know that Gulager had dropped to protect his body. The trollhunters made a run for it down a dark aisle. Somewhere up ahead was a bridge—there was always a bridge—but for once that was not part of the plan.

Jack grabbed me by the front of the shirt. My medallion tightened around my neck.

He searched the sky for signs of dawn.

"Shelter," he growled. "It won't be night for long."

26.

Tub didn't look happy to see me. He glowered from his bed-room window.

"Unacceptable, Jim. It's four. In the *morning*."

"Back door," I whispered. "Now."

He was even unhappier to find me in his backyard along-side two trolls throwing anxious glances at the sky while Jack struck a menacing pose next to the decrepit swing set. Tub leaned against the doorframe and exhaled morning breath, scratching at his bed-head bouffant.

"You kids have fun tonight?"

"It's going to be light soon," I said. "They'll turn to stone."

"See, that sounds like something worth seeing."

Jack shifted just enough so that his scabbards clattered intimidatingly.

"No jokes," I said. "There's no time. I need you to . . ." There was no other way except to just say it. "I need you to take ARRRGH!!!."

Tub laughed once.

"The gigantic ape-monster? In Grandma's house? You need to have your head X-rayed, kid."

"You can hide her from Grandma way easier than I can

from Dad. Just help me out here. I'm taking the others. I'm doing my part."

"It's *all* your part, Jim. You're the big-deal trollhunter, remember? I'm just some kid who, I don't know, is pretty good at video games, I guess? Why would a big, famous hunter like you want the help of an amateur like me? Thanks, anyway, but I think I'll pass."

"Then don't do it for me! Do it for her. It's not her fault she's stuck out here. But if we don't get her inside in two or three stones—a half-hour, I mean—she's going to die. You want to live with that? You want to come out here in the morning and see the pile of rocks?"

"You're an asshole."

"Call me whatever you want. Just take her in."

ARRRGH!!! tilted her head.

"Boy human. Have peanut butter. For eating?"

Tub's lips closed around his thick braces as he deliberated.

"I'm going to go ahead and assume she said something about my great prowess as a warrior. In that case, fine. For her, I'll do it. Just get her inside before the neighbors wake up."

Getting through the door was the easy part. ARRRGH!!! popped her arms out of place and didn't restore herself to full girth until we were inside the house. There was an optimistic moment during which we thought this was going to go well. It didn't last. ARRRGH!!! began reaching for every knickknack in the living room with a delighted look on her face. An entire shelf of ceramic children plummeted to the floor. Tub started mumbling about glue, where was the glue?! A row of delicate wicker decorations was the next casualty, ripped to shreds by a single curious claw. Tub's focus switched to the vacuum cleaner—somebody get the vacuum cleaner! When ARRRGH!!!

started munching on a vase of plastic flowers, I gave her a push toward Tub's bedroom. She got the message, but on her way punctured a vinyl sofa cover with a toenail.

I pointed at a spot on Tub's carpet for ARRRGH!!! to sit.

She did so with a smile and set about tasting everything within reach.

"Game controllers!" Tub cried. "Not food! Bad troll! Bad troll! Wait, wait, no, don't—don't eat—those were my favorite shoes! You can't—no, I need—oh, man, you gotta be kidding me! You know how much that hard drive cost?"

Tub bolted from the room without explanation. In the meantime I did my best to wrench Tub's possessions from ARRRGH!!!'s paws before they were popped between her grinding teeth. Blinky was no help; he was enraptured by a shelf of sci-fi DVDs and enthusing about the historic importance of this library of human/alien contact. Jack, meanwhile, had yet to move from the front door. He regarded the homey family room as if it were a jungle concealing its predators.

Random objects began sailing through the open window. It was Tub, hurling junk he'd collected from his neighbors' backyards: a bundle of chicken wire, a couple of jolly lawn gnomes, three upended flower pots, an entire bush ripped out by the roots and dripping dirt. Then he crawled over the sill and I pulled him in.

"Stuff for her to chew on," he grunted. "This is worse than having a cat—"

He froze. I did, too.

A feline screeched.

We caught only a glimpse of calico tail before it vanished down ARRRGH!!!'s throat. Tub pressed the back of his hand against his forehead like a Victorian damsel.

"Cat #20! Jim! That was Cat #20! Sweet lord, Jim, she's eating Grandma's cats!"

ARRRGH!!! licked her lips and plucked up another cat as if it were a peanut.

"Cat #36! No! Not Cat #36!"

A short-lived yowl later, Cat #36 was history. Tub clutched his skull in despair. For reasons we couldn't understand, the cats were drawn to the snack-happy troll and kept winding about her legs, stroking their whiskers against her stiff black fur.

"Cat #23! Shoo! Shoo! Cat #40, for the love of all that's holy! Run!" Tub grabbed my arm. "This isn't going to work! They only respond to their real names!"

"Then use their real names!"

"You know I lost the list!"

"Find it!"

"It's in here somewhere—oh, no! Please, anyone but Cat #39, that's Grandma's—"

ARRRGH!!!'s long tongue smacked at the furry remnants of Cat #39.

Tub dug his fingers into his scalp.

"Why do the stupid cats keep coming into this den of death?!"

Jack leaned into the room. His barbed gloves carved four scrapes through the paint by Tub's light switch. He nodded at Tub's TV set.

"Turn it on."

Tub and I fell over each other in a race for the remote. A minute of fumbling commenced, during which at least one more cat met its untimely end, before we were able to summon an infomercial from the dead screen, a shouting guy with a headset hawking some kind of new-and-improved mop. Tub lowered the volume, while I messed with the set to achieve a much blurrier screen.

"Not too much static," Jack said. "It's not healthy."

ARRRGH!!!'s grin slackened as she began to notice the flickering images. Seconds later, five tendrils of drool fell from her jaw. Now that it was within reach, I took hold of the car tire still impaled on her left horn and yanked it off. It went bouncing through the room, scaring away the remaining cats before obliterating a decorative table in the hallway. ARRRGH!!!'s paws relaxed and a chubby tabby bounded from its palm prison.

Tub dropped his body onto the edge of his bed. He prodded with a toe at the chicken wire and lawn gnomes. Bits of cat fur hung in the air. His lips moved silently as he calculated the deaths. It added up to one big problem with Grandma; he'd have to come up with a hell of an excuse, and I didn't have time to help.

"Sorry, Tub," I said. "I didn't mean to—"

"Just get out, Mr. Trollhunter." He sunk his face into his hands. "Grandma wakes up early on Mondays."

27.

Jack stood at the far edge of the living room, staring through his goggles at the altar above our electric fireplace. He panned slowly across his own school photos, examined his milk carton portrait, and lingered over a shot of him and his brother with their arms wrapped around each other in a sandbox. I watched from the dark hallway outside my room, afraid to interrupt.

Blinky sidled up alongside me, the heat of his slime warming my cold skin. Together he and I had cleared out my closet so that he would be able to crouch within it during the day, covered with a sheet from the linen closet. He was concerned about the imminent dawn, yet took a moment to speak of Jack.

"Tact, courtesy, patience," Blinky said softly. "These qualities are as foreign to your uncle now as were our troll ways during his first season underground. Even the scantest of aboveground scents, like those of blossoming flowers or baking bread, odors which I understand are comforts to your kind, reduce poor Jack to trembling. Why do you think he wears his mask, even here?"

"He could come back," I said. "We could adopt him or something."

"Would you adopt a wild animal and expect anything else than to be bit? Jack has become a creature of rock, mud, cave, and sewage, far more at home within our glorious squalor than in your rudely lit land of sharp corners and stultifying sterility. You have read the human fable of Never Never Land? So is the troll world to Jack. The accomplishments so treasured by humans are rituals of which Jack shall never partake. There will be no school graduations. There will be no first kiss. There will be no driving a car. There will be no family. Being denied this has created within Jack a great rage; that is no secret to anyone who has seen the business end of his blade. However, it is a *useful* rage. He would not be the warrior he is without it. He knows this and has accepted it. A tragedy, to be sure, but a necessary one."

Blinky left my side to tuck himself within the safe confines of the closet.

In my bedroom I kicked off my shoes and ripped my arms from my hoodie. I felt something in the pocket and withdrew a crumpled piece of paper. It was the flyer of the missing little girl with purple glasses. I looked at it for a while, thinking of the changelings, the rust trolls, and all the other beasts amassing for invasion.

I returned to the living room. Sunlight was beginning to leak through the cracks of the fortress, making it obvious that Jack was no longer there. I felt a flash of concern before noticing Dad's bedroom door was ajar. Then I felt even greater concern, hurried over, and inserted my head.

Jack was standing over the bed, looking down in a posture of heartbroken wonderment at the wrinkled old man, once upon a time a little boy called "Jimbo." He reached out with a tentative hand to stroke his brother's face, but stopped when he remembered that his fingers were covered with sharp tacks. Jack's goggles fogged over.

Dad's body made a somnambulant jerk. Something quivered in his throat.

Jack had no problem grabbing *me* with those sharp gloves. "The schmoof," he said. "You won't want to see this part."

Together we stood in the living room watching a peach glow paint the walls and ceilings. It was Monday morning. That meant work for Dad, school for me. School—how could I face those bland hallways and ignorant faces knowing what I knew now? It seemed a century ago when Tub and I had been trash-compacted in lockers, fallen from gymnasium ropes, and rolled around in a parking lot to evade the bouncing ball of Steve Jorgensen-Warner.

"There's an attic," I said. "Dad hardly ever uses it. You could hide there."

"No."

"Or maybe the garage? We'd just have to cover you up with—"

Dad yawned from his room.

Jack looked at Dad's door with more fear than he showed when facing a troll battalion.

"I'll be back at midnight," he said.

"You can't go back to your cave. The rust trolls—"

"I'm a *boy*." He said it like he was trying to convince himself of the fact. "I'm not going to turn to stone. Just give me some of your clothes and I'll wander around town. Sit on a park bench. Like a kid. Just like a regular kid."

"Fine," I said. "But this isn't 1969. Adults see a thirteen-year-old kid by himself, they may ask questions or call the—"

"I can take care of myself." He snapped his gloved fingers. "Clothes. Now."

28.

Pinkton was all over me about neglecting my homework. Homework? I tried to recall the meaning of the word as she stood at my desk and ranted while the rest of the class crunched the numbers on the board. She warned me again about the big test on Friday and how my fate hung in the balance. I looked penitent but it was an act my body remembered from past conflicts. My eyes were looking past Pinkton at the rest of the classroom.

There were two empty desks.

It meant nothing. I knew that. A bug was going around. Wasn't there always a bug? Between classes I focused on the festival decorations to avoid noticing banks of lockers that may or may not have the right number of students opening them. There was a single empty desk in biology. Nothing strange about that. Two people were absent from American lit. Hardly unusual. I considered talking to Tub before gym class to get a second opinion, but he dressed with atypical speed. He didn't just look angry, he looked exhausted. That stiff black hair he pulled from his braces and brushed off his clothes was familiar.

Later I called out to Tub in the hall but was drowned out by a throng of cheerleaders shilling for Steve Smackers. Principal Cole had purchased a warehouse full of these cheap noise-makers two years before to offset a deficit in the sports budget (plans for that new jumbotron might have had something to do with it). Constructed from hard foam and painted in Saint B. red and white, each set was made up of two paddles that made a deafening noise when slapped together. They were beyond irritating, and local football fans took to them like monkeys to poop. With Steve's rise as a star, they had been dubbed "Steve Smackers"—pretty savvy marketing for pieces of crap that went for fifteen bucks a pop.

It was almost by accident that I found myself at play practice after school. I had meant to rush home to check on Blinky when my eyes fell upon a series of *Shakespeare on the Fifty-Yard Line* posters that led me to the auditorium, the only place unplagued by Steve Smackers. Mrs. Leach was holding court before the gaggle of actors, carrying on about what an insane tradition this was, and how no one could expect halfway decent Shakespeare with only a week of rehearsal. The kids all stared at her in alarm—what, exactly, had they signed up for?—until she wore herself out, clapped her hands, and said that we'd begin with act 1, scene 1, though we'd skip the intro, since both our Sampson and Gregory were absent.

Nobody but me found that ominous.

The first big event was the duel between Benvolio and Tybalt. Benvolio, played by a flamboyant theater guy named Jasper, and Tybalt, played by a heavy-metal kid named Frank, made for pretty believable foes until the fencing foils were drawn. Jasper, having been in a dozen productions, improvised each thrust and parry with comical exaggeration, while Frank, in his first role, whipped his foil around like he was swatting flies, losing it more than once in the front row of seats.

Mrs. Leach shouted instructions to make the fight simpler, shorter, and less hazardous for the audience. Still, Benvolio and Tybalt continued to lose control of their foils and land on their asses, and each time they fell our over-eager Lord Capulet shouted his big line: "What noise is this? Give me my long-sword, ho!"

Kids were snickering. Mrs. Leach was in despair. Both fighters were bruised and winded. Something had to be done.

Licking cool-ranch flavoring from her fingers and swigging from a can of grape soda, Claire traipsed out between the duelists. She was a vision of Juliet seen through a steampunk lens, clad in black flight pants rolled up to midshin that exposed six inches of skin before her combat boots took over. Her herringbone pea coat was unbuttoned, revealing brown suspenders that dangled from her hips. Bracelets made of multicolored electrical cable gathered at her wrists, and dual ponytails intertwined to slap at her back like the supply hoses of an oxygen mask. Her round cheeks were bunched into one of her mirthful smirks.

For the first time that day, I did not think of trolls.

"Your weapon, gentle Benvolio," she said, holding out her hand.

Jasper shrugged and turned over his foil. Claire bounced it in her palm, testing its weight.

"Sufficient."

The blade whirled through the air in a figure eight, then another. Her ponytails danced.

"Adequate."

Her boots hopped to their rubber toes and she scuttled forward and back, the foil whirling through the air like a lasso, above her head, at her sides, as low as the floor.

"Tolerable."

Claire extended her weapon and playfully tapped the foil held between Frank's hands. He gulped and extended it as far from his body as he could. That was when all sense of reality went flying out the window and Claire Fontaine became a warrior goddess. With her blade whistling, she struck Frank's weapon from six different angles, each of them executed with an extravagant form that would look good even from the cheap seats. Between blows, she called out bits of advice.

"Circular attacks! Easier to follow the action!"

Frank grimaced and held to his sword for dear life.

"Footwork! Three steps, Benvolio! Three steps, Tybalt!"

Jasper watched her feet, making frantic mental notes.

"Act! This is a play! Recoil from the blows, gents!"

I was as slack-jawed as the rest. She choreographed a routine right then and there, and made it so believable and comprehensible that the whole cast was dying for a go at it. At last she disarmed Frank with a twist of her wrist. His foil went clattering to the stage, and Claire lowered her own. She exhaled upward, blowing loosened strands of hair from her sweaty forehead. She saluted Frank with her can of soda and took a drink. Not a drop had been spilled. Everyone was hushed until Lord Capulet remembered his favorite line.

"What noise is this? Give me my long-sword, ho!"

The applause thundered, from me louder than anyone. The gleam in Mrs. Leach's eye betrayed a rogue hope that she might just pull this off. The noise died out until a single clapping sound continued from somewhere in the auditorium aisle. We all turned to look, shading our eyes from the stage lights. The clapping had a remarkable consistency, as if it might continue in that manner until it drove you mad. In fact, it wasn't clapping at all.

"Marvelous." Steve Jorgensen-Warner kept bouncing his ball. "I've never seen anything like it."

Claire blushed and pointed the toes of her boots together as if self-conscious about her exposed calves.

"Lessons," she said. "Mum and Da had me in fencing for six years."

"I'm so glad they did," Steve said. "It's just magnificent."

The drama dorks were breathless, caught off guard by this intrusion of flirting into their after-school geekery. Only Mrs. Leach frowned. She didn't trust a sportsman infiltrating her hallowed sanctuary.

"Can we help you, Mr. Jorgensen-Warner?"

Steve flashed his movie-star grin. With feet trained on the court and field, he took the stage steps in three agile jumps, the ball smacking upon each step. Thespians, not the most coordinated bunch, murmured in appreciation. Claire's eyes were on the star athlete the whole time.

"There's a bit of an emergency with my grades." Steve faked an abashed smile. "Coach said there's a point system I can use to boost my average so I can play on Friday. Geez, *everybody* is counting on me to play. The whole town, seems like. Anyway, Coach gave me three options."

He took the ball under his arm and removed a folded piece of paper from his back pocket. Mrs. Leach took it, flapped it like a fan until it opened, and read it aloud.

"A: Trigonometry Contest. B: Build a Solar Panel Science Project. C: Theater Understudy."

"Coach said it was like being on the bench. I swear I won't get in the way. I just want to help out however I can."

Rarely in life does one get to witness such expertise in disarming a hostile adult. Few teachers at Saint B. could rival Mrs. Leach in day-to-day bitterness, and yet she melted right there before our disbelieving eyes. She folded the note and put it in her pocket. What, was it going into her personal scrapbook?

"Of course, Steve, we'd be happy to have you. It never hurts to have understudies. Your timing is perfect, actually. We have to get our Romeo into costuming. Jim, lend Steve your script for the balcony scene while we get you fitted."

So went the cruel twist of fate that led to Steve Jorgensen-Warner exchanging romantic verse with Claire Fontaine, high up in the balcony set, while I stood in a side room wiggling into a blouse, a pair of tights, and a peplum skirt as two student costumers pinched me in places I would have preferred to go unpinched and sighed about how they'd need to find some heels to offset my shortness. Was I good at walking in heels? They wanted to know. I nodded—sure, sure, anything to speed through this debacle.

From the stage I could hear the interplay of Claire and Steve's sweet nothings. Claire, of course, staggered everyone with her tranquility and poignancy. Infinitely more surprising was Steve, who bashed through speeches the same way he bashed through defensive lines. His reading exuded utter confidence, the quality most lacking in high school actors. Even his mispronunciations were forceful—it was his way or the highway, and everyone loved it.

"Very nice," Mrs. Leach said. "How do you have this memorized already?"

"No big deal," Steve replied. "Comes from memorizing sports plays, I guess."

"Well, it's very impressive. Keep going."

This was getting out of hand. I had to get in there, and fast, before Steve stole the part right from under me. The laces on my heels were only halfway tied before I stumbled out beneath the bewildering glare of the stage lights.

"I'm ready!" I announced.

Giggles erupted from all sides. I kept charging across the stage even as I began to suspect that my purple skirt and silver tights didn't cast me in the best light when compared with Steve Jorgensen-Warner, who looked rather rakish in blue jeans and a shirt—definitively not a blouse—opened to the third button. He dribbled the ball casually with his left hand.

"Let's just have Steve finish," Mrs. Leach said.

Something was wrong with my feet. I couldn't stop my momentum.

"No, it's okay," I said. "I got this, I'm ready to—"

My high-heeled ankles flopped to the side and I rammed into Benvolio and Tybalt, both of whom lost their foils; seconds later my right elbow socked the ear of Friar John and my flailing left hand grabbed one of Lady Montague's breasts. By the time she screamed, I was careening out of control. Steve, watching me in bemusement, and Claire, looking down at me from the parapet, were but blurry impressions before I went headfirst into the balcony set.

You wouldn't think a human head could punch through plywood, but that's what happened. The base of the set spun halfway around and I heard a board crack. In seconds the

"You are about to witness possibly the most vile ritual in all of trolldom."

entire thing was groaning and folding shut like a suitcase. I pushed against the plywood, unplugging myself from the collapsing wood just in time to see the set pitch toward the orchestra pit.

Like someone caught in a burning building, Claire kicked through the railing of her balcony and leapt for the safety of the stage. I think in that moment we all imagined her beautiful body being hopelessly mangled. But Steve stood there as if nothing out of the ordinary was happening. He adjusted his body to catch her as he had caught endless types of passes in his career, and she swung around in his grip like a ballroom dancer, her arms naturally clasped behind his neck.

There was a final smash as the balcony crumpled to lumber and scattered across the pit.

Everyone stood silent, blinking and panting.

Mrs. Leach knocked a fist to her chest as if beating back cardiac arrest.

Claire looked up at Steve, eyes wide and thankful.

Steve grinned.

My heart sunk.

He was still bouncing the ball with his left hand.

"What noise is this?" Lord Capulet said. "Give me my longsword, ho!"

Claire laughed the only way she knew how. Steve, understandably surprised by her volume, held her more tightly. Relieved guffaws tore through the assembled cast and crew, and they hung upon each other, delighted survivors of an event soon to go down in Saint B. Theater Department lore.

Roughly twelve years later, from the feel of it, rehearsal ended. I told myself that my foibles had been for the best: trollhunters had no time for school, much less extracurriculars. I told myself to forget about it, go home, hunt trolls, come back the next day, and tell Mrs. Leach first thing that I was quitting.

Removing a pair of tights was a new challenge for me, and by the time I returned to the auditorium I was the only one left. I slipped through the side exit and, once outside, watched Steve suit up and jog across the football field beneath the dead black rectangle of the jumbotron, while the practicing pom-pom squad clacked their Steve Smackers in appreciation. It left me numb. Steve *was* everything and he *had* everything. Not only was I no one, but I had no one—not Claire, not Tub, not Dad. The only path forward was to give myself fully to the night.

29.

That evening we began to win. The fragments of my life's failures—video games left unconquered, hobbies abandoned, sports left to guys much bigger—all perfectly interlocked to supply me with everything I needed as a trollhunter. My whole miserable life, rather than being a waste, felt like it had been training for this.

None of my fellow warriors needed to comment upon the change in me. We all felt it, none more so than the Gumm-Gumms, whose softies we pierced and whose gallbladders we harvested for burning. Our first conquest that evening was with a quartet of Wormbeards: hulking, bulbous creatures whose objectives were to whisper demoralizing insults to children while they slept so that the children would be compelled to run away from home, sad little sojourns that always ended while passing beneath a bridge.

Wormbeards were so fat around the middle they could roll themselves at you like runaway boulders. They achieved impressive speeds that way, and I don't think I'll ever forget dashing down Jefferson Street with Jack, Blinky, and ARRRGH!!! at my heels, chasing a rolling gray blob as it bulldozed mailboxes and road signs and a single fire hydrant. I burst through the jetting water and threw Claireblade like a javelin. It sunk into the Wormbeard's spine and he unballed, denting two cars with his outstretched paws. The next morning the damage would be blamed on a hit-and-run driver. Only we hunters knew the truth.

We tried to intimidate the Wormbeards into revealing Gunmar's location. They used their dying breaths to laugh at us. Using ARRRGH!!!'s nose and Jack's astrolabe, we raced from bridge to bridge trying to divine the secret opening to the Gumm-Gumm lair. Every door we took led us through sewer pipes and long-forgotten caverns, but sooner or later we'd find ourselves back in a bland Saint B. suburb under assault from another troll lowlife.

Tuesday morning came fast enough to make me want to vomit. I plodded through hallways decked out in red-and-white crepe paper and in gym class flat-out refused to climb the rope because of my sore muscles. Tub didn't say a word in my defense while Coach Lawrence wrote me a detention slip. I carried that worthless slip of paper all the way to play rehearsal, where I was unintelligible with exhaustion. Mrs. Leach had no choice but to call in Steve, and I was sure Claire preferred him anyway. With a mixture of relief and remorse I sunk into an auditorium chair, sedated by the knowledge that my skills were the kind that had to stay hidden. Just a few hours more and I'd prove it.

The Yarbloods were the smallest trolls in the known universe. Complained about in everything from Sumerian pictographs to Egyptian hieroglyphs, these legendary nuisances were no larger than mosquitos and fed upon children who played outside too late. The Yarbloods attached themselves to hair like lice and burrowed into a child's skull to cause illness.

We followed Jack's astrolabe to their latest hunting ground: a local orphanage.

Jack slathered a sour-smelling slime upon the upper lip of any kid we found within the grips of a fever. This slime made the kids need to defecate; we hid in the hallway while the first boy stumbled to the bathroom. Afterward we ran in and Jack commanded me to reach down into the toilet. I did it without question until my arm was submerged in toilet water up to my shoulder. I felt it, some kind of clog, and wrestled with it for a minute before yanking out a lump of white, mice-sized trolls clinging to one another with claws and teeth. The Yarbloods had grown quite a bit before they'd been pooped out.

Unpleasant to catch for sure, but pretty easy to kill.

Sergeant Gulager crawled by in his cruiser as we were leaving. By the dashboard light I could make out his drawn face as he drained the latest in what was probably a long line of cups of coffee. After seeing ARRRGH!!! with his own eyes in the junkyard, no doubt he was questioning his sanity, and yet he had a community to protect. So he was up every night, just like me, doing what he thought was right. I thought about him as we trollhunters spent the next few hours burning gall-bladders behind a vacant warehouse.

Wednesday came as it always did, though I'd have been hard-pressed to tell you the day of the week if you'd asked. The only way I was keeping track of time was by the rising number of missing students in each class. Though I ignored Pinkton's math, I made calculations of my own, adding up the vacant desks. It was no different at play rehearsal. Where was our Mercutio? Our Friar John?

Then, in a crash, it was night. Meet the Zunnn—their dingy drawstring bags told you all you needed to know. They were out to nab kids for Gunmar, plain and simple. The Zunnn fought as a team, rushing at us with arms locked like rugby players and wearing matching jumpsuits dyed with red and green stripes and helmets constructed from the skulls of larger trolls. It was rather intimidating, truth be told, but their bash-and-smash technique was no equal to four well-wielded swords, a few dozen whipping tendrils, and a member of the ARRRGH!!! family fortified by a three-course meal of cats. Even as they were losing, the Zunnn belted out their minor-key fight song. To counter I began shouting bits of Shakespeare coming to me from out of nowhere.

"Take the measure of your unmade grave, fiend!"

Off went a pouch of softies.

"Alack, there lies more peril in mine eye than twenty of thine swords!"

Off went a pair of hands.

"O! she doth teach the torches to burn bright!"

Off went a head, still wearing its helmet.

Never had a trollhunter slayed with such style. Even my companions were stunned. Soon the squad of Zunnn was no more and we spent the rest of the night on another fruitless search for the Gumm-Gumms. More than once we had to hide to avoid the zealous eyes of Sergeant Gulager. He was everywhere, all of the time, and I was duly impressed. He wanted to help, that was obvious. But even heroes had their limits. This fight was not for him.

30.

When we got home, I didn't think much of the light and sound coming from the TV. I packed Jack's lunch, as I did each morning before grabbing a couple of hours of sleep, but when I found him he was glued to the television. At first I couldn't make sense of the wobbly, low-resolution footage, but then I recognized trolls, and not just any trolls.

The footage stabilized and I saw Blinky and ARRRGH!!!, standing in what looked like a kitchen, their faces smeared with peanut butter. The next thing I heard was human voices. My voice. Tub's voice. I went lightheaded and gripped for something to keep me standing. Nothing was there and I staggered, far enough to see the cables leading from the TV to a teddy bear—the nanny cam that I had forgotten about.

Dad sat on the sofa, watching it in a stupor that suggested he'd been watching for hours.

Jack didn't need to say a word: he'd forgotten to apply the schmoof. The packed lunch fell from my hand with a paper-bag crinkle. The noise broke through Dad's trance, and with aching slowness he reached for the teddy bear. The grainy footage blinked off and was replaced by early-show video of a sunken-eyed Sergeant Gulager refusing to confirm that more than four kids had disappeared.

"Individuals cannot be considered missing until they have been gone for twenty-four hours," he said.

"In light of these disappearances," asked the reporter, "should the Festival of the Fallen Leaves be canceled for the first time in San Bernardino history?"

"Of course not," Gulager said without emotion. "There is no reason for panic."

Dad modulated his breathing before turning our way.

"We must band together as a community," Gulager said from the TV.

Dad stood. The sofa springs creaked. He was much taller than Jack.

"We must show unity in the face of strife," Gulager insisted.

Dad took a single step. His eyes swam with tears of confusion.

Beside me, Jack was nailed to the floor.

"Jack?" Dad whispered. "Is it really you?"

"Jimbo," Jack said.

There was a pause, filled with the babble of a commercial break.

"I'm sorry," both brothers said together.

Dad reached out to Jack, but his hand floated upward of its own accord. His eyes followed his hand, and his neck began to roll backward. Then, with the first lancets of morning light poking through the chinks of the steel shutters and jabbing the counter on which was propped a framed milk carton photo of the brother lost forty-five years earlier, my dad, Jim Sturges Sr., originator of the Band-Aid method of glasses repair and uncredited inventor of the Excalibur Calculator Pocket, fainted.

31.

Eighty-eight percent. Pinkton had drilled the number into me for weeks. The math test was the next day, and that was the grade I needed. But all I could do was apply the merciless percentage to other events in my life:

Eighty-eight percent chance that I would not be playing Romeo.

Eighty-eight percent chance that Tub would never speak to me again.

Eighty-eight percent chance that Gunmar the Black would return.

Eighty-eight percent chance that I would die upon the field of troll battle.

Eighty-eight percent chance that Dad had lost what was left of his mind.

I'd left Dad and Jack in the living room. Dad's unconscious body had been transported to the sofa before I threw myself in the shower for a quick rinse. By the time I emerged with a fresh set of clothes, Dad was awake but hunched on the edge of the sofa, facing away from Jack and whispering to himself that he was being tricked, someone was trying to trick him. Jack, looking young and innocent in my baggy hand-me-downs, gave me a distraught look. Would Dad call Sergeant Gulager? Principal Cole? Would he find some way to prevent me from trollhunting just a single day's time before the Killaheed's completion?

Jack wanted me to blow off school and help him with this brother situation—it was well outside of his comfort zone of hunting and killing. But I found the reunion of long-lost siblings too intense, too personal. At least at school I could lose myself in the Steve-Smacking clamor of kids with nothing on their minds beyond the game the next night. I grabbed my backpack and didn't look back until I'd caught the bus.

With Pinkton's 88 percent ringing in my ears, I made a pit stop at my locker for my math book. I found myself longing to trash-compact myself, just so I could take advantage of the privacy for a nap. It was while I weighed the pros and cons of this plan that I heard a cruel laughter down the hall. It wasn't enough to convince me to move. Even the smacking of a basketball failed to incite my interest. What did it were the snatches of words in that cool, finely articulated voice.

"Ten dollars is the new price," I heard. "Inflation."

Just down the hall, Tub's head was wrenched beneath the arm of Steve Jorgensen-Warner. It was a reprise of the scene in the Trophy Cave, but with the fun added bonus of a fare increase that Tub would never be able to satisfy with his grandma's pitiful allowance. I was heading toward them before I knew what I was doing, pushing aside rubberneckers. I wasn't the same guy that I had been a week before, not even close.

With both hands I shoved Steve in the chest. Until that moment I'd never realized the extent of his muscle density: he didn't budge an inch. But the action garnered the desired effect. He pitched Tub to the side to regard this newer, more interesting victim. A cymbal clash announced Tub's head-on collision with a locker, but I kept my eyes trained on the enemy and his bouncing ball.

SMACK, SMACK!

"Jim, thanks for reminding me," Steve said. "I've been meaning to ask if you'd be willing to participate in our daily toll. It's a great program with lots of keen benefits."

"Lay off Tub."

SMACK, SMACK!

"I'll take that as a yes. Why don't we start right away?"

"Lay off everyone. Everyone's sick of your crap."

SMACK, SMACK!

"Are they? I hadn't noticed. Seemed to me it was the opposite."

"They're just scared of you. I'm not."

SMACK, SMACK!

"Scared? Why should anyone be scared? I'm the guy who's going to score the winning touchdown tomorrow. I'm the guy who's going to do a quick costume change and per-form some play in the middle of the field. All night it's going to be me up there on the jumbotron. I don't do it for per-sonal glory, Jim. I do it for the school! People appreciate that. They're only too happy to give a few bucks here and there for the cause."

SMACK, SMACK!

"That's my role," I growled.

"You did look cute in your skirt and tights, I'll give you that. Tough break. Don't worry, I'll be sure to give your Juliet a big, wet kiss from the both of us."

"Why are you so interested in Claire all of a sudden?"

"Why?" Steve repeated. "Why *not*?"

He laughed. In comparison, I realized that my voice had become wheedling. The dull weight that had heavied my fists seconds before was gone. Weakness snowballed. Onlookers were chuckling and it hurt like it used to. I hung my head and turned to find my books where I'd tossed them aside. My only successes came in the dark of night; I should have known better than to try to take on Steve in the light of day.

"You're a dobber, Mr. Jorgensen-Warner."

All heads, including mine, turned toward an accented voice that sounded considerably less adorable when it was crackling with fury. Claire had dodged through the crowd and stood there in her familiar grays and greens, her beret tipped at a wartime angle. The only things pink about her this time were her cheeks, inflamed with rage.

Steve's laugh was uncertain.

"I'm a what?"

Claire came within striking range.

"I'd soon as kiss a chanty wrassler like you as I'd shag a goat in a rot outhouse."

"Shag a . . . ?"

"You try and give me a nookie badge and you'll find yourself with a keeker, you daft muppet. Jim is twice your Romeo. Say otherwise and I'll play fisty cuffs with your hooter and kick you in your baw bag."

"You'll play *what* . . . ? With my *hooter* . . . ?"

"Look at you, you're right gliffed, ya bas. What, you think I'm a quine? More like a radge! I'll dance the slosh on your napper and do a number on both your wallies *and* your walloper. Then you'll be crying to your ma, you will."

"Wallies? Walloper?"

Pent-up slang from her homeland, long boxed up, came

pouring out in a stream as incredible as it was indecipherable. You could intuit some meaning—kicking him in assorted sensitive areas seemed to be the basic gist—but mostly it was violent emotion delivered by a girl whose easygoing attitude had always been her most notable trait.

She was right up in Steve's face when she lashed out with a foot and kicked the basketball all the way down the hall. His eyes went wide and his right hand formed into a fist. We all saw it. Claire pointed at it—her bravado knew no bounds!—and laughed as if it were a child's pinwheel.

"Aw, yer maw cares, you shite-tongued zoomer! Best remember my way with the sword before you go waving your puny knuckle pouch."

Chiding laughter, so fickle in high school hallways, now tottered in Steve's direction. He'd never been the target of ridicule and was baffled. He looked at each chuckling face as if it were a personal betrayal. His handsomeness separated into ugly pieces of panic: beady eyes narrowed to stony glints, sharp teeth bared in a defensive sneer, and his thick body compacted as if bracing for a tackle. Then he made the wisest choice he could. He sucked down his anger and turned tail. He might rule again, but that day was lost. He took off after his basketball and looked pretty childish while doing it.

The rubberneckers dispersed, repeating snippets of Claire's tirade guaranteed to be incorporated into local vernacular. I let out a giant held breath and turned to help up Tub. There was a dent in the closest locker, but he was gone. I was disappointed, though I couldn't blame a guy for wanting to flee a monster. I was familiar with the instinct.

Claire, though, was there, and when the bell rang she wasn't startled. She gave me a level consideration.

"Mr. Sturges," she said.

"Ms. Fontaine?" I tried.

She nodded sagely as if judging my response adequate.

"You seem a bit different, Mr. Sturges."

"So do you," I said.

"Oh, that?" She rolled her eyes. "You should hear me when I bump my knee."

"I'll never bump your knee. That's a promise."

"I heard Ms. Pinkton today. About your troubles. About the eighty—"

"Eighty-eight percent," I finished. "Yeah."

"I'm not half-bad at numbers, Mr. Sturges."

"I know. It's very impressive."

She rolled her eyes again.

"I mean, I can help you, you scaffy skenker."

"No, please." I held up a hand. "None of those words. I can't take it."

Her smile was glorious and her laugh as loud as ever.

"Let's meet tonight. Eighty-eight is nothing. I can get you to ninety."

"You . . . you want me to come over?"

Her smile faltered.

"I'm sorry. You misunderstood. You can't come over."

"Oh. I'm sorry. Uh. Well. Great. Thanks?"

"Relax, Mr. Sturges. It's not you. My house just isn't a good place to visit. In general. But I could come over to your place. I've told Mum that tonight is the final rehearsal, and I know she can convince Da that it's going to be a late one. You and I can walk together after the final run-through, set up at your house, and get right to the numbers. I know a few tricks that'll kablooey your brain."

"I'm—" The concept of turning down any offer from Claire Fontaine was a difficult one. But the truth was the truth: I needed sleep, even if it was just two or three hours, because when the sun went down, the final hunt was on. We had only one night to find the Gumm-Gumms before the Killaheed reached its completion. I sighed and continued. "I'm not coming to rehearsal."

Her disappointment was evident. I appreciated it. If I was bailing on *RoJu* that night, there was no hope of my salvaging the role. She'd have to act opposite Steve, the guy she just humiliated in front of the entire school. For a moment I wondered if she might walk away from the whole deal. But then her expression sharpened. That's the kind of girl she was—she'd decided to *relish* acting opposite Steve. It was a challenge, and if she delivered her lines just right, maybe she could show him who was boss more than once.

"All righty," she said. "Six o'clock. Sturges household. What do you say?"

The simple question was riddled with risk. Nobody but Tub had ever visited the steel-plated, camera-protected stronghold of my home. An eight-eyed creature was hiding in my bedroom closet. My dad was on the precipice of total breakdown upon the arrival of a supposedly dead older brother who'd not aged a single day. And once it was dark enough, a band of sword-wielding weirdoes would come together in my living room to track down the infamous villain who'd taken at least a dozen kids in the past week, who knew my name and wanted me as well.

There were a million reasons to say no to Claire except one: I'd been waiting all my life to say yes.

32.

Claire Fontaine knocked at my door twenty minutes late, rosy-cheeked and complaining about all the "festival rubbish" that was making the whole town look like a little kid's birthday party. I went "heh-heh-heh," a laugh so forced that I creeped myself out. Thankfully, she came inside anyway. I closed the door behind her and reached for the first of the ten locks, ready to whip through the repertoire of *click, rattle, zing, rattle, clack-clack-clack, thunk, crunch, whisk, rattle-rattle, thud* before stopping myself. Not with her watching I wouldn't. I was braver than that now.

I left the door unlocked.

Claire missed nothing. Within seconds, she'd zeroed in on the metal shutters, the three security consoles, and the dangling wires of the kitchen ceiling fan, which still hadn't been replaced. She asked after Dad and I had to plead ignorance. He was gone and this was not normal. Dad spent no more time at San Bernardino Electronics than was required. Again I offered my "heh-heh-heh" and again she overlooked it. She bounded through the kitchen and flung her pink backpack upon the dining room table, and moments later we were pulling out textbooks and strategically arranging pencils and paper.

The first hour was useless. I kept smelling her and feeling the heat from her body and repeating in my head that I had a girl at my house. Not just a girl, but *the* girl. So it came as a surprise when numbers, correct ones, started imprinting themselves on paper as if my pencil were possessed. After another hour of Claire's arithmetical trickery, insight was slashing through my brain as swiftly as the first blades of morning light through Troll City. Maybe I'd surprise Pinkton after all.

"Your da's going to be upset? Is that it?"

My face was so close to the page I could smell the pencil lead. I looked up into a bag of chips, which Claire pushed aside so she could see me.

"What do you mean?" I asked.

"You've been checking the front door all night."

"Have I?"

"Like you're expecting him to come busting in with a tire iron and bash in our heads."

"Sorry," I said. "He wouldn't use a tire iron."

Her eyes widened. "Oh? What would he use, then? A cricket bat?"

"No, no, no. He's not going to use anything, period. He's not going to attack us. I can't believe we're even having this conversation. Dad works in *electronics*. He mows *lawns*. No one's getting their head bashed in. I'm just—it's weird, because he normally doesn't work late. He'll probably just be surprised to see you when he gets here, that's all, because I don't, you know, have a lot of people over."

"Yes, I noticed the defenses. Terrifically imposing. Are we expecting an invasion?"

I shrugged. "There's always something. That's what Dad would say."

"Is there? Always something, I mean? Is America all that dangerous?"

"Depends on where you go." I pictured the space beneath my bed. "There are bad areas."

"This street didn't look like a bad area. Unless the gang members here wear sweater vests."

"It's not a bad area. Dad's just . . . excitable."

"And how does your mum feel about this? Most women I know aren't in love with the steel-shutters-and-barred-windows look. To each her own, of course."

"Yeah, she didn't like it either."

"She's gone?"

"Yeah."

"Dead?"

The frankness with which she asked this caught me off guard. I dared to look at her for several consecutive seconds and detected nothing besides an earnest desire to know. Her lack of shyness inspired me to behave likewise.

"She left us when I was a kid."

"Why did she do that? Nice boy like you. Husband who wouldn't use a tire iron on anyone."

I grinned. "It was just . . . *this*." I gestured at the barricades. "That's my theory, anyway. She and Dad were having some issues, I was old enough to know that, but I never knew it was that bad. One day she was here and things were pretty normal and the next day she left."

"You don't hear from her?"

"Nope. After she left, my dad said a few things, not a whole lot, but I got the impression she had a strange past, you know? Like she was maybe in jail or something? I'd believe it. She was smart but kind of devious, too. She probably married Dad because he was safe, different than the rest of her life. But she can take care of herself. I bet she went and got herself a new name and a new ID, and is off getting sick of a whole new husband and little kid. Mexico, maybe. Or Hawaii. Or just some small tropical island somewhere."

"That's sweet of you."

"What's sweet of me?"

"To imagine her somewhere beautiful like that."

This made me stop and think. I did, in fact, picture my mom walking barefoot along a beachfront, dodging sand dollars and starfish, inhaling the salt smell and trying to find glimpses of her old life in the red sun setting behind a lush green mountain. These fantasies were dry of emotion, and for the first time I wondered if I had drained them to protect myself.

"I was home sick the day she left," I said. "I was there when she walked out. She didn't say a thing. She just undid all the locks and walked out. After a while, I got up and locked the door behind her. I was just a kid; I thought that's what I was supposed to do. So I don't *feel* sweet, you know? I locked the door behind her. It was the day before my birthday, the first of May, and I was like, well, if she's not going to at least stay for my birthday, then screw her."

"May second is my birthday, too," Claire said.

"Seriously?"

"Inverness, Scotland, May second."

"Scotland? I thought you were from, like, London."

"London! Good god! Don't you know a Scottish accent when you hear one?"

"Well, they're similar, right?"

"*Similar*? You say that in the Highlands, mister, and you'll be spouting a bleeder."

"Sorry! I didn't—I guess I don't know my accents as well as—"

"Hey, we ought to have a party together in May."

"A party? Two seconds ago you were going to punch me."

"Though I'm a full year older than you. My guests might be a little more mature."

"At least you'd have guests."

"What about Tobias? He's worth three or four guests, I'd wager."

"Tub and I aren't really talking at the moment."

"Mr. Sturges," she sighed. "So much gloom!"

I set down my pencil atop my math and turned to her.

"I honestly don't see how you do it. I've been here all my life and I'm like a disease. You've been at our school for like two minutes and you've got friends falling out of your ears. You yell at cool kids in the hall and you're a hero instead of getting stomped? You've got two parents who sign you up for cool things like fencing lessons? It blows my mind. What is that like? Seriously, what in the world is that like, to have a life so . . . *nice*?"

Claire had been twisting a lock of deviant hair around a finger. She let it go and it sprung back to her cheek like the staysail of a boat after being severed. Her expression was not one of offense or anger but rather of darkened curiosity, as if weighing whether I was prepared for a truthful response. I judged that I wasn't, but it was too late: she removed her beret and shook out her hair, which leapt in all directions, a regiment of serpents to back her up. Then she lifted that pink backpack from the chair, set it upon the table, unzipped it, and withdrew the last things I'd expected to see.

Clothes, pretty ones, the kind of ensemble that would vault a girl like her into the popular crowd the instant she walked through school doors. A svelte pink dress with teal trim and matching hair ribbon. A pair of heeled shoes, two sparkly earrings, a tangled strand of pearls. And loads of cosmetics: eye shadow, lipstick, blush, nail polish, and several other containers I wasn't qualified to identify. The last item she removed was a well-used jar of makeup remover. She held this for a moment longer as if it carried the most significance.

"We do have a nice life." She spoke carefully. "We have a nice house. Mum keeps it nice because that's how Da likes it. We have nice hobbies. It's not just fencing lessons I've been instructed to take, it's piano, voice—all the best diversions for some Scots out to be an upstanding American family. We have nice food—turkey, potatoes, greens. Da likes us to have nice food, he makes sure that's understood. And we dress very nicely. Very nicely indeed. I'd say if you were to stop by our place and peek in our window around dinnertime, you might nominate us for the nicest family in all of San Bernardino. Perfect for postcards and TV sitcoms—all we're missing are the spunky little dog and wacky neighbor."

The pink backpack sat between us on the table like an engorged insect on a dissection slab, cut open and spilling its ugly secrets.

"Monsters don't always look like monsters," she said.

Who knew this better than me? Blinky and ARRRGH!!! had been walking nightmares just days before and now were my most trusted friends. Meanwhile, other beings who looked perfectly normal moved through life in simulated benevolence: the Steve Jorgensen-Warners of the world, the Professor Lempkes, the Nullhuller changelings that, according to Blinky, ran most of Washington. Perhaps Mr. or Mrs. Fontaine fit into the same category, demanding a personality from their daughter that she'd been forced to invent.

"I'm sorry," I said.

"Don't be. You didn't say it out of meanness. You said it because you think of me living in a make-believe place as wonderful as that of your mum, even though neither of us deserves it. You're a good person, Mr. Sturges. A bit gloomy, but good."

"Okay," I said. "I like when you say it, anyway."

If I am lucky, I will live to be an old man, and when I'm lying there on my last pillow with bleeping electronic equipment hooked up to measure the exact distance to my death, there will be a few choice memories that run on repeat in my brain, because I won't want to leave life with any other thoughts but the sweetest. What happened next will be one of those memories.

Claire Fontaine, the sort of girl confident enough to one day take on the world and be the equal of those of the highest rank, thought enough of me in that moment to reach out with both hands and encircle my wrists. The raw ends of her electrical-wire bracelets poked into my skin. The adamant tips of her fingers crawled up my forearms and then pulled me closer. Her hair, as wild as ever, touched me long before anything else, and I remember the spider-web tickle of each follicle against my cheek. Then she was too close for me to keep in focus and she became the world's most beautiful blur.

For all my fantasies, I'd never really thought about how soft lips feel when pressed against other lips.

My phone made sure we didn't enjoy it for too long. Claire sat back with an eyebrow raised as if judging my performance as unconventional but precocious, and I blinked at her for a few seconds before rustling through the pocket of my coat for the stupid ringing piece of junk that so badly needed to be destroyed. My stomach lurched a bit. It was Dad, so I held up a wait-a-second finger to Claire, stood up, and answered the phone while heading into the dim light of the kitchen.

"You okay?" I asked.

He sounded depleted. "I can't answer that, Jimmy. But I'll be home later. I didn't want you to worry. There's some meals in the freezer you can heat up. I think there's a cheesy garlic lasagna. Maybe a broccoli and beef. You like those. Go ahead and eat. It's just been a challenging day and there's still a few things I need to think about before I come home and . . . I don't even know what happens then."

"Things are weird right now," I said. "I know that. But we can deal with it. You haven't even met the others yet. All right, I admit, that's going to be pretty weird, too. But if we just all get in the same room, we can explain the whole thing to you, okay? Just as soon as the sun goes down."

"Sun's already down," Dad said. "I'll be home eventually. Take care."

The call went dead. For a moment I was unsettled by his detachment, but that was replaced by the information he'd passed along: it was indeed dark out. I leaned over the kitchen sink and ducked beneath the steel shutters. The floodlights were flickering with moths, a sure sign that they'd been on for some time. The hours had slipped away. I laughed to myself. Math had never been so diverting.

Claire screamed.

It was a guttural noise, as if she were trying to break away from an unwanted embrace. Something wooden exploded, followed by the gonging of stricken metal. Then came the sound of running, way too many feet, followed by a horrible series of sounds: a musical snap like the tearing of guitar strings, the muffled ripping of several thick layers of fabric, and the splinter of lumber being chomped between teeth.

"Claire!" I called.

The name still reverberating from my kissed lips, I sprinted into the dining room, pausing only long enough to note each disaster: Claire gone with no trace but her beret; her chair rolling across the floor in a dozen pieces; a massive dent in the corner of the table where something huge had kneed it on its way out; and the white birds of our math problems making slow, doomed descents. Her pink backpack was missing—she'd managed to grab it, though what good it might do her was beyond me.

In my bedroom I blundered into a snowstorm of mattress guts. A mouthlike hole had been burrowed straight through the center of my bed—the mattress, the springs, everything. I leapt to the edge of the hole and saw the last few motions of the floorboards as the secret staircase locked itself away.

Claire's screams echoed from below, caught in the phantom space of the hardwood floor, the concrete foundation, the clay, and on and on, deeper and deeper, world upon world and fear upon fear.

I threw myself into the cavity of the bed and drove my heels at the floor, shouting for it to open. The chewed-off edges of the box spring scratched at my upper body as I fell to my knees and dug at individual boards with my fingernails. I might be a trollhunter, but I had no idea how to open that door, and without such knowledge right that second, I was worse than worthless.

My screams for Blinky hammered off the flat surfaces of my room. The troll slithered from the closet with the sound of a birth of snakes, his eight red eyes blinking away curds of sleep. I kept clawing at the floor as I felt tentacles, too many to push aside, wrapping around my torso and lifting me out of the cratered bed.

"Let me go! We have to save her!"

I wriggled in midair before my feet touched down amid drifts of mattress foam. Blinky's appendages had my body encircled from behind, and the more I fought to be set free, the tighter he squeezed. Slime oozed from between tentacles as he began to speak in a dapper, infuriating tone that I didn't want to hear, warning me that waiting beneath these boards was an ambush—he had written all about the strategy in volume twelve of his dissertation.

Though I didn't want to believe it, I *heard* them and I *felt* them right through my feet, a seething swarm of Gumm-Gumms just beneath the floor, cackling and slurping in expectation of sinking their teeth into fresh teenager. Claire was gone to their unspeakable hands, taken to unimaginable places, and it was my fault. I moaned and reached for my swords to cut something, anything, just to relish in the breakage.

Blinky's eight eyes lowered before me like wilting flowers and shone at such wattage that I had to shield myself from the brightness. Then the ancient troll inhaled and I felt against my back the warm beats of multiple hearts and the inflation of at least four giant lungs. A sound rose from somewhere inside his guts. It began low, like the boom of a train crossing distant tracks, but then added the higher octave of whale shrieks and the shrill clanging of bicycle bells rang by boys outrunning the death of summer, the end of childhood, and all other manner of gluttonous beast.

What it was was a call, one loud enough to be heard across the neighborhood, provided that you had the right kind of ears. My medallion began to burn and I could smell the singed skin of my chest. Beyond the pain, though, the translation was forceful and clear, and it made me catch my breath.

"TROLLHUNTERS!!!"

Blinky held me and howled, and I howled, too, sending a prayer out to Claire, to all of the missing: *hold tight.*

PART IV

The Battle of the Fallen Leaves

33.

Jack banged through the unlocked front door, took one whiff of acrid air, and ran to my room, where he pushed the remains of my bed to the perimeter. Blinky then spread his tentacles so that the entire floor was carpeted with his mucoid flesh. I climbed on top of my dresser to get out of the way. The tip of each tentacle crinkled as if sniffing out a varmint.

"ARRRGH!!!'s nose is better suited for this task," Blinky apologized. "On the upside, though, I do have seventy-four of them."

This gave me hope until the tentacles ripped away like tape. Blinky backpedaled to the safety of the closet, hacking up fizzing troll phlegm that began to eat away at several items of my discarded clothing.

"The scoundrels are piping up the vilest of odors to throw us off the scent! Strawberries! Vanilla! Azaleas! Coffee! I fear I shall faint like a corseted maiden! Or vomit most forcefully! Or both in impressive concurrence!"

"We attack," Jack said. "Right now. But we need a different door."

"Anywhere but here!" Blinky moaned. "Or regurgitation will be the evening's sport!"

"I know the place," Jack said. "But we need to *move*."

There was no argument. Jack strapped on his armor, the metal parts snapping and ringing, harbingers of combat. I kicked aside the clothes sodden with troll puke and chose a shirt and pants that I wouldn't mind dying in. Blinky handed me Cat #6 and Claireblade, and they felt heavier than ever before.

We swept through the living room, and I grabbed the doorknob. It turned but the door didn't open. All ten locks had been thrown. I began the unlocking regimen before realizing what this meant. I turned around and there was Dad, clutching his battered briefcase, his face patched with stubble, his clothes matted, his unbuttoned left cuff link stained from whatever fast food he'd been living off for the past day.

Dad's reaction to seeing an actual troll was so subdued that I worried his brain might politely explode inside his skull. To minimize his size, Blinky folded as many of his appendages behind him as he could. Jack, meanwhile, kneaded the mask in his hand, clearly wishing he could put it on to avoid this encounter. Dad exhaled and inhaled as if both were being done at gunpoint, and reached out to the shelf above the electric fireplace for stability. Various pieces of the Jack Sturges Collection were toppled.

Dad gazed at his brother's school photos while he spoke.

"Jack," he said. "Why did you come back?"

"I had to," Jack whispered.

"Then don't leave." Dad's voice broke. "Stay here with me. I still have boxes of your clothes. I can buy bikes for the both of us, the best they sell, red for you and yellow for me. I've still got your radio. We can ride and listen to music, Jack. We can shoot our lasers. We can pedal so fast we won't have time to remember any of the bad things that happened. We can grow up together after all! Doesn't that sound like a dream?"

"I can't grow up, Jimbo. Not with you. Not with anyone."

Dad slammed his fist onto the shelf. It shook and the framed milk carton picture fell to the floor, where the glass shattered upon the hearth. Jack jumped and Blinky gasped. Dad whirled around, his face streaming with tears.

"I'm lonely up here, Jack! Stay with me. Or take me with you."

"Jimbo . . ."

"Wherever you go, I'll go; it's what I should've done years ago!"

"I can't—"

"Take me! I'm ready!"

"You're not—"

"I'm the big brother now, Jack! You have to do what I say!"

"You're too old!"

Jack's shout rattled the locks upon the door and made the steel shutters hum. We stood there as the cruel echo made its excruciating exit. Dad's taut expression of shock reshaped into folds of grief. He lifted a hand dotted with the first liver spots of old age and touched the jowls that in recent years had elongated his cheeks. The hand continued up past the worry lines carved into his forehead to the scalp that had long before given up its hair.

"Then I'm overdue," Dad said.

Jack's hand clenched his mask.

"I'm sorry," he mumbled.

We hitched up our weapons and turned toward the door.

"You're taking Jimmy?" Dad asked. "You're leaving me and taking my son?"

"Dad," I said. "I have to go."

"I forbid it," Dad said, emboldened with the concept. "There's danger—have you seen the news? Danger everywhere!"

"I'll bring him back," Jack said.

"And if you don't? What then? You'd be tearing apart what's left of this family. When it's in your power to put it all back together!"

Jack paused with his tack-edged glove on the doorknob. He looked at his boots for a moment and I could see him measure the truth of what Dad was saying. That night's mission might be one of suicide, and even if that meant a troll invasion and the destruction of the entire continent one city at a time, perhaps it was still unfair to rob a father and son of those precious last days.

"This isn't up for debate," I snapped. "I'm going."

"Jim," Jack said. "You need to think what we're about to—"

"I don't have to think. That bridge will be finished tomorrow. Kids will die. Kids I know. And we're sitting here discussing it? Look, it's like what Tub said, except I didn't believe him when he said it. This is what I'm here to do, Dad. This is the only thing I'm good at. There are times when you have to do the right thing, no matter how scary. Both of you should know that more than anyone! If I don't fight now, *right now*, when am I supposed to fight?"

Jack was staring at me. It was a look of warning, then of questioning.

I did not budge.

Slowly a sad smile crept across his lips. He nodded, once.

"We fight," he said.

"Fight?" Blinky laughed. "Too humble a word for our despoilings and devastations!"

They were the color of dried blood, equal parts orange, brown, and red.

Dad collapsed onto the sofa with mannequin stiffness.

"Your Shakespeare," he monotoned. "What about your play?"

With practiced fingers I undid all the rest of the locks. Then I saw the keys to the San Bernardino Electronics van hanging on a hook beside the door. We were behind schedule and wheels would sure help us catch up. I took them before I could think better of it.

"I'm heading over to the field tomorrow to give it a final mowing," Dad continued. "Make it all look nice for your play."

I ushered Blinky into the night, then Jack, who threw a final, regretful look at his brother. I put my hand upon the die-cast vehicles that covered his torso and pushed him down the steps. I took the doorknob and swung the door behind me, pausing for just a moment to watch my dad stare blankly at the dead TV. This could be the last time I saw him. I wanted him to turn around and tell me that he believed that I could do it.

"I'll come back, Dad," I said. "I'll try. I'll try really hard."

"Yes, of course." He did not look at me. "See you tomorrow night at the play. I know you'll be fantastic."

34.

It hurt to leave. But hurting was something every family that had lost a child knew about, and if the trollhunters had one job above all others, it was the ending of that hurt one way or the other before it became something that could never be salved.

That night Jack fulfilled a long-held fantasy: he drove. Ripping the keys from me and saying that he knew as much about driving as I did, he leapt into the driver's seat while I loaded Blinky into the cargo area that usually held Dad's mower. Once I was strapped into the passenger seat, Jack lurched the van forward, punching a nice, neat hole into the garage door.

"Mistake," he said. "My mistake."

He reversed through the lawn and kept going until the tires had munched up a flowerbed across the street. By this point, though, Jack was having a blast, his eyes sparkling with the kind of intensity I'd only seen in battle. He shoved the gear into drive and stomped on the gas. Once the spinning wheels grabbed hold of the pavement, we accelerated through a cloud of burning rubber, Jack whooping with uncharacteristic glee.

He drove the same way he rode his bike back in 1969: headlong, at top speed, and improvising every step of the way. By the time we heaved to a halt in Tub's driveway, we'd only dented three cars, demolished one topiary light, and snapped a sapling in half. Jack honked the horn and Blinky used a tentacle to throw open the side door. The van chugged; every fiber in my body was in motion.

We saw movement at the back of the house. Jack gunned the engine, ready to roll. ARRRGH!!! hulked her cautious way along the side of the house, blotting out the yard lights as she approached the van. Once more, it seemed there was no way she'd fit, and yet she did, turning the entire back compartment into a stinking lounge of black fur upon which Blinky sat. She seemed to find being inside a human's vehicle almost as novel as Jack did. I adjusted my mirror and noticed something glinting from ARRRGH!!!'s mouth. I turned around in my chair.

Proudly she pulled back her furry lips and grinned. Wrapped around each gigantic, lethal tooth was the same chicken wire I'd helped Tub pull through his bedroom window four days before, expertly tightened by metal screws.

"Braces," Tub said.

He stood on the driveway decked out in his best approximation of a ninja: black tennis shoes, black sweatpants, a black hoodie, a belt made from a red curtain sash, and an oversize fanny pack holding his gear, probably not throwing stars and nunchakus but who really knew. It was unfortunate that the fanny pack was lime green, but I still was impressed. Tub pointed at his own braces.

"She liked mine." There was no disguising the satisfaction

in his voice. "She's actually more aware of her looks than you'd think. So I hooked her up. Not bad, huh? She'll have the best choppers around in just, you know, maybe a couple hundred more treatments. But that's nothing in troll years, right?"

ARRRGH!!! extended her muzzle from the side door and rested it upon Tub's shoulder. Her blasts of breath wobbled his mountain of frizzed hair. Absently he patted her on the nose like he'd done it a thousand times, which I realized, he probably had. At once I felt terrible and inspired: this friend whom I'd left to deal with this frightening creature had performed so much better than I'd thought possible.

Five yellow claws wrapped around Tub's considerable gut and lifted him into the back of the van. There was a bruise on Tub's jaw from where Steve had thrown him against the locker, but it was nothing—he looked more certain of himself than at any other point in his life. He grinned at me, showing all those glorious braces.

"You watch my back, I watch yours," he said. "It's only fair."

He offered up a hand and I took it.

"My ninja," I said.

"My trollhunter," he replied.

I don't think Jack was thrilled about having another kid to look out for. But he clenched his teeth and popped the van into gear. The bottom scraped against the driveway with the additional weight. Blinky shut the side door with a tentacle while another appendage curled around Tub's neck affectionately. I felt a sob catch in my chest. We might all be headed to our deaths, but this right here was a family, no matter how unusual it might be.

Off we roared, peeling away strips of lawn and knocking

bumpers from cars that, according to Jack, should've been parked closer to the curb. Tub shook off the blows and unfolded from his fanny pack a laminated artifact of Dershowitz lore.

"The cat list!" I cried. "You found it."

"Yeah, well, it wasn't hard to find once all my video games had been eaten. But I'm happy to report that the killing spree is over. Notice there's no cat hair stuck in those fancy new braces? I've converted our friend to cheeseburgers."

"Pickle," said ARRRGH!!!. "Onion."

"Right, she likes them with pickles and onion."

"Paper. Is flavor best."

"Yeah, she likes the wrapping paper left on, too. FYI, you don't want to know how much two hundred cheeseburgers cost. My god. Point is, she didn't mean anything by eating all those cats and she's done with it."

"Cat no for eat. For chew."

I translated and Tub's face fell.

"No, no, no. We've been over this. You can't *chew* them either, okay?"

ARRRGH!!! gnashed her metal-covered teeth, trying to make sense of it.

Tub sighed and snapped the laminated list.

"I thought a brief eulogy might be in order?"

He cleared his throat.

"For those brave felines who fell in the fight for freedom, I recite these names so that we will not forget that adorable, undeniable sense of curiosity that got them all eaten."

"Make this quick," Jack said. "We're almost there."

"And now for the naming of the deceased. Curly Fries. CSI. Midichlorian. Dow Jones." Tub shrugged. "Grandma watches a lot of TV." He continued. "The Wayans Brothers. Bridezilla. The Secretary of Agriculture. That's So Raven. The Cat Formerly Known as Prince—"

"Parking now." Jack grunted as if bracing for impact. "Parking—parking—hold on—"

Jack did indeed park, or, as I would've put it, sideswiped a shoulder barrier until both driver's side wheels were punctured. The van jerked to an unhealthy halt, and the engine coughed until it died. I felt bad for Dad but for only a second: Jack pulled down his mask, planted his hands on the edge of the window, and leapt out.

I heard him land on his feet in a pile of dead leaves and hurry away. The other doors were already opening and so I followed. There was a bank leading down to a dry canal bed, but getting there meant trudging through overgrown weeds. These slowed me down, as did several decades of trash tossed from the street. Only when I had reached the bottom with the others did I realize the significance of the location.

It was the Holland Transit Bridge.

35.

Though I'd heard my dad speak of the location all of my life, I'd always avoided it. It was easily done: for a generation, people had eschewed it because of a nasty urban legend about a boy being eaten beneath the bridge in the '60s. And then, in the 1980s, a freeway bypass ended its usefulness as a thoroughfare.

Now it existed as the last respite of homeless junkies. I stepped into its shadow and warily examined the chunks of cement dangling overhead by thin iron rods. More empty beer bottles than I'd ever seen had been tossed next to a concrete wall covered in graffiti: demonic beings who bore resemblance to ARRRGH!!!, as well as nonsensical yet ominous declarations like *Harpakhrad Lives!* The structure was in deplorable shape but held the portent of ancient ruins. Something important had happened here, you could feel it.

Jack wandered about with his astrolabe as one does when trying to find a phone signal. ARRRGH!!! snuffled her nose along every clammy surface, giving experimental licks to mold and bird droppings. Blinky's tentacles pushed and prodded for any door that might be hiding in plain sight. Minutes went by, then half an hour. Tub and I sent each other private telegrams of panic until Jack kicked at a pillar, sending pellets of cement skidding down the canal.

"This is the place! I know it is!"

"Gumm-Gumms," Blinky concurred. "I feel them with my every beautiful pore."

"I can't single out the door. I just can't."

"The Machine, Jack. Remember the Machine and the will to fight shall prevail!"

The discussion was interrupted by a soft thud. ARRRGH!!! was hunched over the wilted cardboard box that she'd tossed to the ground. Dirt scritched against concrete as the box shifted around on its own. Jack did not hesitate: he withdrew Victor Power from its scabbard and bolted for the box as if meaning to run his blade through its center.

ARRRGH!!! held out a gentle paw to block him.

"Choice none," she said.

"Balderdash!" Blinky cried. "I shall double my efforts! Triple! Quadruple!"

ARRRGH!!! picked up the box with a bashfulness that begged for forgiveness.

Jack's warning crunched from his boom box speaker.

"I'll cut it out of your hands, I swear!"

Spittle trickled down ARRRGH!!!'s chin as she gave her human friend a smile of metal-packaged teeth. Then she reached carefully into the box and withdrew the Eye of Malevolence. The yellow orb flopped inside the cage of her hand, its long stems whipping like strings of wet seaweed. A high-pitched, babyish squeak emitted from somewhere inside the feculent flesh.

The thing wanted fed.

"Hold her down!" Jack commanded.

He wrapped himself around ARRRGH!!!'s left arm but was nowhere near strong enough and in seconds found himself dangling from the bicep. Blinky knotted his tentacles around both legs but he did not look especially optimistic. Tub gave me a desperate look and we both took handfuls of stiff black fur.

The Eye of Malevolence dug its long, stringy fingers into ARRRGH!!!'s face, and that was it for the trollhunters. Jack's armor crashed loudly when he hit the dirt. Blinky was thrown into a pillar, setting off a small avalanche of crumbled cement. Tub and I found ourselves rolling over and over, locked in a terrified embrace. I put on the brakes and saw the Eye's soft body pulsating as it leeched away our friend's sanity.

A door to the troll world opened in one of the pillars. I was about to announce this news before dozens more began creaking open and snapping shut from every part of the underpass: the belly, the walls, the ground beneath our feet. ARRRGH!!! had done her job, but the Eye had countered by opening additional passages to confuse us. For a bonus we received a deranged ARRRGH!!!; she lurched at her former partners, taking out chunks of concrete and canal bed and sending refuse into the air like filthy insects.

Blinky's tentacles picked up a dozen jagged pieces of rock.

I withdrew Cat #6. Would we have to hurt her? Or worse? Or would it be the other way around?

Only Jack, I noticed, had not armed himself. He stood motionless with his hands at his sides.

I pulled Tub closer to the action.

"Jim! No! Bad timing! She's in a mood! Reschedule! Reschedule!"

"Boost me up!" I shouted. "Now!"

"Oh god oh god oh god oh god," Tub mumbled as he ran up behind the marauding ARRRGH!!!, kneeled down, and laced his hands together. I planted my foot into Tub's makeshift sling and he launched me upward, as he'd done a hundred times in the past. For a delirious instant I was airborne and then my face was full of fur. I wrapped my limbs around an arm muscle bigger than me.

ARRRGH!!! jerked the arm as if shooing away a pest but paid me little mind as she cornered Blinky. For me the ride was like being churned up and down on some vomitous carnival attraction. I pulled my face from the carpet of gamy hair, took two handfuls of pelt, and began surmounting the shoulder. The Eye of Malevolence slurped outward to cover ever more of the troll's face, digging a couple of stems so far into her nose that they reemerged from her mouth, looking as if they'd made a wrong turn.

A troll door opened from the concrete and knocked Blinky to the ground in a spill of tentacles. ARRRGH!!! bellowed and took advantage of the moment, placing a giant foot on either side of the Lizzgump scholar and raising a fist for the killing blow. I aimed Cat #6 but was too far from the Eye to strike.

Seconds before Blinky was to be crushed I became aware of a song.

The sun slides into darkness,
At midwinter stands it still
And out the trolls of Christmas come from the hollow cave
*   and hill.*
Since Saturn penned the Titans
Imprisoned in the earth

The children of the gods return to walk the winter earth.
Shrieking and capering down they whirl
When the veil is thinned to the underworld.

The melody was fragile and inexpert, but it was this very roughness that brought poignancy to the wistful tune. I took a handful of fur and leaned to the side to find Jack coming closer, his mask and astrolabe dangling from either hand, his swords stashed across his back. The kid warrior, unbelievably, was singing.

Shouting and galloping down the sky
Comes Odin's band, the Jolerei.
'Tis Death to see them, thunder rolls
O'er this poor lost band of hungry souls
The veil is thinned to the underworld.

ARRRGH!!!'s right arm shot out like an out-of-control garbage truck. It passed inches in front of Jack's face, whipping the astrolabe from his hand and sending it clattering into the gutter among the broken bottles. Jack took a single swallow of fear before continuing the song.

Crockery shattered and feasts spoiled sorry.
This must be the work of the callicantzari!
From down the Greek mountains these winter trolls scurry
To carry off children born of winter's hurry.

ARRRGH!!!'s infested snout twitched with a distant memory of this lilting melody. She lowered her fanged head to get a better look at this curious little being, and then her hairy forehead peaked in surprise as Blinky's voice, a distinguished tenor, joined in on harmony.

If you'd ward off their mischief, build your Christmas fire big
And hang upon your mantel the jawbone of a pig.

Just picture it. Forty-five years before, there was Jack, just months after leading the trollhunters to victory over the Gumm-Gumms, finding the glow of battle fading as October and November passed into December. To a kid, Christmas is Christmas, and the urge to return to his family must have been overwhelming. Thankfully there was an old song about the holiday known to few trolls outside of their foremost scholar, and Blinky sang it to the little boy while ARRRGH!!! cradled him in her furry arms—their first family ritual. Bonds forged by war are one thing. Those formed by love are something else.

It was easy to climb a troll so still.

The Eye of Malevolence flicked my way at the last instant, the red veins fattening to the size of my forearms and the pupil widening into that tempting pool of darkness. Not tempting enough—I chopped with Cat #6, severing half of its stems. The holiday song cut off as the Eye gobbled in pain and withdrew its tendrils from its host's body. ARRRGH!!! spat until eye stems were flying everywhere and hitting the ground like bisected worms. With the same paw that had threatened Blinky and Jack, ARRRGH!!! ripped the Eye from her face, along with a great deal of fur. She threw it against a cement pillar, and it hit the ground with a wet splat.

ARRRGH!!! fell into a sitting position, wrapping her hands around the boulder embedded in her skull. Jack hopped onto her legs and stroked her face despite the pus leaking from her eyes and the blood draining from her lips. Blinky, too, slid forward to run a gentle tentacle over the fresh wounds. I lowered myself to the ground and leaned against the sticky pelt to catch my breath.

It was by chance that I saw the Eye of Malevolence crawling like a slug and leaving a trail of translucent slush in its wake. What none of us had realized was that all of the doors to the troll word had shut except one. I stammered and stamped my foot. One of Blinky's eyes took note; seconds later I had the attention of all eight.

"Corpulent one!" Blinky shouted. "Follow that Eye!"

Tub and I looked at each other.

"Me?" I asked. "Him?"

"Avoirdupois child! Zaftig boy!"

"Him?" Tub asked. "Me?"

"Heavyset! Stout! Husky! Go! Go! Go!"

"Husky! Husky!" I pushed Tub. "That's you!"

Tub's expression hardened into a righteous one and he bared his metal teeth. Braying like a sick donkey, he picked up a softball-sized hunk of concrete and charged. The Eye doubled its inchworm speed. As fast as Tub moved—and I'd never seen him move faster—the Eye outpaced him and the tail of its eye stems slithered through the door seconds before Tub got there. The door began to swing shut, but Tub tossed the chunk of concrete and it landed in the door's path, blocking it.

"Hell yes!" Tub shouted. "Did you see that? Did you guys see that?!"

"O-ho! Ha-ha! Hee-hoo!" Blinky cried. "You have not failed us, pudgy warrior! Fellow hunters, gather round, for it is nigh time to hunt!"

While we panted for breath, Blinky extended each of his tentacles and quilted them, over and under, into a shifting, liquid pattern that seemed to capture the entire nighttime in its net. I found myself at a cadet's attention. Blinky at last began to speak, softly at first, but with a rising, rousing grandiloquence.

"There will be no more despair—no, friends, not tonight. If sorrow or regret or anger chills your bellies, permit me to warm you with the whiskey of anticipation. Oh, how each of my four stomachs roils to smell troll blood darkening the underground mud. There may have been scores of trollhunters in wars past and only five of us here tonight, but so much greater will be our glory. Follow me now, with courage the size of the fabled Old World mountain trolls! Follow me with your blades whetted sharp enough to split the very oaths of vengeance that fall from our throats! Look around you, soldiers! These are the nights of legend! These are the grim circumstances that inspire the greatest of songs! And when we destroy the destroyer, brothers and sister, we shall be fêted like kings and queens in the Promenade of Victors!"

My chest swelled with pride.

"The Promenade of Victors!" I shouted.

"To watch as they carve our names in the Tower of Truth!"

"The Tower of Truth!" I echoed.

"Or, alternately, into the headstones of the Graveyard of Glory!"

"The Graveyard of . . . hang on, the *what*?"

"Either fate we shall welcome as eagerly as a stein of boiled bile!"

"Yes." Jack unsheathed his swords. "Yes!"

ARRRGH!!! brought herself to unsteady legs. "It be yes."

"Urrrmmg, bleennhh, plaarff," Tub griped. "Don't mind the guy without a translator."

The trollhunters rushed for the door. I took a breath and stared at my battered sneakers, hoping for a similar burst of bravery. There, lodged between a dented flask and a foam container stained with barbecue sauce, I saw the mangled remains of the astrolabe. I kneeled down to gather them.

"Don't," Jack said. "It belongs here."

His eyes were blazing but calm. I looked from him to the bridge that towered above us to the rest of this dingy, littered catacomb. It was as broken as Dad, but it also had provided us a way to put all of the wrong things right. Jack held out a hand. I took it around the forearm, preferring the circled notebook wire to the tacks of his glove, and after he helped me up, we stood in place, gripping each other a few seconds longer than necessary. History had witnessed stranger hand-clasps of brotherhood, but not many.

Before the door sealed shut behind me, I caught a glimpse of a lone vehicle that had opted to use the Holland Transit Bridge. It was a large shipping truck and the metal sides of its trailer bed had been dented from the inside as if something in there were fighting to be freed. The truck's general direction suggested that it was heading toward the area of town best known for its shopping district, its well-kept parks, and, perhaps most notably of all, its world-class museum.

36.

We cornered the Eye four hours later in a cave toothed with stalactites. It didn't thrill us to discover that the Eye could scale rock faces like a spider. Tub, in a fit of bravery, grabbed for it and was whipped with its stem—poisonous, we discovered, when the welt began to inflate. The injury slowed us, and the Eye squeezed itself through a one-foot drainage pipe with the sound of a straw sucking up the last liquid in a glass.

Without the Eye to chase, without the astrolabe, without a healthy ARRRGH!!!, the wrong turns multiplied until we were lost. Frustrated and tired, we turned a blind corner to find ourselves in a tunnel bisected by a ray of light—it was morning already. ARRRGH!!! and Blinky retreated like spooked livestock and I could see the rocky stiffness that had already set in their joints. They were in pain, but neither Jack nor I permitted them recovery time.

The arrangement was awkward: ARRRGH!!! led with her nose, but because of the danger of sunlight, Jack, Tub, and I had to walk in front. It was slow and arduous, and as we continued along a downward labyrinth of forgotten sewers and abandoned mines, the air grew colder and thicker. When we came upon yet another tunnel that split in three directions, it was Jack who sat down on a boulder and held his masked head in his hands. The trolls stopped, too, out of ideas.

Their despair was contagious. I squatted and stared at the obdurate rock between my shoes, thinking of everything I was missing back in the brightly lit human world: Pinkton's math test, preparations for the big game, the final ragtag rehearsal for a play now missing its female lead,. the fitting of the head stone into the Killaheed Bridge, and whatever panic or self-delusion Dad was going through. We'd been down here for almost a day. Hope was dwindling.

Tub's voice surprised all of us.

"Huh," he said. "Don't normally see a whole lot of pink down here."

He was pointing near my feet. I shifted my gaze a few inches and saw a scrap of polyester still clinging to a rubberized zipper. It was pink and I'd seen it a thousand times before.

"Claire's backpack," I said.

"Claire's backpack?" parroted Tub.

"Claire's backpack!" I leapt to my feet and flapped my arms at the despondent trollhunters. "Claire's backpack! Claire's backpack!"

Their glances were easy to read: the Sturges kid had finally gone insane. I laughed, rather insanely, and ran down the center tunnel. Just before the light from Blinky's eyes ran out, I spotted a second pink scrap, this one a silky fabric fringed with lace. It was the dress she wore at her da's request, the one she hated, the one she was now tearing to pieces. She might as well be tearing up all the lies of her past life, for this was life and death, and she was fighting with what weapons she had on her.

I marveled at the turn of events as the rest of the gang

gathered behind me. It would be the bold breadcrumbs of a sixteen-year-old girl, not the combined talents of a trained regiment of trollhunters, that would lead us to Gunmar.

And they did. We followed Claire's pink clues through hidden crevasses and over unlikely crags. Pinpoints of sunlight slowed us at times, but the sun couldn't stay up forever. When it set, Blinky and ARRRGH!!! were renewed with the vitality of the night, and they scampered across treacherous terrains as only underground dwellers could. The blood pounded in my ears and my skin prickled in anticipation of battle. I can't speak for Tub, but I'm pretty sure he felt the same: I'd never seen the guy look so alive.

The tunnel tightened like a closing fist before releasing us, one at a time, into a limestone cavern as wide as a hockey rink. Tall, contorted objects jutted at haphazard angles from the ground. We walked among them in silence until we were surrounded. Blinky kept his eye-light low. There were no living creatures about and yet I felt a frosty dread.

"The Cemetery of Souls." Blinky was hushed with reverence. "So long have I heard whispers of this fabled place, though never did I dare dream of seeing it with my own eight eyes. But of course the Hungry One would position himself so as to relish the agony of those who died the most painful of deaths."

"What's the most painful way to die?" I asked.

"See, Jim?" Tub said. "That's the kind of question I could live without."

"Being caught in sunlight," Blinky said. "It is said that the pain goes on for decades."

"Is that why they were given these weird gravestones?" I asked.

"Gravestones?" Blinky raised several of his mournful eyes. "These are not gravestones."

The glow of his red eyes intensified and revealed the terrible truth.

These were not monuments to fallen trolls, but rather the trolls themselves. Multiheaded and multilimbed bodies twined into postures of ultimate torment, jaws caught wide open in eternal screams, arms and tentacles and wings raised in final failed efforts to shield themselves from the dreaded light. I was so stunned that I kicked aside a few stones by accident, which was fine until I remembered that they were not stones at all. They were horns, ears, fingers, teeth.

I returned each of the stones to its rightful spot.

We passed through the rest of the Cemetery of Souls without further comment. By the time we reached the end, it felt as though I'd witnessed the genocide of an entire species. The last of Claire's pink scraps was speared on the stone antlers of a troll who'd died on all fours, and I took a knee so that I could remove the inappropriate color.

My fellow trollhunters were waiting up ahead. It took me a moment to realize that the light flickering across their bodies was not originating from Blinky. In fact, the illumination came from the chamber that awaited us around the bend: deep, fiery reds; white-hot razors of yellow; churning brown smoke that curled around their ankles like affectionate rodents. I didn't need to see for myself to know that we had found the Gumm-Gumms.

37.

Black oil dripped from above in long, sticky threads that burned like ant bites when they touched skin. The walls seeped white pus that crawled to the ground like fattened worms. Each step we took eddied the hot steam shooting from shuddering contraptions of delinquent metal. The clangorous moans of these devices added to the wail that thickened the air into fog.

We climbed over a berm of melted steel and found ourselves behind a conveyor belt, a crudely sewn patchwork of stained textiles that shuttled cargo into a large tin funnel. At the moment the belt was empty of everything except greasy stains, but nonetheless I followed the progress. The funnel fed into a thundering box the size of a treehouse, held together with railroad spikes and constructed from miscreant metals: a dented go-cart frame, a child's red wagon, a neon sign from a strip club. Scorched wires snaked in and out, while virulent fumes poured from electrical circuits gone haywire. The box shook like a laundry machine about to explode and I could hear from inside it the whirring of saw blades and the music-box plinking of a grinder churning through gristled remains. It all led to a spout on the other end.

A gloved hand took my shoulder.

"The Machine," Jack said. "Be sure you really want to see."

His goggles gave up nothing but didn't need to—the force of his grip said it all.

With Tub at my side, I climbed over a hill of decayed pinball machines to get a closer look. A corroded pipe held aloft by spindly stilts ran from the Machine, and from inside it I could hear the squish of pulpy matter. It stunk like death, but I leaned toward a section of pipe that had been rusted away.

Inside was meat, a lumpy sausage equal parts red muscle, white bone, and gray tendon mashed together with the multicolored gristle of internal organs. The fleshy sludge slugged through the pipe in uneven spurts as the Machine shoved it along. The kaleidoscopic viscera dazed me, and so I was caught unaware when the meat squirted forward and revealed something else sunk into the ground flesh.

A girl's barrette.

Vomit lurched up my esophagus.

The little girl with purple glasses from the flyer was all I could think of, and I dropped my face into the Machine's steam and let it bead upon my face like tears. But Jack was there in seconds to push me back toward the pipe, a cruel thing to do. All at once I wanted to kill him, I wanted to dig my teeth into his neck and pull out his throat in a wet chunk.

The tacks in Jack's gloves dug into the sides of my head. Blood streaked down my cheeks.

"Look at it!" he demanded.

"I hate you! I hate you!"

"The Gumm-Gumms are infecting you! This whole place is toxic! Will you look?"

"I'll kill you!"

"Just look!"

The tacks in my scalp forced my head within inches of the pipe and I choked on the smell. I couldn't help but see what he wanted me to see: loose teeth, embedded in the meat, white as pearls. This made me all the sicker until the meat rolled and I saw that the teeth were tiny and pointed.

"Rats!" Jack shouted. "The meat is mostly rats!"

Within the threads of muscle I saw a long pink tail.

"Can't you smell it?" Jack demanded. "This meat is ancient. Left over from the last war. He's had to cut it with animal parts to keep him strong until the Killaheed is finished. Which means your friends aren't in there, not yet. You've got to pull it together, Jim."

He let up and pointed at the rickety tube that rose high into the air on rusted risers.

"Follow that meat," he said.

We dove through black smoke and emerged in a bowl-shaped arena surrounded by natural rock columns. The meat conduit passed over our heads like a miniature roller coaster, dripping rank fluids onto our cheeks before rising even higher on swaying, deteriorated poles. We craned our necks and stumbled across a desert surface to follow the pipe. It criss-crossed the space above us in the most illogical of paths before reaching a dirt plateau twenty feet off the ground. Here the pipe angled sharply downward and was lashed to a Y-shaped brace by a knot of barbed wire. From the open end of the pipe, clods of meat plopped like wet dog food into the open mouth of Gunmar the Black.

Hope drained from the trollhunters as if each of us were being bled.

Even without the plateau, the Hungry One would've

outsized us all. He sat upon a throne of yellowed bones collected from the 190 kids who died during the Milk Carton Epidemic, and with long icicle teeth he gobbled at the meat that spattered across his face and chest.

The "Black" of his title was metaphorical; his skin glistened a deep, blistered red. With each swallow, his limbs convulsed along several unexpected joints—two elbows to each arm, a scabby, wrinkled knee on each leg, and all of them adept at bending in any direction. His crooked spine elongated and retracted like a periscope, rifling the thick porcupine spikes that ran from the back of his head all the way down his back. Luxuriously he spread the six arms that sprouted from his sinewy chest, each of which was encumbered with seeping tumors, except for the topmost left arm, which, as promised, was a weathered block of wood marked with his numerous kills.

Gunmar's jaw dropped open to reveal the mangled tongue that he'd been chewing on in resentment for over four decades.

"SSSSSSTURGESSSSSS."

We turned away from the voice's warm gust. My pulse thundered to hear my family name so spoken, and when I next looked, Gunmar was using a single claw to tickle the Eye of Malevolence. Gunmar's left socket had long before sealed over with scar tissue, but the Eye looked perfectly content to sit upon its master's shoulder like a parrot.

"Hey, Jim," Tub whispered.

"Yeah."

"If we couldn't beat the eyeball, how are we going to beat, you know, all the rest of the parts?"

"See, Tub?" I replied. "That's the kind of question I could live without."

"Jim! Up here!"

Never again would I mistake a Scottish accent for an English one. I zeroed in on the source of the cry and found Claire to the right of Gunmar's throne. Not Claire exactly, but her head. Yes, for a few surreal seconds I believed her severed head was calling to me, which I took to mean that I had just been killed and was in fantasyland. But no, she was alive, though for some reason I could only see her face poking over the edge of the plateau. Behind her I saw the twisting heads of other kids, at least a dozen of them. There was no cage, no other trolls but Gunmar—why weren't they running?

From behind us came the squeal of unlubricated metal gears. From above, the sputter of a pipe pushing along its last specks of sausage. The Machine was empty and in need of fresh fuel.

ARRRGH!!! patted the boulder lodged in her skull.

"Gunmar! Fight! Now!"

"FIRSSSSSST," Gunmar rasped past his forked tongue, *"MY FRIENDSSSSSS."*

Emerging from beneath the shadow of the plateau was a dizzying gallery of trolls, horrors of doubled jaws and compound eyes and swaying silica. They dragged clubs and bludgeons and chains. The braids of their hair were hardened by dried blood and their bodies had mutated from residing too close to Gunmar: scabs birthed extra eyes, sores sprouted extra fingers, rashes gleamed with newly grown teeth. There were Nullhullers, Ğräçœjøïvõd'ñûý, Wormbeards, Yarbloods, Zunnn, and scads of other weak-willed rogues that made up this new generation of Gumm-Gumms. So it was with surprise that I overheard Jack's mutter of disbelief.

"That's it? That's all there is?"

"Underestimate Gumm-Gumms at your own peril," Blinky warned. "Perhaps the Hungry One has not had sufficient time to amass the number of followers we'd estimated. Let us take this as good news and leave it at that, eh?"

Jack clashed together his swords. "Agreed."

He unleashed his battle cry and the other trollhunters did the same. In a practiced motion they fanned outward in triangle formation, ARRRGH!!! to the right, bowling over three Gumm-Gumms with a single fist; Blinky to the left, tripping up foes with his whiplike tentacles; and Jack on point, swirling his swords like lassos. Instantly the atmosphere thickened with the whump of pounded muscle, the clash of colliding weaponry, and the invigorating ripping noise of softies being separated from necks.

Dust billowed up from the warriors, and Tub and I used it to scurry around the periphery of the dome. We couldn't see three feet in front of us, but used our feet to gauge drop-offs and our hands to push aside brambles of metal. Against the backs of our necks spattered the gore to which I'd grown accustomed: cold slivers of troll skin, hot jets of arterial blood, the sticky mesh of softie tissue. The cries of captured kids grew louder as we neared, a sound that battled against the entranced moan of the Gumm-Gumms:

"Killaheed. Killaheed. Killaheed."

The bare face of the plateau split the befilthed air like a ship emerging from fog.

"We're here," I sighed.

"Great," Tub said.

Then a lone creature materialized from the smog. Across its chin was a cross-shaped scar. It was the nasty little troll that had weaseled away from me beneath the tire pile at Keavy's

Junk Emporium. With its unrivaled sense of smell, this rust troll had tracked me through the dust and smoke and viscera. It snapped its towering body like a bullwhip and hissed a mist of venomous oil from its crude slash of a mouth.

"Correction," Tub said. "*Not* great. This is *not* great."

"I got this skinny bastard," I growled. "Stand back."

Never before had I drawn Claireblade and Cat #6 with such operatic flair. I believe I saw the rust troll flinch before the tiny gems of its eyes hardened and it writhed sideways. It came fast to my left, but I parried Cat #6 with Jack's favorite move, Fling the Poop, and when the troll accordioned and sprung to my right, Claireblade enacted another of Jack's patented salvos, the Blue Jean Surprise. But the troll was wily, dodging the swords and whipping gashes through both legs of my jeans. I cried out in pain and came at the rust troll with both swords swirling.

I had the *Grācæjøïvōd'ñûy* against the side of the plateau, and yet my blades rang off the stone with enough force to shake my entire skeleton. The damned thing danced around each strike, mocking me with its coughing laughter. Giving into brute instincts, I clubbed madly, forgetting the rabbit and python in favor of the bull. It was a rookie mistake. The rust troll bit me on one wrist, then the other, and in a flash I'd been disarmed, firelight flashing off my blades where they had stabbed themselves into nearby dirt.

The troll lassoed my waist and flung me against the plateau. My forehead hit rock and I slumped to the ground. The thing's mouth unzipped and venomous tar dripped down the cycling rows of chainsaw teeth. It darted up my legs, light as an insect, and leaned in to deliver the killing bite.

A sharp silver point popped out from between the rust

troll's eyes and then twisted, grinding whatever brain the troll had into shavings. The edge of a scalpel then burst through its open mouth, knocking out several of its triangular teeth. Then I heard a high-pitched whine and watched in disbelief as a tiny circular saw cut through the lower third of the troll's body, splitting the gallbladder, which voided a gush of blue ooze. The troll went stiff for several seconds and then released its reservoirs of inky poison through all of its pores, forever wasted as it sopped into the dirt. The troll fell limp as a leaf.

Tub stood victorious, his hip sack open, gripping in both fists the most disturbing weapons I'd ever seen, hand-fitted tools forged of pitiless steel and callous chrome. He switched off the whirring handsaw and grinned.

"Dr. Papadopoulos," Tub said, brandishing the dental devices with pride.

"You stole them?" I asked.

Tub shrugged. "Thought maybe it was my turn to cause a little pain."

Together we hurried around the edge of the plateau until the screams of the abducted kids were directly above us. Now that the Machine was empty, it could be a matter of minutes before Gunmar made a meal of one of them. I stared up at the sheer face, wondering how we'd scale such an impossible wall.

Tub grabbed my shoulder.

"Good news, bad news time."

"Good news," I said. "And make it real good."

"I found a way up."

"That is good. Very good. How bad could the bad news be?"

Tub winced, turned aside, and pointed.

Two thick black cables trailed up the side of the plateau and over the top.

"God, no," I said. "Anything but ropes."

"We can do this, Jim."

"We couldn't do this in regular old gym! Much less a troll inferno!"

Tub stuffed Papadopoulos's instruments into his pack and zipped it shut. His grin was as cocky as a globe-trotting swashbuckler's.

"All those times I fell in gym class? I was faking it to piss off Coach."

"Really?"

Tub's grin straightened.

"No. But it sounded good, didn't it? Let's pretend that it's true and climb these bastards."

He clapped me on the neck and jogged over to the cables. By the time I got there he had two handfuls and was bracing his feet against the rock as if rappelling. I kicked aside a stack of human bones and grabbed the other one, scrambling up several feet before a familiar dread seized me. My blistering palms began to slide down the hot cable, and my spine began to twist, the final signal that I was a goner.

My left foot slipped from the rock and I experienced the vertigo of a plummet. It was a familiar feeling followed by automatic bracing for pain. But it didn't happen—a strong hand caught me by the lower back and held on just long enough for me to wedge my foot back in place and find new grips on the cable. I looked over to find that it was Tub who had saved me while holding aloft his entire weight with just one hand.

"Not this time," he panted. "This time we make it."

It was all I needed to hear. I put my chin to my chest and ascended: two feet, three feet, four feet. Tub's foot hit an unfortunate crag and he began to spin, but I kicked off from the wall and was able to steady his rope with my left hand. There was no time for thanks. Our sneakered toes found notches. Our muscles held true. Most important, our willpower didn't flag. For a time, the clamor around us wasn't screaming kids or dying trolls or even the laughing of gym class rivals, but instead the cheers of believers who rooted for us to make it all the way to the top, which we did.

We gasped into the dirt until our eyes found each other and our faces split into miserable, hysterical grins. It was the frenzied calls of the kids that compelled us to push our bodies to sitting positions. Gunmar the Black was fifty feet away, towering above us on his bone throne, his red skin crawling across his body as if it had its own intelligence.

Tub and I crawled on hands and knees toward the kids. Claire's dirty, exhausted face was the first I saw, and I pressed a finger to my mouth to keep her from crying out my name. She bit her lip and nodded. As soon as Tub and I crested a small rising, it became clear why we could see only her head.

Each kid had been buried in the dirt up to her or his neck. It was bad enough that they'd been paralyzed this way rather than kept inside of a cage, but the real hell of their situation became clearer as I got closer. Their mouths were crusted with unidentifiable slop, evidence that Gunmar had been fattening them with tasty stuffing before making sausage of them in the Machine. These children and teens hadn't been buried, they'd been *planted* so that the rich dirt and underworld clay could properly season their bodies for the troll palate.

There was nothing to do but dig with our bare hands. Claire was the last one planted and therefore the easiest to remove, and within thirty seconds I'd scooped away enough dirt for her to wiggle herself free. She pressed her filthy face against mine in a quick hug before scrabbling over to the next kid and tearing at the ground to release him. Tub and I set to freeing a little girl I recognized despite the lack of purple glasses. I whispered to her that it was going to be okay. My fingertips bled against rock as I dug.

The more kids we released, the more diggers we had, and within ten minutes we were cowering behind a hill alongside seventeen begrimed others. The murk of the battleground below had cleared enough for me to see the tireless advance of the trollhunters. Perhaps due to their brainwashed state, the Gumm-Gumms were not the best of fighters—ferocious, yes, but undisciplined in the face of a coherent attack. And, as Jack had said, there just weren't anywhere near enough of them— only two dozen remained. It was time for ARRRGH!!! to make her move.

Pressing both blood-matted paws to the dirt, she took a swinging, simian leap, launching her body through the smoke and landing in front of the throne. Brimstone swirled around her like demonic insects as she rose to full height—less than half that of Gunmar. She swiped to the left with a paw, destroying the Machine's final length of pipe, just to show the Hungry One that she meant business.

Gunmar's humungous jaw grinded and the stake-sized teeth fought for placement. His single eye blazed as he rose from his throne. Six sausage-stained arms, including the wooden one, spread open as if preparing to greet his attacker with an embrace. The Eye of Malevolence leapt from Gunmar's shoulder and scuttled in gleeful circles through its master's boiling drool.

ARRRGH!!! unleashed a roar so tornadic it generated a

storm of dirt. Behind the corkscrews of grit, the trollhunter widened her stance and stomped closer to Gunmar. Rocks rained from the walls and the Machine squealed in protest. The storied foes were within striking distance—the legend of snarled black fur, the myth of all-devouring appetite. Inconceivable muscles flexed; rancid breath poured from open throats; the pestilent air was charged with the electricity of the anticipated first blow.

And then the Killaheed Bridge was completed.

We knew it the instant it happened. The world around us went pure white for an unknowable number of seconds and every sound was silenced: the clacking of the Machine, the whining of the children, the chanting of the Gumm-Gumms. We became weightless, as if yanked into the sky by parachutes, and there was the usual slight elastic sting of passing through a dimensional doorway, except that instead of walking forward we were soaring without direction. When color drained back in, soft like the lifting of eyelids, what I saw was not the soot and shadow of the underworld but the startling green and white of a manicured field beneath floodlights. Sound came back to me just as gently, the twittering of referee whistles, the dull collision of protective gear, the collective gasp of a huge crowd of people, and a single hissing voice that overwhelmed it all:

"IT ISSSSSS FINISSSSSSHED."

38.

So this is the story. With two minutes left to go in the biggest game of the season, at the culmination of the Festival of the Fallen Leaves, after a week of missing children that had citizens desperate to cheer for anything, the Saint B. Battle Beasts were up by six points thanks to the superhuman heroics of Steve Jorgensen-Warner, though the team was down several key players and struggling to stave off a comeback by the Connersville Colts, who were at midfield and driving. Not one person at Harry G. Bleeker Memorial Field rested on her or his butt; they danced upon the feet of the saved, clapping their Steve Smackers with such furor that the environs became a deafening world of madness—so mad, in fact, that it took the townspeople a good minute to register the white blast that shot throughout the neighborhood and the scattering of grotesque monsters that were deposited upon the turf.

The second-down-and-six play, a sweep to the right with number thirty-three of the Colts getting the pitch, dwindled to a halt as the halfback came up against not the expected Saint B. cornerback but instead a yellow troll wearing a vest and swinging a barbed mace. The halfback stopped, thought for a second, and offered up the ball. The troll, discombobulated

*From the open end of the pipe, clods of meat plopped like
wet dog food into the open mouth of Gunmar the Black.*

but also hungry, took the ball and crunched it between its boulder teeth.

The abruptly cut-off sentence of the announcer reverberated through the speakers—he was unequipped with the vocabulary to describe such an unusual play. The jumbotron operator finished a full-color animation but lacked the wherewithal to begin the next, and the pixels faded out until the screen was as empty as a blackboard.

The silence was not absolute. Popcorn continued to pop in the snack bar and sloppy make-out sessions continued beneath the far end of the bleachers. But soon even these noises ceased and the human beings of San Bernardino met for the first time the trolls of San Bernardino. Pieces of hot dog fell half-chewed from gaping mouths. Children carried upon shoulders were dropped. Trombones, tubas, and other instruments gave a last blurt before falling from the hands of band members.

I stood from where I had materialized at the forty-yard line and gazed over the rows of blank faces. In the distance I saw a final lightning flash coming from the Historical Society Museum. The completed Killaheed had pushed Gunmar the Black through the barrier of worlds and brought the Gumm-Gumms and trollhunters along with him. I had to wonder, though, if Professor Lempke had aligned the head stone a bit off-center, seeing as how we'd emerged just down the street.

Gunmar crouched on all his limbs like a triceratops, his head swinging mistrustfully from side to side. Caught beneath the bright white lights, he looked more unreal than ever, a gnarled gargoyle set down amid an orderly world. In other areas of the field, Jack, Blinky, and ARRRGH!!! rose to their feet, shaking off lightheadedness.

Football players of both offensive and defensive inclination began to backpedal to the sidelines. To the Gumm-Gumms it must have looked like the slide of delicious food off of a tilted plate. Almost instantly the air went rotten with the stink of salivating mouths, and the Gumm-Gumms began creeping across the treacherously even terrain toward the bleachers, tails whipping, claws extended, jaws dropped in anticipation.

Gunmar drew himself to full height, yawning with the volume of an air horn and striking with his quills one of the overhead banks of lights. It detonated, sparks rained down, and the Eye of Malevolence chased each one like a puppy.

Way too late, somebody screamed.

Linebackers, wide receivers, coaches, and water boys alike backed themselves into the grandstand before climbing over the railing. Mrs. Leach and her cadre of underqualified understudies hid behind the painted castle sets stacked near the end zone. Sergeant Gulager, fixed in his traditional spot near the ambulances, stared blankly as if he'd been expecting disaster all night but not at this scale. With their noses to the air, the Gumm-Gumms stormed through a thicket of scattering cheerleaders, grabbed hold of railings with tentacles and paws and pincers, and tossed their slimy, scaled, or leathery bodies into groups of families, young couples, and kids who'd shown up just for the junk food.

The crowd split down the middle and surged toward either exit, but paused upon hearing the piercing cries coming from the field.

Scattered across the gridiron were the town's seventeen missing children, shielding their eyes from the lights with grubby hands and searching through the chaos for their families.

The people stopped fleeing.

They did this under threat of death from terrifying creatures beyond their imaginations. Most of these people didn't have a missing child in their immediate family, but almost all of them knew someone who did. Though hardly to the scale of the Milk Carton Epidemic, the Internet Epidemic was in full swing: social networking sites had been blanketed by posts from parents attaching photos of their missing kids and giving the details on the last reported sighting, and these posts had been faithfully reposted by friends.

Now there were the missing children, *right there on the field*.

They'd all heard the sound bites from Sergeant Gulager on local TV, about how the community's best chance of defeating this crisis was by pulling together. And so they did. With backpacks, seat cushions, and bare fists they faced the Gumm-Gumms, and within seconds the bleachers were a sea of flailing limbs of both human and troll variety. Football players from both teams got into the act, ramming helmets into troll stomachs and absorbing savage attacks through shoulder pads.

It was an inspiring, though hopeless, display. In just one minute, blood-red slashes appeared across dozens of defending arms, and the frightened and confused humans turned to the most desperate of maneuvers, scurrying through the gaps in the bleachers and curling into fetal balls, while the trolls continued to rip and slobber and swipe.

Gulager ran down the side of the bleachers with his sidearm raised—but what could he shoot at? Every Gumm-Gumm was locked in close combat. Gulager tripped on a pair of discarded Steve Smackers and went tumbling. He got to his feet, picking up the noisemakers to toss them aside, and then paused, weighing them in either hand. He perked up his head, searched about wildly, and sprinted to where the drama club were cowering within their plywood castle. Gulager accosted Mrs. Leach, who nodded and pulled out the microphone that would have been used to amplify *RoJu*.

Gulager's voice boomed through the stadium speakers.

Not once did he stutter.

"USE THE SMACKERS! PICK THEM UP! THEY'RE EVERY-WHERE! YOU CAN DO IT! FIGHT BACK! FIGHT BACK!"

No ordinary voice could command the attention of a populace so overwhelmed with fright. But Sergeant Gulager had been the man whom San Bernardino had depended on through trials of every sort, and that kind of trust ran deep. Parents and teens and elderly alike reached for the nearest Steve Smacker and delivered their best roundhouse blow to the closest troll. The Gumm-Gumms were flummoxed; the plastic blasts were so much more rhythmic than anything heard in the underworld, and the bright colors were blinding to those who lived among dim shades of brown and black. The crack of the Smackers, what to me had been the most irritating noise in existence, became something else altogether: the sound of hope.

"Jim! Jim!"

Tub and Claire were waving at me. According to the sideline markers, they were precisely thirty-six yards away, close enough that I could read their hysterical gestures at the space above me. Before I could look, darkness fell across me like a heavy quilt. I wrenched my neck and saw the descending form of Gunmar the Black. The ability to react left me and I stood with swords dangling. He fell upon me, trapping me in a six-armed cage. His lips pulled back as if blistering away from his face, and from between his foot-long teeth slithered the tattered remnants of his tongue.

"MORE SSSSSSTURGESSSSSSSESSSSSS."

His spittle rolled down my cheeks like molten lead.

Gunmar's wooden arm received a solid blow—Jack's long-sword. The blade got stuck halfway in but succeeded in pushing the arm out from under the gargantuan monster. Gunmar's titanic torso slammed to the turf but I was already rolling out of the way, passing beneath his empty eye socket before emerging back into floodlights. Jack grunted, yanking his sword from the wood and tumbling backward with the effort. Gunmar transitioned to a squat and examined the new notch on the wooden arm.

"YESSSSSS. MUSSSSST HAVE NEW KILL."

ARRRGH!!! struck Gunmar at a full gallop, ramming her horns into his ropy chest. Gunmar choked in surprise, staggered back a few steps, found his footing, and then used those same horns to lift his attacker into the air and slam her to the field. ARRRGH!!!'s brawny body sounded like a pitiful bag of bones. Gunmar reached down to choke her but she came alive just in time, taking the hands by the wrists and diverting them. But there were three more hands where those came from, and each of them fought for the privilege of strangulation.

Tentacles fastened around Gunmar. It was Blinky, with what looked like every one of his hundred limbs. Gunmar fell back from ARRRGH!!!. For a moment it looked as though Blinky might force the larger troll to the turf. But the spines along Gunmar's back sprung outward like a regiment of bayonets and I heard the excruciating sounds of several of Blinky's tentacles being torn in half.

Still, the fighting historian clung to the villain long enough for ARRRGH!!! to struggle to her feet and mount another head-on attack. Gunmar released a boom of laughter and began operating his double-jointed limbs to fight both enemies at once. It was an awesome display of power: six arms fought a trollhunter on each side with bewildering speed while the spine telescoped and retracted to dodge fists, twice causing ARRRGH!!! to sock Blinky in the head.

"Lummox!" Blinky spat. "The Hungry One! Not me!"

ARRRGH!!!, as if in apology, leapt and caught Gunmar's head between two crushing paws. Gunmar's tongue whipped across her face, leaving pink stripes of acid burn, then he opened his cavernous mouth to bite off some of her face. But one of his teeth struck down upon ARRRGH!!!'s new metal braces and snapped in two. Gunmar wailed—his first sign of pain. ARRRGH!!! clawed at Gunmar's remaining eye in hopes of blinding him for good, while Blinky slithered his tentacles into new formations, grabbing hold of individual quills and pulling Gunmar backward.

Jack looked at me through his goggles and held up a fist. I nodded and withdrew my swords, and with the screams of the crowd as our battle hymn, we charged. Gunmar's lowest arm lashed out as if it had eyes of its own, and though Jack ducked beneath it, I was not as quick and had to meet it with Claireblade. The top half of a yellowed claw, as big as a skateboard, was severed and embedded in the field. The damaged red hand curled its fingers into a fist and hurled itself at me like a boulder. I dodged to the left and swung downward with Cat #6, cutting the thumb all the way to the bone.

The fingers went rigid, striking me hard enough to knock the wind out of me. I landed spread-eagle upon the turf, and as I gasped for air I saw Jack rise to a crouch directly beneath Gunmar. Dodging the troll's shambling legs, he unsheathed Doctor X and held it with both fists below Gunmar's stomach. My heartbeat quickened. If Jack's aim was true, it could be an injury that changed everything.

Everything did change, but not for the better.

Jack drove his blade into the right side of Gunmar's gut and then dragged it left, opening a huge gash. Gunmar howled and twisted with such force that both ARRRGH!!! and Blinky were thrown aside. A hard spray of scarlet blood and yellow liquid blasted Jack, but that was expected, and he wiped it from his goggles with the back of his glove.

What was not expected were the dozens—no, hundreds—of tiny trolls that fell from the opened cavity. The first few thumped off Jack's helmet, wiggling and mewling, and Jack just stood there, shocked stupid. But as they continued to pour, Jack backed away, picking the parasites off his armor and flinging them to the ground in disgust. In seconds, the little trolls were everywhere, writhing in the grass, blinking tiny new eyes at the strange world around them.

"The rest of the Gumm-Gumms," Jack rasped. "This is where they were hiding!"

I looked down at a trio orienting themselves at my feet. Each was the size of a baseball and an exact copy of Gunmar: glistening red body, six little arms, a cape of quills flexing experimentally along its back. Worse, each of the beasties appeared to grow larger with each breath, as if the smell of so much human meat were enough to fortify their young bodies.

Gunmar shook his torso so that a few more babies fell to the field, and he grinned down like a proud papa. Perhaps that was what he'd been learning those forty-five years in the dark: how to replicate himself and safely carry an army of voracious carnivores into the human world. Emptied, he roared and leapt back into battle with ARRRGH!!!, Blinky, and a very dazed Jack Sturges.

Pain blazed up my leg. One of the baby Gunmars had bitten through my shoe, right into my toe, and I kicked my leg to dislodge it. But the tiny troll held fast, its arms flapping as if enjoying the ride. At last I stomped my foot back onto the forty-yard line, took up Claireblade, and drove it downward. The little red creature dodged right and the point embedded in the turf. I tried again, and this time it dodged left. Finally I reared back and booted it. The onside kick went bouncing across the grass, while blood from my bitten toe began soaking the leather of my shoe.

I scanned the football field and saw hundreds of these fiends, stretching their toothy mouths in newborn yawns and shaking off mucus as a dog shakes off the rain. They were teetering toward the bleachers, learning to walk on their way to their first meal. Several kids rescued from Gunmar's lair were doing their part, stomping these babies to death with their shoes—a courageous effort, though not nearly enough. Even if we had twice the trollhunters, we were outnumbered. Despair overwhelmed me and I looked to the sidelines for some sort of help.

Instead I saw Professor Lempke near the end zone, breathless from having just run from the museum. The fastidious fellow had become an agglomeration of sores. His face and arms were an irritated pink crusted over with dried pus. Like a toddler at a birthday party, he jumped up and down, giggling and clapping his hands. With each clap, wet strings of sickness extended between palms. The entire brutal scenario of battle had him overjoyed, but what held his particular attention at that moment was the kid he hated most in the world: Tobias "Tubby" D.

Tub stood in front of his baffled grandma, fending off the Eye of Malevolence with Dr. Papadopoulos's soon-to-be-award-winning tools. The Eye swung its stem and knocked the instruments from Tub's hands as rapidly as he could extract them from his fanny pack. Tub might have been a goner if Grandma hadn't stepped up and clobbered the eye with what looked like the heaviest purse in human history. The Eye rolled about as if drunk before crashing into a stack of home-team water bottles.

Tub took his grandma by the hand and ran toward the bleachers. The Steve Smackers had allowed the crowd to fend off the Gumm-Gumms for a laudable amount of time, but it couldn't last, and Tub had proven that night to be a formidable fighter.

But he did not enter the fray. Instead he kept running, hand-in-hand with Grandma, around the side of the grandstand until they disappeared from sight. My energy halved. Now I, too, knew how it felt to be left behind. I directed my despairing eyes past the countless baby trolls and their snapping young jaws and over to the mammoth beast that was casually tossing aside Jack and Blinky to focus upon ARRRGH!!!. Tub was not a genuine trollhunter—I tried to remind myself of this hard and true fact—and yet his abandonment felt as monumental as if one of us had fallen.

39.

Seconds later, a familiar freckled face popped up in the score-keeper's booth, followed by an elderly woman with magenta hair who looked like she was in the midst of a record-breaking streak of complaints. Gone were the headphone-wearing announcers and tech staff. This left Tub to pore over some sort of control panel, waving his finger above what I imagined were a thousand confusing buttons. Then, in a moment of divine inspiration, he discovered a huge, perspiring cup of soda on the counter and held it above the electronics. He looked up and I swear he caught my eye. His braces glinted in a wicked smile before he poured the soda onto the control system for which the school had paid so much money.

The jumbotron went wild. I squinted as the screen flared to dazzling life, cascading the stadium with light as it shuttled through a lunatic montage of cartoon animations—kicked field goals and gyrating mascots and a series of inane chants—D-FENSE! GO, BATTLE BEASTS, GO! MAKE SOME NOOOISE! As soda infiltrated the deepest layers of internal wiring, pixels scattered and the words and images fizzled to give way to a single element:

Fuzzy, flickering, beautiful static.

Every Gumm-Gumm in the bleachers stopped what they were doing and turned to face the largest TV they'd ever seen. Their misshapen jaws went slack and drool began to drop. Gunmar, unaffected by the static, roared his disapproval, but his minions could not hear. They leaned toward the screen, intoxicated. The humans remained curled into frightened balls, unwilling to make a move. It was Sergeant Gulager, of course, who led the way, stepping up to the nearest troll, waving his gun in front of the glassy, unresponsive eyes, and then, at his leisure, firing a bullet right through the softies.

The crowd woke up, began to cheer themselves on, and then, in short order, overwhelmed the hypnotized Gumm-Gumms, pouring over the trolls like ants and pinning their comatose bodies to the bleachers. Tub moved like a maestro in the sound booth, drizzling a little more soda here and dumping a lot more there to keep the static at its most lush and frisky. At some point he tripped the audio, and the warble of a dozen different radio stations blared from the speakers in total sonic confusion. I could see Tub fiddling with knobs, but matters were far out of his control.

"Jim! Wake up!"

It was Jack, hollering at such volume that his voice broke into adolescent splinters. He had removed his mask and his pale, sweaty face showed none of the relief I felt. Behind him I saw why: Blinky was rolling around on the turf, whimpering in a register of pain I'd never before heard, a half-dozen destroyed tentacles spewing thick violet liquid. ARRRGH!!!, meanwhile, was backed into a light pole, her hackles raised in bedraggled defense, her black fur shining with blood.

With a blasting laugh, Gunmar used all six arms to lift ARRRGH!!! high over his head. The lights atop the pole released glass shards that stabbed into the flesh of both trolls. ARRRGH!!! wrenched about but was as helpless as I'd ever seen her. Gunmar reared back and threw her huge body twenty yards through the air, a missile of horns and teeth and fur, and into the end zone, where she collided with the goal posts at such speed that they crumpled into tangles of steel. Several feet of dirt and turf billowed upward from the impact.

There was no movement from the fallen trollhunter.

Dirt and grass eddied in the air of the end zone.

"NO!!!" Jack shrieked.

Gunmar's single eye jerked about like a lizard held by the tail.

"YESSSSSS . . . COME TO ME, SSSSSSTURGESSSSSS. . . ."

Jack bawled and ran at Gunmar, looking like a little boy handling a couple of toy swords. I wanted to follow, to be the trollhunter Jack believed that I could be, but my fighter's heart flagged upon seeing the hundreds of baby Gunmars continuing their march, as impervious to the jumbotron static as their daddy was. Their confidence, and size, grew as they closed in on all those yummy tubes of fresh meat packed into shirts, pants, jackets, and hats. Their numbers were irrefutable and they would devour the townspeople as would a plague of locusts.

The decision tore me in half. Help these innocent people about to be eaten? Or come to the aid of Uncle Jack, the closest thing I had to family?

Or so I believed before I heard a familiar noise.

It came from the opposite end zone, a rumble that I felt in my ribs before hearing it with my ears. The pitch rose in intensity until it became the drone of a thousand bees. In the tumult of the moment, the denizens of Harry G. Bleeker

Memorial Field seemed not to notice, but I knew that tell-tale tremor. I had felt it in parks and gardens all across San Bernardino, as well as in the front yard of my own house, where the various pieces of the machine were cleaned, sharpened, and tested upon our poor, over-trimmed lawn.

Dad rode onto the field of play on his golden industrial mower, the oversize back tires powering the eight-wheeled mowing deck, so wide that it took up nearly one-fourth the width of the field in a single swath. All of the dull technical details that he'd pounded into me now became the vital statistics of survival. The seven-gauge steel. The sixteen-inch discharge chute. The six-inch-deep cut. Dad came tearing up the sideline suited differently than his brother Jack but in armor all the same: hair net, allergy mask, goggles, work gloves, steel-toed safety boots, and grass-stained work shirt—Excalibur Calculator Pocket firmly inserted and both sleeves, if you can believe it, buttoned.

For a second I thought the invasion had driven my father over the brink, and that it was a mark of his madness that he'd chosen this moment to give the field a trim. Then I heard the yelp of the first baby Gunmar as it was sucked beneath the mower, the whir of blades as its diced corpse went flying from the chute. A half-dozen more of the beasts stopped their crawling and stared at the oncoming death machine, immobilized by a strange new sensation called fear. The feeling was brief. They went in as hungry carnivores and came out as pulp.

"Dad!" I screamed. "Go, Dad!"

He gave me the briefest of nods before gripping the wheel to jag the mower leftward to catch a couple little Gunmars who'd made it all the way to the sidelines. Seconds later they were applesauce. The mower hurtled at a speed Dad had never before allowed himself, zooming down the sideline like a kick returner seeing nothing but green, and I realized in a light-headed flash that he would get them, all of them, that the baby trolls' conquering instincts were no match for a man with an awesome lawn mower who knew how to use it.

Gunmar shrieked, several of his hands clutching at his own body as if he felt each individual death. He lowered his head and bellowed. Windows in the snack bar and sound booth exploded; I caught a glimpse of Tub shielding his grandma from glass. Memories of that fateful day in 1969 came back to Dad in a burst, and for a moment the mower's trajectory began to list. Then the radio stations fighting for precedence through the loudspeakers gave way to a single oldies station, and as cosmic luck would have it, it was a song familiar to every Sturges on the field that night.

"I stood on this corner, / Waiting for you to come along, / So my heart could feel satisfi-i-i-ied. . . ."

The voices were distorted and pierced with bullets of static, but it was Don and Juan, all right, and Dad took their voices to be the song of the gods, bestowing upon him a second chance to be the man he'd always wanted, and so he bore down, hunching over the wheel and gripping it even harder with those gardening gloves. The mower straightened and the green grass turned a putty color with the mulch of massacre.

I rushed through the slippery pools of mashed troll until I arrived at Jack's side. My shoulder struck his; he looked over and I saw in his eyes the wild look of a kid ready to accept the most dangerous of dares. Blinky was struggling to his feet to our right, but the three of us still looked pretty wretched when compared to Gunmar, who stood shivering above us as if sobbing over the destruction of his infernal litter.

"This may go badly," Jack said.

"I know."

"But you did good. I want you to know that."

"Thanks."

"Jimbo, too—your dad. If you make it and I don't, tell him I said that."

"I will."

Jack grabbed my neck, the most affectionate of touches he'd ever given.

"How about we make this son of a bitch think twice about messing with a Sturges?"

With that, Jack whooped with a warrior's mirth and came at Gunmar with both blades whirling. Blinky heard the signal and charged, dragging his dead tentacles behind. The conscious calculations of every fighting technique I'd learned faded away. I could feel all over my skin the prickle of pure instinct, and I dove under the towering figure, rolling beneath knuckles the size of medicine balls, springing to my feet to slice at one of his heels. The tendon snapped like a rubber band and he stamped in such fury that the twenty-yard line cratered into a car-sized hole. Blinky knotted his tentacles around Gunmar's lowest arms, while Jack used his cutlass to climb up a leg, driving Victor Power to the hilt into Gunmar's knee.

It was the paragon of coordinated attacks, one we could be proud of when we met together in the soldiers' heaven of Valhalla. With a single twist of his body, the three of us were tossed aside like bugs. Back we came, limping and bruised,

and again we were dispelled, this time sporting an assort-
ment of sprains and cuts. My lungs hurt inside of ribs that
I thought might be broken, and when I rose a third time my
knee gave way. I fell with my chin in the turf, leaking furious
tears, looking on as Jack was backhanded to the ground. Pints
of steaming saliva poured over him from Gunmar's jaws.

My bleary eyes landed on the *RoJu* set, familiar to me from
a glorious alternate life where I'd been poised to receive the
applause of the whole town and even get the girl. I gazed at
it for a delicious moment, longing for the comfort of the fake
stones and artificial drawbridge.

That was where I found Claire Fontaine cradling one of
the prop swords in her hands as if it were speaking to her.
She turned it right, then left; she brought it up, then down;
she began to make circles with it in the air, then figure eights,
then patterns too complicated for me to follow. Faster and
faster the sword went, and behind the blur of the blade I saw
her mouth curl into a smile of sorts, as if she'd realized the
purpose of her life at the exact second that it was about to end.

To the disbelief of anyone who saw it, she ran across the
field, sliding through troll guts and dodging Dad's mower,
and reared the prop sword like a javelin. She threw it, holding the release pose like someone who'd done it a thousand
times rather than once. The sword flew through the air with
a whistle and embedded itself in the center of Gunmar's open
mouth.

Gunmar gagged and the waterfall of saliva falling upon
Jack went black with blood. Gunmar reeled in a crazy circle,
clutching for the sword but having trouble fitting his considerable claws inside of his mouth. Jack dragged himself away,
slopping the spit and blood off of his face, and when he saw

Claire jogging up to us, he took hold of Doctor X and threw it at her, end over end.

I yelled for her to duck—Jack had confused her for an attacking troll! But instead, she plucked the sword out of the air and used its own momentum to pull it back with an ornamental flourish. She stared at us with wide eyes, panting in exhilaration. Jack was grinning, his teeth white beneath the dark smear of his gore-splashed face. Even Blinky paused to braid a few tentacles in exultation.

"Trollhunter," Jack said.

"Trollhunter!" Blinky cried.

"Claire?" I asked.

She blinked her eyes at me, bewildered but electrified.

"Hello, Mr. Sturges."

In that moment it all made sense. Claire came from the Scottish Highlands, a hotbed of trolls and trollhunters alike. Her birthday was exactly a year from my own. Her skill with the blade, evidenced upon the theater stage, couldn't have been the result of a few paid lessons. Her trollhunter blood was true and she'd been drawn to San Bernardino via the same subtle pullings of destiny that had brought me here. It was only because she had become so adept at hiding her dual selves, one side from her parents, one side from her friends, that the trollhunters had failed to detect her paladin nature—and that she had failed to recognize it herself.

Claire knocked the mud from her boots with the sword.

It was the behavior of a girl born to fight.

There came a deafening cough, and the prop sword impaled itself into the twenty-yard line.

Gunmar lorded above us, blood streaming from between his teeth and down a torso that, emptied of babies, flapped with loose flesh. He'd lost control and was flailing about, stamping his feet like an infant, flogging himself front and back with his double-jointed arms, quills extending and flattening with the sound of a hundred falling guillotines. He spread his limbs and swooped down at us, big as a fireworks finale.

Trollhunters are born for this, and to do what you are born for feels like nothing else in the world. Each twirl and slide we made provided the survival buffer of a few essential inches. Every second was both dodge and attack, thrust and parry, and sustained by planning three moves ahead. You couldn't call the noise from the bleachers cheers, but the hoarse cries were encouragement nonetheless. And you couldn't call what Dad was doing a victory parade, though he circled in tighter and tighter coils, his golden machine gobbling up every last mini-troll. All of it helped: we fought, our eyes slit, teeth bared, muscles aching, bones singing with the war song of the blade.

Claire was the best of us. Even Jack paused to gape at her fearless climb up Gunmar's vertebrae and how she dug Doctor X into Gunmar's armpit and clavicle, trying for the elusive softies that hid beneath protective plating. We were piranha, nipping at his extremities, and he was caught in an extended state of preparing to ruin us, always lifting his arms for the fatal blow, always backpedaling to get the momentum he'd need to stomp us for good. We had him at the goal line; there was little farther to go. Beyond the goal was a tall chain-link fence and a ravine, but this fight wouldn't get that far and we knew it.

A swipe of a middle arm caught a tangle of Blinky's tentacles. He was lifted from the ground and sent like a bowling ball into the opposing team's vacant bench. In the same instant, Gunmar's wooden arm, slotted with the fresh kill mark, swung through the air like a massive golf club and shot Jack ten feet away, where he hit the turf and curled into an injured ball. I grimaced and stood firm. It was left to me, on the ground, and Claire, holding onto his back.

Gunmar slapped blindly at Claire and squatted so as to catch me between clawed hands. The flap in his gut that Jack had sliced open dropped to my level and on instinct I clambered into it. Gunmar squealed and began pawing at the invader inside his body. The world around me went black and Gunmar's interior organs assaulted my head and shoulders as they jounced in their nets of entrails. A sliver of light entered the body cavity as Gunmar stood and I saw it, the gallbladder, the same as any troll's except larger: an orange thing of leafy texture, the size of a basketball.

I'd had more than enough of threatening basketballs.

I took the gallbladder with both hands but was seconds too late. Gunmar plucked me from his insides like a tapeworm and flung me to the ground as if I weighed no more than Jim Sturges Jr. 2: The Decoy. I laid there beneath the towering monster, unable to move, almost unable to see Claire struggling across Gunmar's shoulder, mere feet from the vulnerable softies. I tried to shout encouragement but I was out of sounds. She looked so small up there, but so sure of herself, too, and when she stood on her feet, balanced on the shoulder of the worst of all living things, her front hand holding the sabre, her back hand outstretched for balance, that was the real moment I fell in love.

It was easy to forget how Gunmar's spine could retract at will. He compacted himself down to half his height and Claire stumbled, dropping Doctor X and sliding through the quills before landing hard on her knees in the end zone. She grabbed them in pain. Gritting her teeth, she looked from between Gunmar's legs and found me staring back, and though both of us were unable to move, we held each other's gaze in case each of us was the last thing the other saw.

Dad's mower stopped in the distance with a defeated cough.

Gunmar the Black had waited forty-five years, but here it was at last: the final demolishing of the trollhunters, no more difficult than a little kid's squashing worms on the playground. Afterward, he and his kind would infest the surface of the earth, gorging themselves on the meat of man and growing fat and surly in the way of the Old World. He lifted a foot over the nearest trollhunter—me—aiming so that when my runny guts squirted out they would bleed into those of the hundreds of his slaughtered offspring.

The foot never fell.

Leaping from the cratered pit of the end zone, ARRRGH!!! wrapped her arms around Gunmar's neck. A crooked segment of goal post had been driven into her skull and branched out like strange yellow antlers fighting for space alongside her horns. Instantly Gunmar shot upward to his full height; ARRRGH!!! did not let go. Gunmar shook his torso with all of his might; ARRRGH!!! did not let go. Gunmar beat backward with fists connected to hellishly jointed arms; ARRRGH!!! did not let go. Gunmar extended his quills and I saw a dozen of them sink into black fur and emerge bloody from the other side of ARRRGH!!!'s body. Still, stabbed through a dozen times, she did not let go.

Gunmar thrashed like a hog on the killing floor and lifted two fists over his shoulders to grab ARRRGH!!! by the head.

But something was different. Gunmar sensed it and a quick exploration with his fingers revealed that the boulder, the one he'd implanted in his rival's skull decades before, had been knocked free by the fragment of goal post. Before he could register what this meant, ARRRGH!!! removed her right arm from around Gunmar's neck and in that fist was clutched the boulder, that forty-five-year-old symbol of good luck.

Her voice had reclaimed a tone that was intelligent and true.

"My name is Johannah M. ARRRGH!!!," she said, "and I told you I'd get you."

The boulder soared downward and cracked Gunmar's cranium in half. The noise was like the rending of the planet, and it felt like that, too, when he collapsed to both knees. ARRRGH!!!'s grip weakened, the boulder dropped into the grass, and her lacerated body slipped from the quills. She crumpled to the turf, a limp pile of blood-soaked fur.

Gunmar's body swayed and his six arms tried to push his skull back together to cover the exposed brain. His manifold hands, though, became confused and tussled with one another before giving up. Then the mighty lord of the Gumm-Gumms, the Hungry One, He Who Sups of Blood, the Untangler of Entrails, Gunmar the Black wavered in place for a long moment before dropping to his back with all the ceremony of a chopped tree.

40.

Jack left it to me to do what decades before he'd failed to do: deliver the killing blow.

Claire helped me over to the still convulsing body, and Blinky boosted me onto a thigh. Once there I found it simple enough to traverse the landscape: the tarn of blood gathered at midsection, the ravaged gut, the hills and valleys of the ribcage. I took a seat on the boiling red skin over his heart and felt myself lifted up and down with each uneven hiccup of his pulse.

Weariness, not victory or relief, engulfed me. I placed the tip of Claireblade over the throbbing patch of skin and felt a newfound sympathy for Jack. Defeated, the troll beneath me felt not as evil as he did obsessed, led by an inescapable hunger that consumed his every atom. I listened to the reedy breaths struggling up his throat and watched the shredded tongue loll from the corner of his mouth. His single eye stared upward into the night sky, while the Eye of Malevolence nuzzled the empty socket.

I blinked my heavy eyes at the crowd of people. They were quiet aside from the sounds of seventeen tearful reunions.

There were no pictures being taken: as I'd learn later, all of the electronics in a three-block radius were fried the instant Gunmar went down. Most of the faces I didn't know, but all of them seemed certain of one thing: this monster that had taken their children must be destroyed. The task felt beyond my capabilities and I looked elsewhere for help. I found Ms. Pinkton, who was shaking her head as if apologizing for even considering giving me less than 88 percent. I found Sergeant Gulager, too, his rumpled hairpiece and thick mustache splattered with softie effluvium. He gave me the smallest of nods.

Jack and Claire leaned on their swords and waited. I spotted Tub, returning to the sidelines with his arm around his grandma's shoulders, and the look he gave me was absent of judgment: this was the burden of being asked to lead. Only Blinky paid my decision no mind. He sat with his tentacles wrapped around ARRRGH!!!, whispering into the fur the kind of complicated, arcane ceremonial recitations known only to brilliant scholars sending off great warriors into the next realm of unknowable adventure.

I remembered what Jack had asked me once.

It's a terrible thing, isn't it? To be dragged under?

It took only a few slices to carve out Gunmar's heart; the leathery, tubed organ skipped around in an attempt to dodge my blade. After that was done, I broke through the crustaceous skin of the softies and turned them to gelatin. Then I ducked into the stomach cavity and removed the gallbladder, tossing it to the turf for later burning.

Surviving Gumm-Gumms watched from the bleachers, their spell of slavery broken, watching their once-master's vivisection as if uncertain about how they'd arrived in this peculiar place overrun with humans. They rolled horned heads and fluttered bony wings, decidedly uncomfortable as they looked around for the nearest bridge.

I slid off Gunmar's hip and was caught by Claire and Jack. Dad was there, too, and brought me in to his chest. His shirt smelled like grass, like home, and when I smiled I felt the stiff edges of that stupid old calculator pocket. No, not stupid. Brilliant. He'd worn that thing for thirty years and it had yet to show a single indication of wear or tear. That pocket was a work of genius.

I looked up at Dad, thinking I might apologize, but was rendered speechless. The stress lines of his forehead had shallowed and the worry lines of his cheeks were all but gone. His smile seemed to open parts of him that had long been locked, just as I knew the steel shutters and locked doors would open for good once we returned home. He patted me on the face, the odd gesture of one unaccustomed to tenderness, and so I patted his cheek in return. The last scabs of the schmoof were gone.

"Nice mowing," I managed.

He took off his glasses to wipe his face. He noticed the dangling Band-Aid and threw the whole thing onto the turf.

"I've had lots of practice."

With our arms around each other's shoulders, we hobbled across the field toward Blinky, whose tentacles were smoothing each blood-snarled whorl of black fur. Tub was already there, sprawled across the hide of his dead friend, his face buried in her masses of hair, one hand dangling over the goal-post antlers.

Blinky's voice was hoarse with emotion.

"An entire volume of my history shall be devoted to this

warrior. No, no—such rudimentary canonization would be insufficient. Her memorial shall be a comprehensive history all of her own. Yes, a biographical work of dedicatory power so encyclopedic in its recountings of heroism that even the dimmest of illiterates will believe they might reach out and stroke luck from her boulder. My measly life has but another several hundred years left before it ends. Yet I cannot imagine a better way to run out my golden years."

Jack put his hand on the nearest tentacle.

"We need to get her underground," Jack said. "Before the sun—"

"No."

The refusal was muffled because it came from a mouth lost in folds of fur. Tub raised his head to reveal a face ruddy with tears. He shook his head with such determination that his bouffant rocked like a bush in high wind. He stood, his ninja-wear smeared with Gumm-Gumm slime, his lime-green fanny pack empty of Papadopoulos's savage inventions, yet with a confidence that looked good on a kid who just a week before was giving up daily fivers. He spoke softly into Blinky's ear—or his best guess of where one might be located.

"An idea most unusual," Blinky whispered, "but a requiem unforgettable. Plump midget, you have humbled me with your elegiacal instincts. When they think back upon this day, which they will, and often, it will be your contribution that will be remembered first, and fittingly so. It is poetry, and you, my corpulent comrade, are a poet."

Tub understood none of this, of course, but shrugged anyway, and Blinky whispered the plan to Jack, who squinted across the field as if measuring the difficulty of the task before nodding his agreement. Without explaining the goal, he arranged us on all sides of ARRRGH!!!: Claire and Tub at one leg, Dad and I at the other, Jack at the right arm, and Blinky at the left. At Jack's call we attempted to drag the great troll from her position midfield. Panting and groaning and sweating, our attempts earned us less than a first down.

Then I felt another pair of hands at my side and looked up to find Sergeant Gulager. He took hold of a horn so that ARRRGH!!!'s head wouldn't drag across the turf. More people followed: Principal Cole, Coach Lawrence, and Ms. Pinkton, all goggling in disbelief at the arm they lifted from the ground; Carol the museum cashier, the man with the dyed black goatee, and his little girl whom I'd first seen on a flyer lifted up a foot; Mrs. Leach and her thespians took up an entire left leg; and then, in a single wave as if responding to a referee's whistle, the entire varsity squads of the Saint B. Battle Beasts and the Connersville Colts assembled to lift the torso.

None of the players knew what they'd witnessed that night or if they'd wake up Saturday morning to find this had been a wild fantasy brought on by concussion, but at that moment they were moved by a sense of *right*, and so they lowered their shoulder pads, flexed muscles trained in weight rooms, and lifted.

The body traveled the entire length of the field as if by miracle, with the noble, snouted face pointed at the stars. When we reached a spot just past the end zone close to the street, Jack gave a signal and we set the body in an upright arrangement. As Jack gathered yard markers and first-down poles to prop up the arms, I began to understand Tub's plan. Tears sprung to my eyes and I backed way, afraid to be so close to something so beautiful.

ARRRGH!!! was posed in a stance so lifelike I expected her to wink at me one more time. Her crouch made it look as if she were about to spring forward, while her open jaw suggested the earsplitting roar that would never again be heard. Right now it was the macabre posing of a corpse, but in a few hours, when the sun crested over Mount Sloughnisse, she would turn, quite painlessly, into a stone statue. Hers would not be one of those sad things lost in the Cemetery of Souls; hers would memorialize the site of the Battle of the Fallen Leaves and serve as a reminder that the worlds of human and troll could operate in friendship rather than in the age-old cycles of animosity and carnage.

Harry G. Bleeker Memorial Field had always been missing a mascot, and what better icon to represent the Battle Beasts than this one?

We made our way back to the midfield, the football players dispersing into the crowd of people who were only now beginning to rub their eyes and pat their pockets for car keys, objects they barely remembered how to use. Tub wandered over to check on Grandma, though she seemed quite pleased. Everything, after all, had been at a suitable volume for the hearing impaired. Only Sergeant Gulager stood in place, hands on his hips, surveying the normal-looking people of his town who'd performed so far beyond expectations.

"We shouldn't let those people go."

It was Jack, cleaning Victor Power against the bike chains surrounding his shins.

"Why not?" I asked.

He gestured at the motionless mountain of Gunmar the Black.

"We'll need all the help we can get to haul that body underground before morning."

"They'll help," I said.

"Who?"

"The Gumm-Gumms." I pointed them out. "I think they'll do whatever we ask."

"Yeah, maybe."

"Something tells me they'll be open to the non-human-eating message, too."

"I suppose you're right." Jack sighed. "You know the closest bridge?"

"I do."

"Well, all right. Let's get this thing started."

"Okay, but—give me just one minute?"

Jack followed my gaze and smirked. He sheathed his sword. "Take two."

Claire was crossing the field, splashing her hiking boots through the gunk blown out by Dad's mower but not looking disgusted in the least. Her fatigues were crusted with unspeakable fluids and her face was a smudgy mix of mud and blood. And yet she was radiant, her tangled hair bouncing behind her, beaming with the same abandon that I'd been enamored with long before we'd shared a single word a week ago in math class.

She stopped a few inches away and scraped dried blood from Doctor X as another girl might toy with a ring.

"Look," I said, "I'm sorry."

"Sorry? About what?"

"About everything. About letting you get caught. About not realizing you were like us."

"It all ended well enough," she said. "A bit sticky, perhaps."

"And the play. I'm sorry about the play."

She laughed, that loud bray that made me feel like butter.

"The play? Are you serious, ya silly gowk?"

"That accent, I'm telling you." I shrugged. "You would've been great."

"It *was* a lot of lines to memorize for nothing."

"Tell me about it."

Claire gave me a sly sidelong glance.

"Good pilgrim, you do wrong your hand too much, / Which mannerly devotion shows in this, / For saints have hands that pilgrim's hands do touch, / And palm to palm is holy palmers' kiss."

She held out a small white hand stained with blood.

My stomach fluttering with nerves, I took it.

"Have not saints lips, and holy palmers too?" I asked.

"Ay, pilgrim, lips that they must use in prayer."

"O, then, dear saint, let lips do what hands do, / They pray—grant thou, lest faith turn to despair."

Claire moved closer. The frayed ends of her coat brushed against my chest.

"Saints do not move," she whispered, "though grant for prayers' sake."

"Then move not while my prayer's effect I take. / Thus from my lips, by yours, my sin is purged."

Beneath shattered lights, atop a ruined field, surrounded by an audience of battered survivors and the mangled dead, we kissed, and kissed again. While I closed my eyes and sank into a dark enjoyment, two random thoughts pricked at me like a pesky mosquito. Did someone deal with Gunmar's gallbladder after I'd tossed it to the field? And where, come to think of it, had Professor Lempke gone?

Those worries were lost as Claire ran her hands over my back. Warmth sealed her body to mine and in the dizzy nirvana of the moment I felt her teeth scrape across my lips as she continued to murmur Juliet's most lovelorn of lines.

"Then have my lips the sin that they have took."

I kissed her cheek, her eyelids, raised on my toes to kiss her forehead.

"Sin from thy lips?" I said into her hair. "O trespass sweetly urged! / Give me my sin again."

Her arms tightened around me in a hug that was every bit as crushing as a Claire Fontaine hug ought to be. I wheezed happily within her grip, feeling her trollhunter heart beat opposite mine, the taste of her warrior's lips still salty upon my own. I looked through blowing wisps of her hair to find Tub at the sideline next to Grandma, making fake gagging faces through a wide grin that gleamed with the latest in dental technology.

To my surprise, Steve Jorgensen-Warner stood there, too, unaware of Tub's presence, staring at the field of battle with a face drained of emotion. His uniform was grass-stained from play but free of gore, leading me to believe that he'd managed to hide away during the skirmish and was only now crawling out to absorb the aftermath. Tub looked at his former tormentor, who no longer looked as intimidating as he once did. I had a feeling that my friend was done paying a toll, and might, in fact, reclaim the Trophy Cave as his own.

Tub regarded Steve for a long time. Then he examined the random pieces of football equipment scattered at his feet. Then, once more, he looked back up at Steve, as if an idea was forming that was every bit as brilliant as tuning the jumbotron to static. Tub gently guided Grandma aside before kneeling down and picking up one of the helmets of the Connersville Colts. Only when he stood up again did I realize what had been staring me in the face all night.

The emblem printed on the Colts' helmets was a horseshoe.

And what had Blinky once said about horseshoes?

Iron works best, but in a pinch, anything of horseshoe design will suffice.

Acting upon instinct that would make any trollhunter proud, Tub pressed the helmet against the forehead of Steve Jorgensen-Warner. To say that he reacted would be the kind of understatement worthy of a punch to the face. Steve howled as if the mere touch of the emblem had torn him in half, which, a second later, it did. His blond hair self-scalped as a reptilian ridge asserted itself through his skull, and then his face, the lure that had hooked many a lovelorn high school girl, ripped down the center, splitting his forehead to reveal a bone-studded faceplate that spat out both eyeballs in favor of silver orbs that glimmered with coal-hot fury. Steve's cheeks slopped away like two uncooked hamburger patties and his jaws exploded in a shower of teeth to make way for a massive gray mandible. The football uniform parted like a robe and thin ribbons of human meat began melting to the turf in favor of the hard, gray musculature of a changeling troll.

Claire and I broke our embrace.

Steve, his true form revealed decades before he could mature to a position of global power, screamed at the moon. Tub got out of the way, his work there done, and he motioned for Dad to quit with the heroics for one night and give the professionals room to work. Dad nodded, turned to Jack, and gave his little brother a go-ahead nod.

To my right, Jack unsheathed his sword with a satisfying *zing*.

To my left, Blinky chuckled, ready to win one more for ARRRGH!!!

Claire gave me a final air kiss and dropped me a devilish wink before using her blade to slice the night into dozens of beautiful shards that dazzled her fellow trollhunters as much as it infuriated the thing that used to be Steve. It was with a weary sigh and more than a few protesting muscles that I took my place beside her, beside all of them. This had been one hell of a long night. But I knew by then the truths of my trade as well as any trollhunter who'd answered the call. Long nights were just part of the deal.

They went in as hungry carnivores and came out as pulp.